Out of Tune

Read these other books
by Gail Nall:

Breaking the Ice

Best. Night. Ever.
(with coauthors)

and with Jen Malone:

You're Invited

You're Invited Too

Out of Tune

Gail Nall

ALADDIN M!X

NEW YORK LONDON TORONTO SYDNEY NEW DELHI

m!X
aladdin

ALADDIN M!X

Simon & Schuster Children's Publishing Division
1230 Avenue of the Americas, New York, New York 10020
First Aladdin M!X edition November 2017
Text copyright © 2016 by Gail Nall
Cover illustration copyright © 2016 by Eda Kaban
Also available in an Aladdin hardcover edition.
All rights reserved, including the right of reproduction in whole or in part in any form.
ALADDIN and related logo are registered trademarks of Simon & Schuster, Inc.
ALADDIN M!X and related logo are registered trademarks of Simon & Schuster, Inc.
For information about special discounts for bulk purchases, please contact Simon & Schuster
Special Sales at 1-866-506-1949 or business@simonandschuster.com.
The Simon & Schuster Speakers Bureau can bring authors to your live event.
For more information or to book an event contact the Simon & Schuster Speakers Bureau
at 1-866-248-3049 or visit our website at www.simonspeakers.com.
Cover designed by Jessica Handelman
Interior designed by Mike Rosamilia
The text of this book was set in Adobe Caslon Pro.
Manufactured in the United States of America 1017 OFF
2 4 6 8 10 9 7 5 3 1
Library of Congress Cataloging-in-Publication Data
Names: Nall, Gail, author.
Title: Out of tune / by Gail Nall.
Description: Aladdin hardcover edition. | New York : Aladdin, 2016. |
Summary: When twelve-year-old Maya's parents sell their house and move the family into an RV
to travel the country, her only goal is to return home to audition for the singing competition show
that is sure to propel her to country music stardom.
Identifiers: LCCN 2015046573 (print) | LCCN 2016022993 (eBook) |
ISBN 9781481458177 (hc) | ISBN 9781481458184 (eBook) |
Subjects: | CYAC: Singers—Fiction. | Families—Fiction. | Country music—Fiction. |
BISAC: JUVENILE FICTION / Social Issues / Friendship. JUVENILE FICTION /
Performing Arts / Music. Classification: LCC PZ7.N142268 Ou 2016 (print) |
LCC PZ7.N142268 (eBook) |
DDC [E]—dc23 LC record available at https://lccn.loc.gov/2015046573
ISBN 9781481458160 (pbk)

To Eva—may you travel the world
but always find home

Chapter 1

93 days until *Dueling Duets* auditions

Dad putters up to our house in an ancient, rust-spotted motor home. He's grinning like he just watched the Tennessee Titans win the Super Bowl—and that's when I know he's completely lost it.

I'm in my room, practicing for the most important moment of my life, when I hear the thing through my open window. I stop right smack in the middle of singing to my reflection in the mirror and run downstairs. Mom's acting like a traffic cop. She motions Dad this way and that to keep him from plowing down the mailbox. I stand on the sidewalk next to my little sister, Bug.

Mom windmills her arms. "CUT THE WHEEL!"

"What *is* that?" I ask.

"An RV. Maybe we'll go camping every weekend now!" Bug stands on her bare tiptoes as she tries to see inside the ginormous hunk of metal Dad's driving.

"I *know* it's an RV. I mean, why is it here?"

"Stop. STOP!" Mom pounds on the door.

The thing jerks to a halt. Dad climbs out and struts around the front to meet us on the sidewalk. He kicks the front tire like he just drove home a Mustang instead of the ugliest RV on the planet. My best friend Kenzie's brother drives an old red Mustang with one brown door. He kicks the tires every single time he gets in the car, as if they're going to pop or something before he drives off.

Dad stands with his hands on his hips and beams. "So what do you think of our new home?"

"Our what?" I ask.

"This rig," he says as he pats the side of it. "It's our new home on wheels."

He really has gone crazy. I glance at Mom. She's smiling too.

"We're going to *live* in it?" Bug practically squeals, as if she's six instead of nine.

Is crazy contagious?

Dad rubs his hands together, the way he always does when he's cooking up some awful plan to ruin my life. "It'll be fun! We'll camp all over the country." He and Mom link elbows, and they look at each other all gooey-eyed.

I hold up a hand. "Wait. Let me get this straight. We're going to live in this thing like it's a house?" I knock on the side of the RV and wait to see if it'll collapse in a dusty, rusty heap and end this whole whackadoo idea.

"We talked about moving a few months ago, Maya. Remember?" Mom says.

"I remember. And now we're going to camp all the time!" Bug's face lights up.

My stomach feels swirly. Of course I remember. Mom and Dad announced that they were thinking about moving, but I assumed that meant to an apartment or something. And then *Dueling Duets* announced it was going to hold auditions right here in Nashville this summer, and then Jack asked me to audition with him, and so I didn't really think much more about the whole moving thing. Mostly because I never thought it would be to something like *this*. "What about our house?"

"We're going to sell it. No more mortgage payments."

If Dad could smile any wider, his lips would be touching his ears.

Mom puts her hand on my shoulder. "We can't afford the house anymore. Dad and I needed to act before things got really bad."

"And this is so much better than some old apartment!" Dad adds.

I cannot believe this is actually happening. I eye the RV. "But if we sell our house, where will we put our stuff? No way will it fit into that."

"We're going to simplify," Mom says.

"Simplify. . . . Meaning get rid of a bunch of things?"

"Yup! Isn't it great? Come aboard." After a couple of good yanks on the door, Dad disappears inside. Mom and Bug follow.

I'm still standing on the grass next to the curb. Sell our house? Live in this piece of junk? Camp out all over the country? And—I can barely even think about it—miss my one shot at *Dueling Duets* and ultimate fame and fortune as the newest and brightest star of country music?

No. Way.

"I'm *not* going!" I yell into the RV.

I cross my arms and wait for an answer. I shouldn't

have been surprised that Dad chose this awful thing over something normal, like a cheaper house or an apartment. Ever since he got laid off in January, he's been acting weird. Like spending tons of time reading library books about nature when he couldn't find a new job. And whittling this tree limb he found in the backyard into a walking stick. He also stopped shaving for a couple of weeks, until Mom refused to leave the house with him. When I asked Mom if Dad was ever going to get another job, she'd get this sad look and start talking about regrets and unfulfilled dreams.

"Hello? Did you hear me?" I call through the open door.

Still no answer.

I grip the handrail and climb the steep steps. The RV smells like old bananas and mothballs. Kind of like my grandparents' house, if they ate bananas 24/7 instead of tuna and pickles.

I move past the front seats into a living room–type area, where Mom, Dad, and Bug are standing around and jabbering. It's brown. All brown. Brown couch, brown armchairs, brown floor. Even the ancient TV is mounted in a brown metal frame on the wall.

"I need to ask Aunt Kim about new upholstery," Mom

says as she whips out her phone, like that's going to improve this place.

This is *not* the home of someone destined to win *Dueling Duets*. Well, maybe if it was all glitzed up and had my name splashed across the side, like a tour bus. But even Kenzie's brother's old Mustang is better than *this* thing. "It's the same color as dirt," I whisper to Bug. "The Dirt Den."

Bug snorts. "Look!" she yells as if I'm not standing right next to her. "This is where I'm going to sleep." She scrambles up a ladder from the Dirt Den to a little nook with a bed that sits over the front seats. There's even a miniature (brown) curtain to shut off the world's tiniest bedroom from the rest of the (brown) trailer.

Mom sinks into one of the (brown) chairs as Dad marches down the length of the RV. I trail after him and check all the corners for cobwebs. Because there is no way I'm sharing this thing with spiders. If I was going, that is. Which I'm not.

"Kitchen. We can have cozy little meals right there." He points to a table with two narrow (brown) benches that look like school bus seats. I take a step closer. They smell like school bus seats too. I bet there's old gum stuck to the bottom.

Dad takes a single step up from the kitchen into the middle section of the RV. On each side of us is a bed set up high with a ladder, and a row of drawers and a cramped closet underneath. This would be pretty fun for a sleepover or a weekend trip. But *not* to live in all the time.

Then I realize there's only one bathroom.

"No. No way." I stand in front of the Polly Pocket–sized room complete with a little accordion door and cross my arms. "We can't live with just one."

Bug appears beside me. "Yeah, Maya takes FOREVER in the bathroom."

I elbow her. "I do not."

"Yes, you do. We'll all have to go out the windows while we wait for you to put on your silly mascara."

"You don't know how hard it is to get right!" Mom just started letting me wear mascara when I turned twelve. It's really tough to put on without getting tons of clumps in your eyelashes or stabbing out your eyeball.

"Girls, enough." Mom's voice echoes from the Dirt Den.

Across from the bathroom, there's a closet, and then in the very back of the RV is a bedroom.

"How come you and Mom get a whole bedroom and we're—*supposedly*—stuck with little cubbyholes?" I ask Dad.

"Because we're the parents and you're the kids and that's just how life is," Mom shouts from the front.

I check out one of the hallway beds again. The mini-closet is barely a closet, and there are hardly any drawers in the dresser. Where will I put my books? Or my stuffed cat collection? All my notes from Kenzie back before we got cell phones? Or my signed posters of Carrie Underwood, Taylor Swift, and Miranda Lambert? I go to sleep every night with the Talented Trio of Treble (or TTT, for short) watching over me. I know Taylor's not so country anymore, but that's where she started out.

Simplify, Mom said.

Right. There's no way I'm giving away or selling the stuff that means the most to me. They'll have to find a place for it, that's all.

Then something even more important occurs to me. Actually, two more important things.

"What about Hugo?" I can't leave my cat. "He's ancient. He won't know what to do without us."

"We won't leave Hugo behind. He'll live here with us." Mom joins us in the tiny hallway.

I feel a little better, until I remember they're turning my entire life upside down.

"Mom! There's *Dueling Duets*, remember? I can't miss it!"

She tilts her head and chews her lip, like she's thinking of the right way to tell me more horrible news. "I know you were looking forward to that, honey. I'm sorry."

"I've been practicing so much. And Jack is depending on me. I have a *responsibility* to be there." Mom's big on responsibility.

"We won't be here, Maya. Jack will still have time to find another partner. And you know how many people will show up for those tryouts. It's unlikely you two would even make it to the front of the line to audition. And if you did, you'd be up against people much older than you who've been singing for years and years."

Okay, first, Jack finding another partner? Not going to happen. Jack asking me to sing with him is pretty much the best thing that's ever happened to me. And two, I can't believe Mom doesn't think we'd even make it onto the show. Of course we'd make it! *If* we get to audition.

My phone buzzes. It's a text from Kenzie, asking what I'm up to tonight. "What about Kenzie?" I can't imagine not seeing my best friend in the world every day.

"You can still talk to her. We aren't moving to Timbuktu," Mom says before following Dad and Bug outside.

I glare at her. Texting and Skype are *not* the same thing as seeing Kenzie every single day.

I look at my phone again, but there are no words to tell Kenzie what's going on right now. So I trudge outside to find my psycho family behind the RV. Dad's in the middle of explaining how he'll hang a rack for our bikes. Which, if Dad does it, means it'll be hanging at an angle and our bikes will be kissing concrete.

"And we'll tow the pickup truck behind us," he says. "This is so exciting, girls. It'll be something you'll always remember."

Sure, like the flu. Or that time Dad chaperoned the school mixer and started headbanging to some old rock song.

Bug throws her arms around Dad and says, "This is the best thing ever! When do we leave?"

Dad laughs. "As soon as possible. I think we'll head west over the summer, then maybe work our way south for the winter."

"Winter? What about school?" I ask.

Dad grins at me. "That's the best part, Maya Mae. You're going to do school online!"

"No," I say.

Bug grabs Dad's arm. "I want to live in the RV, but I have

to be back for school. I'm president of the science club next year. And there's my Girl Scout troop."

"Sweetie," Mom says to Bug, "you're doing something much bigger than science club or Girl Scouts."

Bug nods. "Maybe I can FaceTime into meetings. And I could collect specimens from all kinds of faraway places and report back to the science club!"

Mom and Dad get crazy happy grins, and they all go inside our real house like some loony family I'm not a part of. I'm by myself, standing in the street behind the motor home, staring at the spare tire hanging on the back. Its cover has this fakey painted nature scene of trees and freaky-eyed deer. In cloudlike letters above the trees, it reads, *Groovy Travels with the Unterbrink Family.*

I imagine the Unterbrink family, watching their 1970 TV in the Dirt Den and arguing over who's been in the bathroom too long. The oldest Unterbrink daughter probably stabbed her eyeball out because no one gave her enough time to put on her mascara. Now she's half-blind and has to wear an eye patch and everyone probably makes fun of her.

We're going to become the Unterbrink family. Me and Mom and Dad and Bug. All shoved into one rolling house.

No bedroom.

No school.

No Kenzie.

No Jack.

No *Dueling Duets*.

The freaky-eyed doe on the tire cover stares me down, and I run for the safety of my real bedroom.

Chapter 2

92 days until *Dueling Duets* auditions

"YOU CAN'T MOVE AWAY!" Kenzie's voice shrieks through the hallway at school the next morning.

I should've texted her last night, but instead, I spent the whole night hoping I was just about to wake up from some horrible dream. "We're not really moving away. More like around. In an RV. Did I mention that my parents are insane?"

"Like a hundred times. YOU CAN'T LEAVE ME!" she screams as we round the corner to the sixth-grade wing.

I really should've texted. Because at this rate, I'll be deaf before homeroom.

"Maya! Seriously, you can't do this. Who will I sit with at

lunch next year? You'll miss everything. CMA Fest! And the concerts in the park. Not to mention School of the Arts, and you *know* Jack's going to get in there. I mean, it's, like, a year and a half away, but still. And *Dueling*—"

"I know. I have no idea how to tell Jack." Mostly because I'm head over heels in like with him. When he asked me to be his partner for *Dueling Duets*, I about up and died. Because he is *that* cute. He plays guitar (which I've tried to do, but am hopelessly awful at), he has this crazy good voice, and he always wears a battered brown cowboy hat over his shaggy dark hair. Except at school, 'cause they have a silly rule against hats. Which they should really change, just for Jack.

"I won't have anything to do without you around!" Kenzie flings herself against the wall outside our homeroom. "Who's going to sing me 'Boot Scootin' Boogie' to make me laugh when I get bored?"

"Who's going to tell me lame jokes and remind me that my hair looks stupid when I braid it?" I wave a braid for emphasis.

"It makes you look like Heidi. Like you just came down from the Alps to sell cough drops."

"See? I won't have anyone to tell me that." My hair takes

about an hour to tame into something that doesn't look like a lion's mane. Most days, I can't get up early enough. I figure Heidi braids are better than wild Simba hair. And maybe they can be my thing when I'm famous. Not that it'll ever happen now, since I'll be missing my one big shot.

"And you know my dad," I say to Kenzie as I drape myself against the wall next to her. "We'll probably end up driving off a cliff somewhere. This whole idea is dangerous to our health." Dad's ideas always fall super short of his expectations—in spectacular ways. Like boat-exploding, bicycle-wrecking, building-falling-down ways. Which is why he should've stuck to working in insurance instead of dragging us all over the country.

"Your dad thinks you're going to camp, like, all the time? What if the RV blows up the way that boat did on the lake?" Kenzie asks, reading my mind. There's a reason we're best friends.

I perk up. "If it does, then I can come home. Even if nothing blows up, it'll probably still be a huge disaster, and we'll come home after a few days. In plenty of time for the pool and *Dueling Duets*." I pull out my phone. Five minutes until school starts. Perfect. Jack usually saunters in with about two minutes to spare.

♪ 15 ♪

"Wait, you can stay with me." Kenzie leaps away from the wall and almost crashes right into Lacey—my least favorite person in the entire school. The feeling is mutual. She glares at Kenzie and me before stalking off to her own homeroom. Kenzie completely ignores her and keeps right on talking. "It'll be like a permanent sleepover. There. Problem solved."

I smile. I can always count on Kenzie.

"Hey," she says, sidling up next to me. "Nine o'clock."

"What's at nine o'clock? Science?" I think I have my science homework done.

"Nooooo, *nine o'clock*." She's tossing her head to the left so hard that I'm afraid she'll get whiplash or something.

And then I see what she means. Jack. Battered brown hat (which will find its way into his locker before the bell rings), jeans, and a lazy smile that's directed at . . . me.

I pull myself out of the puddle I've turned into and smile back at him. He holds up three fingers and raises his eyebrows. I nod, and he waves before disappearing down the hall.

"What in the world was that?" Kenzie asks. "Do y'all have your own language or something? Oh my God, that's so romantic."

I grab her arm and pull her into the classroom. "No, he was just asking if I'm free to practice after school today. And besides, I don't know if he even likes me like that."

I hope he does. I'm halfway through daydreams of Jack-as-my-Spring-Dance-date and Jack-as-my-future-CMA-award-winning-partner when I remember that it's all sort of pointless now.

Because I won't be living here in a few months.

When I arrive at the music room after school, Jack's already inside, strumming his guitar. So I have to take a minute outside the door to breathe, rebraid my hair, and breathe again.

"Hey," he says when I walk into the room.

I almost dissolve into that puddle a second time.

Then I remember that I have to tell him I'm leaving. Kenzie and I discussed every possible way I could tell him. None of them seem to be good ideas at all now.

He pulls a tall stool up to the front of the room and leans against it. "Ready?"

I paste on a smile and say, "Of course!" Which is true. I'm always ready to sing. Well, after I warm up in the bathroom, anyway. No way would I ever want my voice to do something weird while Jack's listening.

We run through the song once, and even though I know it needs work—I came in too early a couple of times, and he messed up the words in the middle—I just know it's going to be amazing in time for the auditions.

Except I won't be here. Unless something blows up, anyway. And I *still* need to tell him that.

Jack's lazy smile looks way less lazy when he sets his guitar down and says, "That song was a really great choice."

"Oh, um, thanks!" My voice comes out a little squeaky, and I immediately go warm from head to toe. The second the auditions were announced, I researched the judges on the show. Chance Montgomery had done a (really, really good) cover of an old Tim McGraw song. Jodene Mitchell had a thing for big songs. And Kevin Benson was distantly related to Taylor Swift. So when Jack mentioned me and him trying out together, I pretty much immediately said we had to do Tim McGraw and Taylor Swift's "Highway Don't Care." Well, after I said yes, of course. It was going to be a sure-fire win for us, and we'd both be off to Hollywood for filming, and then get record contracts and probably a world tour. Together, of course.

Except now none of that is going to happen. I twist the end of one of my braids while Jack picks through the part he messed up in the middle, singing the right words under his breath. His hair falls into his eyes, and he's just so . . . *Jack*. How in the world am I going to tell him?

"Those judges aren't going to know what hit them," he says with that Jack confidence. I mean, he only won the school talent show by a landslide, so he knows how to win a crowd.

"I hope so." It's all I can think of to say.

He blinks at me from under his hat. "Maya, is something wrong? You seem kind of out of it today."

Yes! Everything is wrong! "No, I'm fine. Really. Want to run the song again?" I grin at him like I'm not hiding the worst thing that's ever happened to me.

I have *no* idea how I'm going to tell him. And worst of all, once I do, he probably won't want anything to do with me.

"Maya, Bug! Family meeting. Now!" Mom yells from downstairs that night.

I'm sitting on my bed, Hugo purring in my lap. My beautiful audition top is spread out in front of me. It's perfect—a shimmery silver that looks like the ocean at sunset when I put it on. I heft Hugo off my lap, flop onto my back, and stare at the TTT on my wall. I'd bet a million dollars that Carrie,

Miranda, and Taylor never had to deal with their parents crushing their dreams.

Maybe I'll just stay up here and belt out Carrie Underwood's entire *Some Hearts* album over and over until Mom and Dad agree that this whole idea is pointless.

Mom pokes her head in the door. "Maya? Your presence is requested in the kitchen."

"I'm not going anywhere. I'm protesting." I draw my knees up to my chin and wrap my arms around my legs.

"Maya Mae Casselberry," Mom says in *that* voice.

"Fine." I swing my legs over the side of the bed in defeat. "But just because I'm going downstairs doesn't mean I agree to any of this."

Dad is sitting at our scarred-up table—the one that used to be Grandma's and has teeth marks on one corner from when I chewed on it as a toddler. How can they even think of giving that away?

Bug's eating grapes straight from the fridge and rattling on and on about how she's going to decorate her cubbyhole. I grab my usual seat closest to the door. Mom gently pulls Bug by her long blond ponytail to an empty chair.

I lean back and cross my arms. The chair creaks as the two front legs leave the floor. "I don't see why we have to ruin our lives. I have stuff planned this year. Important things."

Mom leans forward from her seat and pushes down on my knee. The chair rocks down onto all four legs. She gives me a sympathetic smile. "You can still sing, and lots of these campgrounds will have pools. You'll see." She doesn't even mention *Dueling Duets*.

"And what about my voice lessons?" I look right into her brown eyes. We all look the same—me, Mom, and Bug. Blond hair and brown eyes.

"I'm sorry, Maya, but even if we stayed, we wouldn't be able to afford voice lessons much longer."

That's it? No *We're sorry we're crushing the only dream you've ever had*? No *Sorry you'll be doomed to a future life of drudgery in an office instead of a fabulous, sequin-riddled life onstage in front of hundreds of thousands of adoring fans*?

"But how am I supposed to keep my voice in shape?" I've been singing with Marianne Phelps—former backup vocalist for LeAnn Rimes—since I was eight years old and drove my parents crazy by belting out "These Boots Are Made for Walkin'" over and over and over.

"You can give us concerts on the road." Dad grins at me like singing for my family in that rust-pile RV is somehow way better than weekly voice lessons with Marianne Phelps and trying out for a show that practically guarantees a record contract.

"Why can't we leave after *Dueling Duets*?" I say. "Or—better idea—let's not leave at all."

A pained look flits across Mom's face. "I know we're asking you girls to give up a lot."

"I'm giving up the Girl Scout camping extravaganza," Bug says in all seriousness.

I roll my eyes. "That doesn't even make sense. You're giving up camping to go camping?"

"It's the camping *extravaganza*."

"Right. If we have to save money, why can't we stay here and move into an apartment like we planned?" An apartment would not be the same as my house, but at least I'd still be in the same city as Kenzie and Jack and the auditions.

Mom reaches across the table for my hand, but I snatch it away. "I know this is going to be hard for you," she says. "But we're living on one salary, and this makes the most sense moneywise. Besides, it's a lifelong dream for your father and me. We get to live an adventure with our girls. It'll be so much better than an apartment, I promise." Mom makes gooey eyes at Dad again.

Normal parents wait to fulfill their lifelong dreams until *after* their kids have grown up and moved out. Then they buy sheep farms or start bands and play old-people rock. They don't uproot their kids from school and their best friends and *everything* for groovy travels in the world's ugliest RV. Plus, I'm pretty sure it's Dad's dream, not Mom's.

"What about your job?" I ask Mom. If she quits work, then we really won't have any money. We'll have to park that awful RV on the side of the road when we run out of gas and, I don't know, sing songs for change in an old jam jar. And that's not exactly how I pictured my life as Nashville's newest country music star.

"I'm moving into a position where I can do consulting work from a home office. Or an RV office."

Dad laughs, and Mom smiles at him.

Ugh. They're really, really happy about this.

Mom opens up a folder I didn't even notice. She hands pieces of paper to Bug and me. "This is a list of absolute necessities. Everything else is a luxury, and we have very little space. Your job this week is to start pulling things out of your rooms to either sell or give away."

I scan the list.

8 pairs pants/skirts/shorts

8 shirts

8 pairs underwear

1 light jacket

winter coat

3 pairs shoes: tennis shoes, hiking boots, flip-flops

Holy potatoes! I stop reading right there. "Only three pairs of shoes? And one of them has to be *hiking boots*?"

"Three. And yes," Mom says.

I'm about to hyperventilate. I must have at least twenty pairs of shoes. There's no way I can bring only three.

That's it. Kenzie's parents have *got* to agree to let me move in with them.

"Go on upstairs and get started," Dad says. "I'm going out to spiff up our rig while your mom calls the real estate agent. Won't be long now!" He thumps the table and grins.

I drag my feet upstairs and stand in the doorway to my room. Nowhere on that list did it say stuffed cat collection or 249 books or signed posters of the TTT or anything else I can't bear to part with.

I'm not packing up a thing. Not until they make me.

Chapter 3

35 days until *Dueling Duets* auditions

By the time the last day of school rolls around, I still haven't told Jack I'm leaving. I just can't do it.

He finds me in the hallway as I'm cleaning out my locker. Which is full of stuff that's not on Mom's Packing Essentials list.

"Guess what?" he says. "I found us a place to practice this summer. Lacey's dad knows this guy who has a recording studio, and he said we could use space there when it isn't booked."

I blink at him. His blue eyes are extra blue today, and his lazy smile is so cute that it's impossible not to smile back at him. "That's . . . great!" I'm still kind of reeling from the fact that he somehow snagged us practice space in a recording studio, of all places. And how it was Lacey who arranged it. I know she didn't do it out of the kindness of her heart. She's up to something, for sure. I figured that out about three seconds after Jack asked me to audition with him earlier this year.

I was already going to audition for *Dueling Duets* when he asked me. I mean, of course I wasn't going to let this dream moment of finally making it as a country music star not happen, even without a partner. But when Jack asked me to sing with him, it was like all those times I'd stared at him in class (when he wasn't looking, of course) and imagined us singing together finally came to something. I've only been crushing on him since I heard him singing by himself in the music room after school one day last September. Who knew that all it would take was me singing Miranda Lambert's "White Liar" in the talent show for him to notice me?

The second I got off the stage, he looked at me and said, "You do that song better than Miranda." And I couldn't figure out what in the world to say back to him. I'm pretty sure I just stood there with my mouth hanging open. But then, right after English class the next morning, he walked up to my desk (which was right next to Lacey's, so she heard the whole thing), pushed his hair out of his eyes, and said, "So, hey, have you heard of this *Dueling Duets* show?"

All I could get out was, "Um, yes." Then I mumbled something about auditioning for it. When I replay this scene in my head, it's all slow motion. Like the way it is in the movies when they want you to notice every single little thing.

"I was thinking that—if you wanted—maybe we could try out together?" He shoved his hands into his pockets, almost like he was nervous. Which is crazy, because any girl who can carry a tune would *die* to audition with him.

In fact, I'm pretty sure Lacey's eyes fell out of her head when he asked me.

And now, here I am, trying to figure out how to keep this dream going. If Lacey gets wind of me leaving town, she'll do anything to worm her way into my spot.

Jack gives me the address of the studio, and we make plans to meet up in two days. He's super excited about the studio, and I would be too . . . if I didn't know what was coming.

Because this thing is getting more real every day. Most of our furniture is gone. Strangers that Mom and Dad find on Craigslist come to take away our widescreen TV, Grandma's old kitchen table, and the matching couch and love seat. Now there's nowhere left to sit downstairs except for Dad's ancient recliner. Mom insists we do Rock, Paper, Scissors to see who gets it for dinner each night. Everyone else eats sitting cross-legged on the floor.

Mom threatened to take all my stuff to Goodwill if I didn't start packing. No way was I going to let that happen. Operation Maya Keeps Everything is under way. If they're forcing me to give up Kenzie, my school, my house, my comfy yellow-and-white bedroom, and, worst of all, my dreams of performing for thousands with Jack, then I'm not getting rid of anything else that matters.

Dad's standing behind the RV as I carry out a box of books. He's holding a palette—like, a real artist's palette—in his left hand and is painting something on the freaky spare tire cover.

"I'm naming her Gloria," he says as he paints over the Unterbrinks' name.

"Oookay." I shift the box over to my right hip. Really, Bertha would be a better name. Bertha the Beast. Instead, I just say, "'Gloria' sounds like a hippo."

"Shh, you'll hurt her feelings," he says with a smile.

I take a step closer to see what he's painting.

GL

"Dad, you are *not* painting 'Gloria' on the tire cover, are you?"

"Well, we're not the Unterbrinks. So it'll be 'Groovy Travels with Gloria.'"

Because that makes sense.

He whistles "Feelin' Groovy" as he paints. I'm about to ask him why he doesn't put our last name on the cover, when I think better of it. I don't really want anyone associating me with Gloria/Bertha the Beast.

I leave Dad to his artistry and heft my box into the trailer. Bug's hanging out in her cubbyhole. All her stuff fits neatly into two drawers in Mom and Dad's little bedroom.

"Did you know Dad named this thing?" I ask Bug.

She climbs down and runs ahead of me to the kitchen. "Yup. 'Gloria' kind of sounds like a hippo."

Finally! Maybe Bug and I really are related. I give her back a sisterly smile.

"I would've named it Hector. Because I think it looks more like a boy RV than a girl RV," Bug says as she places a can of green beans in the cabinet.

Never mind.

I plug in my earbuds, turn up my favorite girl-power

country mix, and spend the rest of the day dragging bags and boxes full of my life into the hallway cubbyholes. I fill the extra bunk from mattress to ceiling, plaster the tiny wall space next to my bed with the TTT (so what if the posters curve up onto the ceiling?), stuff the drawers until they barely shut, and shove the mini-closets full of clothes and shoes.

Three pairs of shoes. Ha.

Score one for Operation Maya Keeps Everything.

It's a gorgeous Saturday afternoon, and Kenzie and her mom are coming to take me downtown for One Last Big Nashville Blast, as Kenzie calls it. I've changed into a white sundress and my favorite pair of red cowboy boots. I even took extra time to flat-iron my poodle hair so I wouldn't have to braid it. And my dress is just long enough to cover the giant scrape I got on my knee this morning when I tripped over my piggy bank and a pile of blankets while carrying a box into my new so-called bedroom.

"What would you girls like to do first?" Mrs. O'Neill asks when I climb into the backseat of her car.

Kenzie and I look at each other. "Pancake Pantry!" we yell at the same time.

Mrs. O'Neill rolls her eyes at us in the rearview mirror. "I don't know why I even asked."

When we get to the restaurant, Kenzie orders the plain old basic pancakes like she always does, and Mrs. O'Neill asks for an omelet, which is so boring at a place known for its pancakes. I take forever to decide. How can I pick just one kind of pancake when it's possibly my last time ever at the Pancake Pantry? I finally choose chocolate chip, and then I spend the rest of the meal trying to remember every last detail of the restaurant, from the wooden floor to the way it smells, all warm and pancakey.

And then, of course, we go to the Ryman. It's early enough that the church-turned-concert-hall is still open to tourists. And us.

Inside, I run my fingers over the tops of the pew seats. The whole place is filled with this . . . feeling. Like greatness that could come at any moment and take you completely by surprise. It's heavy in the air, and I breathe it in. Maybe—just maybe—if I soak up enough of the ghosts of this place, I'll get my turn to stand on that stage.

"Go on up." Kenzie gives me a little push toward the steps at the front of the house (which is theater lingo for, well, the theater).

Usually there's someone standing near the stage who'll take your picture if you go up and stand at the mic. But it has to be almost closing time, because no one else is here but us.

I climb the rounded steps that lead to the center of the stage. When I turn around, Kenzie and Mrs. O'Neill start clapping and whistling.

As if I need much more than that to break into song at the Ryman, of all places. I close my eyes and sing the first thing that pops into my mind. Which is "Coal Miner's Daughter." And it's as if Loretta Lynn herself is standing right beside me as my voice carries through the theater to my audience of two.

It's perfect.

When I finish, Kenzie and her mom give me a standing ovation. I take a few exaggerated bows before running down the steps and collapsing in laughter against Kenzie.

"See, one dream fulfilled," she says.

We stroll around the rest of the theater for a few minutes, and then Kenzie and I beg Mrs. O'Neill for a walk down Lower Broad.

"Please?" Kenzie asks as we push through the door and head out into the sticky June evening. "It's not even dark yet. And we're already almost there." She waves her hand toward the masses of people moving down the sidewalk.

"I don't know if I'll ever get to walk here again," I add. Okay, maybe that was a little over the top, but still. I need to drink up all the Nashville I can before I have to leave. And Mom and Dad would only ever take me down here in the morning, when it's practically dead.

Mrs. O'Neill sighs, clicks her phone to check the time, and then says, "All right. But only for a few minutes. You know how crazy it gets."

Kenzie and I grab hands and jump up and down and squeal like we've just been given a gazillion dollars. Then we link arms and just stare for a moment at all the neon lights and the people and the honky-tonks with music pouring out into the street.

It's just . . . everything. *Everything* happens here, on this street. It's all of Nashville, smooshed down into a few insane blocks. The sidewalks are already teeming with people. Kenzie and I grin at each other, then step forward and join them, Mrs. O'Neill trailing behind us.

It's a slow walk, because it takes a while to squeeze through everyone, but that's okay. I don't want to move any faster. I want to remember every moment of this, so that when I'm squished up next to Bug in Bertha the Beast, I can close my eyes and relive today. And know that I belong somewhere. Here.

A woman's voice floats out of one of the dives, and we stop to listen. I stand on my tiptoes to try to see the singer over the heads of people, but I can't.

"I've got to find a way to get back here for that audition," I say to Kenzie.

"How?" Kenzie asks.

"I don't know yet. But I'm going to figure it out." Jack and I have been meeting up a couple of times a week at that recording studio. Which is amazing, except Lacey always seems to be hanging around outside the door.

"You know you still need to tell Jack, though." Kenzie pulls me around a bachelorette party.

"Do you think I should if I'm planning to come back . . . somehow?"

"Maya!" Kenzie stops in the middle of the sidewalk, right in front of a couple of guys in cowboy hats playing guitar for spare change. Even though it's still early, the neon signs up and down Broadway are fully lit, and Kenzie's glasses reflect all the different colors. "You *have* to tell him! He's going to figure it out anyway, if you're never around to practice. If you don't tell him, I'm going to take drastic measures." She wiggles her eyebrows.

Before I can wonder what drastic measures are, Kenzie's tugging me into one of those touristy "buy one pair, get two pair free" boot stores.

"Let's get matching boots, so every time one of us wears them, it'll be like we're together," she says with an enormous smile.

My heart is so full I think it will burst all over the place. We find these adorable black boots with pink stitching that look really cute on both of us. Mrs. O'Neill pays for the boots, and I wonder where exactly I'm going to put them in my cubbyholes. I might just have to sleep in them.

As we walk back to the car—Mrs. O'Neill hovering over us like a hawk because she's afraid we'll disappear in the hordes of people swarming down the sidewalk—I feel like I should be happy. I've just had the most amazing night of my life with my best friend. But it's hard to feel good when I think that it might be the last great night ever. Not to mention that I really do have to tell Jack—and soon.

When Mrs. O'Neill drops me off at home, I find Dad hanging around in a T-shirt and his flannel Christmas pants. Never mind that it's summer and about eighty-five degrees outside. Dad rocks the flannel pajama pants year-round.

"Guess what!" he says as I head toward my sleeping bag.

I close my eyes. These days, Dad saying "guess what" usually isn't good.

"The house sold!"

I want to grab Kenzie's hand, but she's already left. Instead, I grip the edge of the kitchen counter.

It's actually happening.

Chapter 4

21 days until *Dueling Duets* auditions

A few nights before we leave, Kenzie shows up to help me deal with the last few things in my room. I find her outside, peeking into the RV.

"If I was stuck with my brother in this thing, we'd probably murder each other," she says from the steps.

I don't say anything back, because someone else is leaning up against Bertha.

Jack.

I'm glad it's almost dark and that he's down by the back tires, because my face is probably six different shades of red right now. He's here. At my house. Well, both of my houses, one of which is a rusty home on wheels that screams GLORIA from the spare tire cover.

Jack. Is here.

"Hellloooo, Maya?" Kenzie waves a hand in front of my face. "Emmeline wants to show me her bunk."

I glance down, and there's Bug, grinning up at Kenzie.

Kenzie never calls Bug by her nickname like everyone else. She says it's because it makes her think of crickets, which creep her out for some reason. And yet, Bug adores her.

Kenzie leans over to my ear. "Drastic measures." Then she nods at Jack.

"What? Why? How?" I whisper. Because I can't seem to make a whole sentence.

"I texted Hannah, who texted Vivi, and you know her brother's like BFFs with Jack," she says. "Anyway, I got his number." She shrugs like this is no big deal at all.

"Wait, you texted him? And, what, asked him to come over here?" I can't even imagine what Kenzie said to him. I really hope it wasn't anything super embarrassing, like *Oh hey, Jack, come over to Maya's because she's sooooo in like with you and wants to show you her ugly new RV-house.*

"Maaaaaybe," Kenzie drawls. "Because you have to tell him. And you can't leave without having time with him that

♪ 38 ♪

isn't about practicing your song." Then she lets Bug drag her into Bertha, and it's just me and Jack outside.

Jack's inspecting the RV. I cringe. *Why* did Kenzie have to bring him here? Now he's going to know exactly how crazy my family is. All I can hope for is that Dad stays inside the house. Because the only thing worse than Jack seeing Bertha is Jack meeting my dad.

"It's like you've got your own tour bus," he says. "Why does it say 'Gloria'?"

If I could crumble into dirt and become part of my front yard, I so would right now. "Um, it came that way," I lie. "Want to go around back?"

He shrugs and follows me through the gate.

"Where are you going on vacation?" he asks.

"Oh . . . well . . ." The words are stuck somewhere in my throat. Instead of trying to find them, I make myself really busy with sitting in one of the swings on our old swing set. Dad sold all the patio furniture, so it's either swings or grass back here now.

Jack takes the other swing. "Florida?"

Kenzie is going to get an earful once this is over.

Also. Jack. Is on my swing set.

I twist my swing around until the chains creak, and then

let it go, spinning while I try to figure out the best way to tell Jack what's really going on.

"Is it a big secret?" He's smiling at me now, shaggy hair peeking out from under his hat.

I sigh and study the grass. And somehow I tell him everything. "But it won't last. I'll be back before auditions. I promise," I say once I finish the explanation.

When I finally look up, he shrugs again. "Okay. So, you'll be gone for, like, a week?"

I nod, stunned that he's not freaking out. "Or maybe two."

His face sort of twitches, and for a second, I think that maybe he's not really okay with missing all this practice time, but then he smiles again. "Text me when you know for sure. Here, give me your phone."

I hold it out to him, and my heart about falls all over itself when his hand brushes mine. He types his number in and gives it back.

Jack. Gave me his number. And I didn't even have to go through half the sixth-grade class like Kenzie did to get it.

I admire the numbers on the screen for a second before I remember that he's sitting right here and this probably looks a little weird, me staring at his phone number like it's made of gold or something. I shove my phone back into my pocket. "We'll practice every day when I get back."

"And we'll kill those auditions," he says. "Hey, bet I can swing higher than you." He tosses his hat on the ground, backs up, and flies into the air.

"Not on my swing set!" I push off, and try not to think about how this won't be my swing set in a few days. And about how I have no plan to get home the way I told Jack I did.

I'll figure it out. I *have* to.

The morning that we leave comes way too fast.

I sit buckled into the Dirt Den Couch, which doesn't look so dirty since Mom covered it with an off-white fabric. We've been driving since eight this morning. Dad hooked up the truck to the back of the RV and was ready to go at six, but no one else was. So he spent two hours washing the outside of Bertha—I mean, Gloria—with a bucket and a sponge. Not that it improved the appearance at all.

But the worst part of the day hasn't been the driving or the waking up early. The most awful part was leaving our house. It looked so sad when we drove off, like the red bricks and the windows and yellow front door were crying.

I grabbed Bug's hand as our house disappeared around the corner. A couple of tears leaked from her eyes, even though she'd never admit it.

The second we left our neighborhood behind, I got to work. With the success of Operation Maya Keeps Everything, it was time to move on to Operation Maya Goes Home. As soon as I figured out a plan, I decided, I was going to text Jack. Just to make sure he knew I really meant it when I said I'd be coming back home.

Now I reread the list I made on my phone:

Operation Maya Goes Home (OMGH)

(In time for Dueling Duets.)

Countdown: T minus 19 days

How to Get Home to Audition with Jack and Win

His Heart with My Voice and Stellar Personality:

1. Convince Mom and Dad this is a horrible idea.

2. Bertha needs major repairs.

3. ?

This is the worst list ever.

Also, I have no idea what "T minus" means, except that really serious people at NASA use it in movies to count down the time until the space shuttle launches. And getting home in time for *Dueling Duets* is even more important than launching into space. I have nineteen days until my dream will either come true or I'll be stuck singing to the TTT on my wall/ceiling forever.

"Did you know Texas has twenty different kinds of scorpions?" Bug asks. She's flipping through this enormous book called *Arachnids of North America*. It's one of a whopping five books she chose to take with her.

"No. Why don't you read something normal? You can borrow the one I finished this morning." I stare at my phone, willing it to buzz. It's resting on Hugo, who's snoring in my lap. Mom made me turn off the sound hours ago. She said the texting ding was giving her a migraine. Not that it's going to buzz any time soon, since Kenzie had to go out to eat with her family. I thought I was hungry too, until Bug started talking about scorpions.

"I like this book. Wow, Texas has nine hundred different spiders. Look at this one!" She thrusts the book in my face. A drawing of the ugliest, hairiest spider ever stares at me from the pages.

I push it away and break into my part of "Highway Don't Care." Not only will that make Bug stop talking, but I could use the practice.

"Maya, *please*." Mom rubs her temples. "And, Bug, enough about the spiders."

Okay, how am I going to stay in audition-ready form if my family won't let me practice?

"There it is!" Dad points out the windshield. "Home sweet home for the next few days." He takes a hard right turn into the campground and stops at a small log cabin.

A short, chirpy woman wearing a fishing hat—complete with hooks and feathery-looking things on it—pokes her head through Dad's lowered window. "Howdy do!"

"We're the Casselberrys!" Dad chirps right back. "Here for three nights. We're going to become official Texas residents."

I roll my eyes as the woman congratulates us. According to Mom, it's cheaper to get driver's licenses and register Bertha here than anywhere else in the country. She read that on some weirdo website where people are all about messing up their kids' lives and moving into their own Berthas. At least Mom and Dad didn't have much of a choice, which makes it a teeny, tiny bit better than if we had plenty of money and they were doing this just for the fun of it.

Anyway, I don't care what Mom's and Dad's licenses say. I'll always be from Tennessee, where I've never even seen a scorpion.

The RV lurches into motion again as Dad creeps along the gravel drive. Bug and I peer out the window at the rows of RVs parked side by side. There's a campfire in front of pretty much every one of them. Kids and dogs run around. The scent of something barbecuing leaks through the windows, and my stomach growls.

"C-16," Mom says as she points to an empty space ahead of us. "We'll have to back in." She looks at Dad. "Can you do that?"

"Of course. No big deal. Let's unhook the truck."

Bug and I use the opportunity to jump out of the RV. The heat hits my face like I just stepped into an oven, and I really wish I wasn't wearing jeans. I stride across the campsite in my new black-and-pink boots and join Bug at the picnic table.

I stretch the cramps out of my legs and watch as Mom backs away from Bertha in the truck. Then Dad angles the RV backward. Mom gets out of the truck to direct him, the way she did when he first brought the thing home.

"What do you bet Dad's going to hit a tree or something?" I ask Bug, who's sitting on the ground checking out the dirt and insect life of Happy Trails Campground, Weslerville, Texas.

"If I had a hundred dollars, I'd bet that." She reaches into her pocket with her dirt-smudged fingers and pulls out two dollars. "But that's all I have."

I wave a hand at her. "No bet. We know he's going to hit something."

"At least he can't take down a building from here." Bug stops poking the ground to watch the Mom and Dad Show.

She has a good point. When Dad first bought the pickup, he backed it into a Krispy Kreme doughnut shop the very next day. The entire side of the building came down, everything raining onto the new truck. I thought for sure we'd all be crushed to death, but no one was hurt. Just the building. And the truck, which still has the dents.

"Hard right! Hard right!" Mom yells as she jumps up and down to get Dad's attention.

Dad finally sees her and turns the steering wheel, just barely missing a tree.

Bug climbs up on the picnic table next to me, and we both watch like we're at a movie. I kinda wish we had some popcorn.

"Now left, left!" Mom waves her arms.

Dad's busy looking off to his right and totally doesn't see her. He inches closer and closer to another tree.

"Left!" Mom's shrieking. "Turn left. Now!"

I grip the side of the picnic table as the RV rolls toward the pine tree.

"Our bikes!" Bug squeaks.

My heart stops as I realize our bikes will be toast if he runs into that tree.

"Dad!" I yell. "Stop!" I jump off the picnic table to try to get his attention. Bug's at my heels. All three of us are leaping up and down and yelling.

Dad turns and sees us. And stops too late.

Crrrunch.

I squeeze my eyes shut.

Someone behind me whistles. I open my eyes to see half the campground watching. I wish I could climb under the picnic table and hide. Just because I knew what would happen doesn't make it any less embarrassing.

Dad scrambles out of the RV as Bug and I run over to check out the damage. The back wheel of Bug's bike is twisted into some horrible misshapen bunch of metal.

"Da-ad, my bike," she says, running her fingers over what used to be a cute little red street cruiser.

For a split second, I imagine Dad breaking down and apologizing for this disaster of a plan, and loading us all up to go home. My fingers brush the phone in my pocket, and I'm mentally texting the good news to Jack and Kenzie. But one little bike-smashing accident won't stop Dad.

"It's okay, Bugby," Dad says. "We'll get you a new one."

Mom shakes her head, and Bug's face sort of melts. We can't afford a new bike.

"You can ride mine whenever you want," I say to Bug. "I don't use it much anyway."

Bug gives me a half smile as she wipes her eyes with her sleeve. Mom looks at me all grateful-like.

I send a quick text to Kenzie about the big Bertha-bike-tree accident. Maybe Dad will do something else really stupid—something bigger that will get us back home for sure. Which is technically Number Two on the OMGH list, but who cares about going in order? The point is to go home.

Dad touches the large dent to the right of the bikes. "Might be able to pound this out without making an insurance claim. Don't know what we'll do about Mr. Deer, though."

The doe on the spare tire cover is still looking all creepy-eyed at us, but her deer husband's head is severed from his body in a perfect U shape. It flaps in the breeze.

"Ugh," Mom says with a shudder. "Can't we just get a plain, cheap one? That thing gives me the creeps. And it has the word 'groovy.' We aren't that old."

"But I painted Gloria's name on it," Dad says. "Maybe Maya Mae can sew it up. She was always good at that."

I fight the urge to roll my eyes. Four years ago, Grandma taught me and Kenzie cross-stitch when she came down to visit. We crisscrossed little x's like crazy for three months straight. *Four years* ago. It's hardly like I'm some kind of sewing genius.

"I think Mom has everything you need in her fix-it kit. Here." Dad works the cover off the spare tire and hands the horrible thing to me.

I hold it between two fingers. "Mom?"

"Just do the best you can, Maya," Mom says with a sigh.

At least the sewing will get me away from the whole leveling-the-RV-and-setting-up-camp routine. I find the fix-it kit and decide that stitching up the scary spare tire cover is better than helping Dad connect the sewer hose.

So as Mom and Dad get everything set up and talk RV repair with other campers, I sit on the picnic table and sew up the holes. But first, I snap a picture of the decapitated deer to send to Kenzie.

"That's not very good," Bug says, peering over my shoulder as I sew.

"Maybe if it's awful Dad will buy a new one." I stab the

buck's neck with the needle. There are so many other things I'd rather be doing right now. Texting Kenzie. Dreaming about Jack. Brainstorming new ways to get home. Practicing. Wait, who says I can't practice? I start humming to warm up my voice again.

"Why are you using hot pink thread?" Bug asks.

I shrug. "It was all Mom had in the fix-it kit. Now, stop breathing on me already."

Bug gives me a shove in the back and scoots off the picnic table. "Hey, check out that girl over there. She has blue hair."

I pick up my humming again and follow where Bug's finger is pointing across the dirt "yard" to the next RV over. Sure enough, there's a girl about my age with blue hair, sitting in a canvas chair and wearing earbuds. And the best part—her RV is even uglier than Bertha the Beast. It's brighter-than-the-sun yellow, and a faded smiley face leers from the side. I take a picture of it with my phone and text it to Kenzie.

"I wonder if she knows if there are any poisonous snakes around here." Bug races off across the dirt.

"Don't bother her," I say to Bug's back.

Before I know it, she's chatting away to the girl, who's looking at Bug as if she has three heads. I sigh, pick up my sewing,

♪ 50 ♪

and go to rescue the girl from my sister. So much for practicing.

". . . and down in the lake there are water moccasins. If you swim in there, they'll swarm and drag you down to the depths, where they'll bite you to death," she's saying to Bug when I arrive.

Bug's brown eyes are as round as the ones on that nightmarish spider she showed me earlier. "Really? I didn't know that."

"She's messing with you, Bugby," I say. Bug loves creepy critters so much, she's probably super disappointed to find out it's all made up.

The blue-haired girl stares me down. "How do you know it's not the truth?"

"Because snakes don't do that?" I'm not entirely sure what water moccasins even are, but the whole thing sounds completely fake.

"You don't know." She smirks at me and sticks one of her earbuds back in.

"C'mon, Bug. Dinner's probably almost ready." I turn to walk back to the RV.

"What *is* that thing? A possessed deer?" Blue Hair asks.

I turn back. "It's this stupid spare tire cover from the back of Ber—, I mean, our RV."

"So you guys are like, what, deer worshippers?" She looks again at the cover, and the corner of her mouth twitches up. "That's . . . groovy."

"We're not deer worshippers. That's not even a thing. It's just an ugly tire cover." I want to tell her that her RV is way more embarrassing than our groovy headless deer tire cover, but I bite my tongue.

"You'd be more interesting if you were a deer worshipper," Blue Hair says.

I don't even know what to say. This girl is seriously weird.

"Shiver, food's done." An older woman with crinkled skin and long gray hair emerges from their RV.

"Your name is Shiver?" Bug asks.

"Your name is Bug, so what's wrong with Shiver?" the girl replies.

Bug grins. "Nothing. I like it."

"Hi, girls." The woman walks slowly toward us. "I didn't realize Shiver had company. I'm Gert, her grandmother. You girls want to stay for dinner?" She holds out her hand like we're grown-ups at a business meeting.

I reach out and shake it as I introduce myself and Bug.

"Are you the ones who backed your rig into the tree?" Gert asks.

Shiver snorts.

I restrain myself from glaring at her. "Yeah, that's us."

"It's hard learning to drive one of these monsters," Gert says. "Is that your mother?"

She's pointing behind us to where Mom's striding across the yard.

"Hi there. Are you making friends already?" Mom beams at us.

Ha. Like Shiver's going to be my new bestie.

Gert cocks her head. "You look familiar," she says to Mom.

"Lori Casselberry, from Nashville. Although I grew up in Louisville."

"Lori . . . Thomas?" Gert uses Mom's maiden name. "Shelly's friend from St. Rose's?"

A look of recognition moves across Mom's face. "You're Shelly's mother. Wow, I read about how RVers run into the same people all the time, but I wouldn't have ever guessed I'd see someone from back home! How is Shelly? I haven't talked to her in years."

Shiver rolls her eyes and jumps up so fast you'd think she'd gotten bit by a red ant. She grabs a black backpack from the table, heads into the RV, and slams the door.

Gert watches her, then turns back to Mom. "Not so great. In the middle of a divorce out in California. Shiver's her daughter. I took her with me this summer to travel, get her away from all that."

"Shiver?" Mom asks.

"Adalie, actually. She's going through a phase," Gert says, with the same look Mom and Dad use when they think something Bug or I like is silly.

"Ah. Well, we're here for a few days. Maybe we can catch up?"

"That would be wonderful." Gert squeezes Mom's hand. "I should check on Shiver."

Mom waves, and we follow her back to the RV.

"Who's Shelly?" Bug asks.

"My best friend from high school. I haven't seen her for twenty years, at least. It's so nice to run into her family here. It's almost as if there was a reason for all of this—your dad losing his job and everything. . . ." Mom drifts off and doesn't say anything for a moment. Then she looks at me. "Maybe you and Adalie can be friends, the way Shelly and I were?"

"Sure," I say in my most sarcastic voice. "That's going to happen."

"You could be a little nicer, Maya."

Mom has a way of making me feel super guilty.

She pulls open Bertha's door to the scent of garlic bread and once-frozen lasagna. I shut the door behind us and lean back against it. Kenzie never missed a lasagna night at our house. We'd eat until we were so full we couldn't move. Then we'd go up to my room and talk, or listen to music and pretend to do homework. Sometimes I'd sing her whatever I'd been working on with Marianne. It was after a lasagna dinner that we found out about *Dueling Duets*, and she convinced me that I had to try out.

I stare down at my just-like-Kenzie's cowboy boots. And I miss her more than ever.

Chapter 5

19 days until *Dueling Duets* auditions

That night, Bug pounds on the door of the closet-sized bathroom. "Maya, get OUT already!"

I spit toothpaste into the sink and rinse my mouth as I stare at my phone, willing Kenzie to text. It's been a whole hour since I last heard from her.

"Maya!"

I open the door and stand in Bug's way, just because.

"Mo-ove," she says as she tries to shoulder past me.

"You move." I wiggle back and forth in the doorway to annoy her.

Mom's face appears from their bedroom. "Maya, out."

"I'm getting out. Bug's in my way."

Mom narrows her eyes.

"Fine, I'm going." I give Bug one last good push and walk the whole three feet to my cubbyholes.

"And pick up those shoes on the floor. Your sister tripped on them," Mom yells from her room.

I toss my cute brown wedge sandals back into the closet. A few other shoes roll out, so I really shove them in there good. Then I run my fingers over my shimmery audition top, just to make sure it's still there. I close my eyes for a second and imagine myself onstage with Jack at *Dueling Duets*, mesmerizing everyone with my voice.

Up in my bunk, I have to push a mess of books and blankets out of the way to lie down. I stare up at Miranda's face and wonder if she ever had to live all squished up with her parents and little sister. Or ever had to stuff all her shoes into a pint-sized closet. Or had to sew up a decapitated deer canvas.

Probably not.

Bug tromps through five minutes later. I yank my little curtain shut. Seriously, there is *no* privacy in this thing. Even with the curtain closed, I can hear Mom and Dad going on and on in their room. I close my eyes and belt out the first few lines to one of Taylor's older country songs, "Fifteen." It's not exactly the same as standing in my room in front of the mirror, but it will have to do. I sing straight up to Miranda, Carrie, and Taylor herself.

"Maya!" Mom's voice echoes from all of ten feet away. "Shush. We're trying to get some sleep."

Right. This isn't my bedroom. At this rate, I'm going to be completely out of practice by the time I get back home. I settle for plugging in my earbuds and listening to Taylor instead.

I don't know when I finally fall asleep, but I wake up with a jolt sometime in the middle of the night. The tiny overhead light is still on, and my earbuds are in even though my music's gone silent.

I squint at my phone. 1:57 a.m. Plus there's a text from Kenzie.

Sry. Had to clean house with Mom.

I click my phone off, pull out the earbuds, and strain my ears to figure out what woke me up.

It doesn't take long.

Ow–ow–ow–owwwwwwwooooo!

"Holy potatoes, what is that?" It sounds like something out of the Halloween haunted house Kenzie dragged me through last fall. I scramble to get out of the bunk, shoving aside stuff I moved when I got into bed a few hours ago. Books crash to the floor as I make for the ladder. Poor Hugo just grunts and resettles himself onto some blankets in the corner.

"Maya?" Dad's sleepy voice calls from their room.

"Dad, did you hear that?" I slip on a blanket and grab the doorframe for balance as I head for the back of the RV.

Ow-ow-ow-owwwwwwwoooo!

"What . . . what's going on?" Mom's voice.

I shove open the door to their room and climb onto their bed the way I did when I was five and scared to death of thunderstorms.

Dad chuckles. "Just a coyote."

"Oh." Mom rolls over and pulls the covers over her head.

"A coyote?" My voice goes squeaky. "Like the one that chases the roadrunner and tries to eat him?"

Dad laughs even harder. He leans forward and pats my knee. "Go back to bed, Maya Mae. Coyotes don't eat people. Just think of it as the song of the wild."

"The song of the . . . yeah." Dad likes to think he knows a lot about everything. But he doesn't always. So I don't really trust him knowing about coyotes.

"I don't like it either," Mom says from under the covers. "But remember that it's outside and we're in here—safe."

That makes me feel a little better. I head back to my bunk.

Ow-ow-ow-owwwwwooooo!

Why does it have to keep singing? Why doesn't it go to sleep like a normal animal? I clutch my arms to my chest as I stand between my cubbyholes. What would Kenzie do? She'd freak out. Kenzie's not so great with the whole camping thing.

Ow-ow-owwwwoooo!

Think, Maya, think.

I reach into one of the mini-closets and find the tiny Louisville Slugger keepsake bat I got last time we visited Grandma and Grandpa. I climb back into bed, keeping the bat in my hands.

You never know when you'll need to conk a coyote on the head.

T minus 18 days. I can't really think of anything new to add to OMGH, and Kenzie hasn't been a whole lot of help. I mean, her suggestions are things like *Develop New Rare Disease That Can Only Be Treated in Nashville* and *Tell Parents Hugo Spoke and Demands to Return Home.*

Kenzie's a little overdramatic sometimes. Which is why

I've always told her she could produce all my future concert tours. But I wish I could think of *something* so I could text Jack with a real plan.

So after an exciting day at the Texas Department of Motor Vehicles and a whole bunch of other boring offices, where Bug and I play nine thousand games of hangman and I read practically an entire book and eventually go outside to serenade the parking lot (who knew that people waiting at the Weslerville, Texas, DMV don't really like hearing half a duet?), we head back to the campground. Mom immediately dives into her laptop to deal with work stuff, while Dad spreads a map out on the picnic table.

"So, what do you girls want to see?" he asks, highlighter poised over the map.

"What do you mean?" I ask as I flip through my favorite book ever. It's called *Everything Y'all Ever Wanted to Know About Country Music—And Then Some*. It literally has every single fact and important person in it. I've studied this book way more than I ever looked at my science book last year. Also, it weighs about nine hundred pounds and would be an excellent weapon against attack coyotes. And it's really good for inspiration, which I could use right now since I still haven't figured out how to get home.

"If you could go anywhere in the whole country, where would you go? Minus Hawaii because we don't have a boat." Dad must think this is hilarious because he starts laughing.

Bug's eyes light up. "Yellowstone. Because of all the animals. We could see a bear!"

I eye my tiny bat, which is lying next to me—just in case. And my book. I'd need something much bigger for a bear.

Dad marks Yellowstone on the map. "Good choice, Bugby. How about you, Maya Mae?"

"Home," I say without looking up from a picture of Patsy Cline, who is practically country music royalty. "To see Kenzie. And try out for *Dueling Duets*." With Jack, but I don't say that out loud.

Dad touches my arm. "Besides home."

"I don't know. Where's the world's biggest ball of string? How about that?"

Bug giggles and grabs Dad's phone. "I'll look it up." In about three seconds, she announces, "The biggest ball of twine is in Cawker City, Kansas."

And Dad actually marks it on the map.

Wow. Great. Whoever heard of Cawker City, Kansas? I should've picked Hollywood. Then I could've sent pictures to Kenzie to show to Lacey, who thinks she's all that because she sings in her dad's furniture store commercials. Maybe that giant ball of twine will come loose and roll right over Bertha. Then we could go home.

"Your mother requested mountains. How about Grand Teton National Park? It's right next to Yellowstone. Two birds with one stone." Dad makes another mark on the map while Bug leans forward to watch.

I flip more pages until I get to Faith Hill, who has an amazing voice and equally amazing hair. And I imagine how much more I'd love Bertha if she was smashed flat from a giant boulder of twine.

"Where do you want to go, Dad?" Bug asks.

"When I was a kid, I loved watching old Westerns with my father . . . ," Dad begins.

I tune him out and wonder what Kenzie's doing right now. While I was crammed into a room with half the state of Texas at the DMV, we texted up until her phone died at the pool.

I close my book and text her now, hoping she's home and her phone is charged.

M! Bad news! she texts back.

??? I type. And wait really impatiently for the response.

Ugh, don't want to tell you.

Tell me! What's wrong? I text back.

At pool today, saw Lacey & she . . .

WHAT????

Kenzie's text comes a minute later. She had a box of Twizzlers & gave 1 to Jack. & then their hands touched for like 5 whole secs. :(

My heart drops. This *cannot* be happening. And now I'm not there and—oh my God!—Lacey *knows* I'm not around and now she's giving him Twizzlers! I knew she was up to something.

The worst part of all of this: Lacey can sing. And if she knows I might not be there for the auditions, she'll snag Jack as her own partner so fast his head will spin.

So this Twizzler thing? Not good.

You should be here, Kenzie writes.

She's right. If I was there, maybe *I* could've been talking to Jack and he wouldn't have ever noticed Lacey and her stupid Twizzlers.

"Maya Mae?" Dad says.

"What?"

He pulls my phone away.

"Dad! This is important! It's about *Dueling Duets*." And about how Lacey is trying to June Carter my Johnny

Cash. I reach for my phone, but he puts it in his pocket.

"No, *this* is important." He taps the map with his high-lighter. "Don't you want to know where we're headed next?"

"Not really," I grumble as I rest my chin on my hands. What I want to know is whether Lacey and Jack were also gazing into each other's eyes as they brushed hands. Or whether they said anything after the Twizzler exchange.

"I wish you'd pay attention," Dad says. He looks kind of . . . sad. Like me not being into this is personally hurting him. Then it's gone, and he smiles and rambles on. "We're going to see the big ball of twine in Kansas, and then on to Cody, Wyoming, where they have real live gunfights—"

"If they're real live gunfights, wouldn't there be dead people all over the place?" I feel like picking a fight, Dad's sad-face look or not.

But he just laughs, like normal Dad. "Okay, replica gun-fights. Then on to Yellowstone and Grand Teton. And from there, who knows? Wherever the road takes us. No dead-lines, no limits." With that, he pops my phone back onto the table, rolls up the map, and heads into the RV. Bug trails after him, going on and on about bison and snakes and something called a yellow-bellied marmot. I smile a tiny bit. As much as I hate it, this whole living-in-an-RV thing is a dream come true for Bug. I don't think I've ever seen her this excited all the time.

I grab my phone and demand more details from Kenzie. But she doesn't have much else to share, except that Jack said, "Thanks," and then Lacey said, "You're welcome."

You have to spy for me, I text her.

Am so on it, she writes back.

I click off my phone and set it on my book. I feel so . . . helpless. Like, what can I do from here? Lacey could be hanging out—no, *singing*—with Jack right this second and stealing my spot as his partner, and there's nothing I could do to stop it.

She's got this light, soft yet strong voice, and she can do pretty much anything from country to Broadway to . . . I don't know. Everything, probably. Not to mention that she's practically perfect. She barely even has to study for tests, her parents have more money than mine could ever dream of, and she always knows what to say. I'm pretty sure she wouldn't have just stood there the way I did when Jack complimented me on my talent show performance. Not to mention that she has hair that doesn't instantly frizz out into a puffy cloud at the slightest hint of humidity (which in Nashville is all the time). This means that 1) I need to practice more and 2) I *have* to get home. Before Jack forgets all about me.

I could text him. I bring up his number and stare at it for a moment. Except I don't know what to say. He'll want to know when I'm coming home, and I don't have an answer for that—yet.

That's it, List Item One from OMGH is going into action tonight. I stuff the phone into my pocket and stand.

"What's that book?" Shiver's next to the table, one earbud in, one out.

"Nothing." I hold the book close to me so she can't read the title. I don't know why, really. Maybe because I'm pretty sure she'd call me a hick for liking country. Or maybe I just don't want to share my most important dream with someone like Shiver.

"Whatever." Shiver stuffs the dangling earbud back into her ear and parks herself at the picnic table.

I'm about to demand to know what's she's doing here when Gert arrives bearing something covered in aluminum foil.

"Good evening, Maya," she says. "I've brought falafel for dinner."

"Fa-what-el?" I wish I could take it back the second I say it. It sounds really rude. Plus, Shiver rolls her eyes so high, I'm sure they'll get stuck somewhere in her forehead.

Gert's laugh is like bells. "Falafel. It's tasty, I promise. I'm going to bring this to your mother." She moves toward the RV, and I follow her with my book and my bat, leaving Shiver camped out at the picnic table by herself.

Which is what she probably prefers.

"Hi there, Gert!" Dad waves as he sets up the grill outside the RV. "Ready for some ribs and corn on the cob?"

Gert laughs again, and Mom emerges from the RV.

"I didn't know they were coming for dinner," I whisper as I grab the door.

"We invited them this morning," Mom says. "Put your stuff away and entertain Shiver."

"Ha." I carefully slide the book onto my bunk, where the TTT can keep an eye on it. I wonder if Taylor Swift ever has to deal with girls like Shiver. She probably has people who do that for her. Anyhow, I don't think there's any way I can "entertain" Shiver. Unless I shaved my head or started bowing down to the freaky-eyed deer on the spare tire cover.

Which is where I find Shiver when I go back outside. At the spare tire, that is.

"Awesome." She points with an earbud at my hack sewing job. The buck's neck is crisscrossed with hot pink thread in a U shape. "It's like Frankendeer."

Well, maybe entertaining Shiver isn't that hard after all.

"Who's Gloria?" she asks.

"Um, the RV. Dad's idea." I shove my hands into the pockets of my favorite shorts and glare at the deer.

"Weird."

Then I guess she's bored with looking at the Franken-deer, because she abruptly turns and heads back to the yard area where Dad's got his embarrassing *Professional BBQer at Work* apron on. Mom got him that thing when he was obsessed with grilling and entered all these barbeque competitions. At one point, there was so much smoked pork in our freezer, it looked like the meat department at Kroger.

Shiver walks right up to the grill and watches Dad. "That's disgusting. I'm a vegetarian."

Dad blinks at her. Then he puts on his Dad smile and says, "That's fine. There's corn and salad, too."

"But you're grilling the corn where the meat's been," Shiver says.

"I . . . am." Dad nudges an ear of corn with his tongs and it bumps right into the ribs.

"Gross."

"Shiver, honey, manners," Gert says from over by the picnic table where she's helping Mom lay out plates and cups.

Shiver rolls her eyes.

Bug looks at me from where she's sitting at the picnic table. I know exactly what she's thinking. Mom would murder us if we rolled our eyes as much as Shiver gets away with. And we'd never in a million years get away with rolling our eyes at someone else's parents.

Shiver plops down in the dirt next to Bertha and plugs in her earbuds. The setting sun glints off something on her nose.

Is that a nose ring? I act like I'm going back into the RV to get a closer look. Sure enough, the world's tiniest diamond twinkles from the side of her nose. How did I miss that before?

And how in the world did she convince her mother to let her get her nose pierced? Mom let me get my ears pierced only last year. Her head would explode if I even mentioned getting a hole through my nostril.

"What are you looking at?" Shiver growls.

"Nothing."

Dad saves me by announcing the food is ready. Bug and I load up with ribs and corn and salad. I even put one of Gert's falafel thingies on my plate to try.

Shiver reaches over my food and grabs a handful of falafel balls. She plops them onto a plate, ignores the rest of the food, and then sits at the very edge of the picnic table bench. Like I have cooties or something.

Mom and Gert talk about old times, while Dad throws in a few jokes. Bug and I eat, and I text Kenzie under the table. Mostly about how she's going to go all super-private detective on Lacey and Jack. Mom's not a big fan of texting during dinner. But tonight she's too distracted to notice.

Which is good, because it's not like Shiver's going to talk to me.

As if I care. I already have a best friend. She's just hundreds and hundreds of miles away.

Chapter 6

18 days until *Dueling Duets* auditions

I wait until Bug and Dad retreat to bed. Then I sit in my pajamas across the little booth-style table from Mom. Time to execute OMGH Number One.

"Maya, why aren't you in bed?" Mom asks without looking up from her laptop.

I fold my hands and put on my best responsible-daughter face. "I need to talk to you."

Mom moves her laptop lid down to look me in the eye. "Well, that sounds serious. Wait, this doesn't involve a boy, does it?"

"No. . . . There kind of aren't any boys here."

"I'm kidding. I know you hate the entire idea of our new life. So spill it." She reaches out and puts a hand on my arm.

I take a deep breath. "I need to go home. I get why we're doing this, because of the money and all. But I have to be in Nashville for the auditions. Jack needs me. If I'm not there, he'll find another partner. I'm sure I could stay with Kenzie's family. I've tried to do this with y'all, but I can't."

Mom gives me a sympathetic smile and sort of pats my arm.

And I know exactly what she's going to say.

"I understand where you're coming from," she says. "But it means a lot to both your dad and me that we're all in this together. Did I tell you about why we chose to do this, instead of finding some sad apartment back home?"

"Because Dad got laid off and is having a midlife crisis?"

Mom laughs. "Well, yes and no. Dad losing his job made it clear that something big had to change for us. But when we were twenty-five years old and spent a month traveling out west, we saw all these families in their RVs and thought, wouldn't that be a great life for a family? And choosing this made our situation seem more like a choice, rather than a necessity."

My mouth is hanging open. The whole time, I thought

this crazy idea was all Dad, and Mom just went along with it to make him happy or save money or something.

"I know it's really hard to understand, but when you're an adult and you feel you have no control over what's happening in your life, any actual choice you can make is so empowering."

She's wrong there. I know *exactly* what it's like to have no control over my life. That's the whole reason for OMGH.

"And that's something your dad really needs right now. A choice, and the opportunity to see a dream through."

I think of the sad look I saw on Dad's face earlier. It was more than just sad—it was almost like I'd crushed his soul by saying I didn't want to be here. And that makes me feel awful.

"I understand this is a huge adjustment," Mom says. "I can't say we'll do this forever. Or even for a year. We'll see how it goes. But we need you here to experience it with us."

There's no way Mom will change her mind, and there's no way I'm going to ask Dad. I already feel like the World's Worst Daughter just for wanting to go home. But how can I choose between my family and my dream? Like I ever even had a choice, really. I feel totally defeated.

"And I am really sorry about the tryouts. But, Maya, you

have *plenty* of time to follow that dream. Trust me, okay?" Mom says as I stand up.

"Mmm-hmm." I don't even try to argue, but those words make me more determined than ever to get home. No way am I losing *everything*. I head back to my bunk to think.

Mom said this might not even last for a year. Except I can't wait a year. My life is going on without me in Nashville. I stare at my silver shirt, which I've draped over a pile of stuffed animals at the foot of my bunk. The auditions are in eighteen— almost seventeen—days. I need to get back, pronto. Lacey's already trying to move in on Jack. Plus, what if I make it on the show and actually *win*? A recording contract equals money. And then I'll have to stay put in Nashville—for my career. Mom and Dad will have to give up this crazy "dream." We can buy a new house, and then I'll have everything and everyone I need—at home.

I scoop up Hugo from my pillow and plop him on my lap. It's settled. I have to get home. So the easy way didn't work. Mom said no, but so what? That doesn't mean I can't come up with another plan. I text Kenzie for more advice.

Fake asthma attack, she suggests.

I don't even have asthma. What if you have emergency & you need me to come help? I ask.

The little texting ding is almost instantaneous. I could fall downstairs & break both legs! & both arms. & maybe my head.

No—that sounds rly painful, I type back.

We go back and forth with ideas until Mom pokes her head through my cubbyhole curtain and demands I go to sleep. I am so over this no-privacy thing.

I snuggle up with Hugo—and my shirt—and will myself to dream up the perfect solution to get home.

Mom waves out the RV window to Gert when we drive off the next morning. "That was nice. Maybe we'll see them again. All those RV forums online talked about running into the same people all over the country."

"That's the beauty of the road," Dad says. "Who knows who we'll meet next."

"Ariana Grande," Bug says.

"That doesn't make any sense," I tell her as I flip through *Everything Y'all Ever Wanted to Know*. "Why would Ariana Grande be at a campground in the middle of nowhere?"

"Maybe she wants to go camping," Bug says. "We could hike and swim and sing camp songs together."

"Right."

We drive and drive and drive. I stare at my OMGH list, wishing any new inspiration to whack me in the head. Bug's scratching away at a notebook.

"What are you writing?" I peer over her shoulder but I can't read her cramped handwriting.

"A list of observations to share with the science club and my Girl Scout troop over Skype." Bug chews on her pencil.

I don't know what she's observing way out here. Number of farms: 1,000,000. Number of cows on farms: 1,000,000,000,000. Number of best friends and cute audition partners and *Dueling Duets* judges: 0.

Mom points ahead at a river. "We're almost in Oklahoma."

"Oklahoma is OK by me," Dad, the Captain of Randomness, says. "Now, where's that sign? We have to stop and take a picture."

Oklahoma turns into Kansas the next day, not that it looks any different. I'm down to T minus 16 days and still haven't come up with any new ideas.

Just spent 2 whole hrs looking at World's Biggest Ball of Twine, I text to Kenzie the day after (a.k.a. T minus 15 days).

Fun? she writes back.

Ha. Ha ha ha ha.

"Home, home on the range . . . ," Dad sings as we fly

down the narrow two-lane road out of Cawker City, home of the World's Largest Ball of Twine, and across flat Kansas.

I tune him out and concentrate on texting Kenzie.

Twizzlers? It's become our code word for *Anything new on the Jack and Lacey front?*

I don't want to tell you, she replies.

I can't stop the sigh that escapes my throat. Mom turns around. "Oh, it's nothing," I tell her. "Just my dreams disappearing into a black hole, that's all. No big deal."

"Maya," Mom says in low voice. Right. No sympathy from her. I go back to my phone.

Are you kidding? TELL ME.

L maybe sort of told J he could be in a furniture store commercial.

No. Seriously? That girl has no shame, at all. And?

He was kinda excited about it. He's gonna sing the store's new jingle. Lacey wrote it.

How can I compete with that? My dad's idea of a "career" is careening around the country in stupid Gloria. Meanwhile, Lacey's hooked the only guy I've ever liked by offering him local fame in her dad's commercial.

You ok? Kenzie texts.

Not really. Any new ideas?

No. We'll think of something.

I sigh again. Really loudly. Mom doesn't turn around this time. Still hoping wheels fall off Bertha.

I look out the window as I wait for Kenzie's reply and try not to think of Jack and Lacey practicing the furniture store jingle together. And Jack asking Lacey to audition with him for *Dueling Duets*. And Lacey singing my part in "Highway Don't Care." Instead, I stare at the landscape outside the window. Kansas is flat, flat, flat. Way off in the distance, one of those tall, round grain silos pokes its head into the sky. Each town seems to have one. Without it, you'd never know there was a town buried in all this tall grass.

Before I can even stop myself, I pull up Jack's number and type, Have you ever been to Kansas? I press send.

Oh. My. God. I can't believe I sent him something that dumb. And now he's not texting back because he's probably like, *Why in the world did Maya ask me about Kansas?* And also probably because he's too busy practicing Lacey's song.

"Ooh, windmills!" Bug points out the window across from us.

I lean forward to see a million windmills guarding a field far ahead. They don't look anything like the windmills I've seen in pictures. Instead of the quaint, fat wooden paddles, these things are tall, thin, and white and have three skinny blades that look like airplane propellers.

I check my phone. No signal. Which means no possible texts from Jack or Kenzie.

All I have to do is find a way home, and I know Kenzie would let me stay with her. But how can I get there? And before auditions?

POP!

"Hold on, girls!" Mom yells from up front.

Chapter 7

15 days until *Dueling Duets* auditions

The RV jerks one way, then the other. My phone flies out of my hand and skitters across the floor as I bump sideways against Bug. Hugo leaps from his spot next to me and cowers under the kitchen table. Magazines and postcards slide off the counters onto the floor. And then I hear the unmistakable thumps of my entire book collection falling like an avalanche off the bunks and onto the floor.

"Watch out!" Mom shouts.

The road moves back and forth on the other side of the windshield, making me dizzy, as Dad spins the wheel.

"Tire," Dad grunts as he manages to slow the RV down. "Think we blew one."

Did my wish come true? Did the tires actually fall off? If we don't die, this will be perfect!

Bertha finally comes to a stop on the side of the road. Dad jumps up and flies out the door.

"Girls, you okay?" Mom twists from the passenger seat to see us.

I nod. Bug sits, unmoving, next to me.

"I'm going to help your dad," Mom says.

When I finally unbuckle my seat belt, I realize my hands are shaking. "Come on, let's go outside," I say to Bug.

She blinks at me but doesn't move. I click her seat belt and grab her arm to pull her up.

"What happened?" she says as I help her to the door.

"Don't know. I think the wheels fell off. Are you all right?"

She nods as we walk down the stairs. My legs feel like jelly, the way they did when Jack told me I sang better than Miranda Lambert.

We thread through knee-high grass to where Dad is kneeling on the ground, checking out the remains of one of the tires. The thing looks like some maniac took a knife to it, slashing the rubber to pieces. So it's not exactly like Bertha tossed her wheels all over the highway, but still. That tire looks really bad.

Bug and I watch as Dad wrestles with the spare. Mom keeps encouraging him and trying to hand him tools. The freaky-eyed doe and the Frankendeer glare at us from where they lie tossed in the dirt.

As minutes turn into an hour, and an hour turns into three, I begin to wonder if Dad will ever get the spare on. A whole two cars have driven by, and I swear there are buzzards circling over our heads, just waiting for us to croak out here in the middle of nowhere.

"What if Dad can't get the tire on? Will Mom call a tow truck?" Bug asks.

"How? There's no cell signal." I show her my phone. "Zero bars out here in the wilderness."

"Then what will we do?"

"I guess we'll flag down the next car that drives by." I pluck a piece of long grass from behind us and use the end of it to write my name (linked with Jack's) in the dusty dirt.

"What if no one stops? Maybe no one else will ever come by. Maybe we can live here! Set up tents in the grass and live off dead snakes." Bug actually smiles at the idea.

I try not to gag. "Someone will come. Eventually." But other ideas play across my mind now. Good ones, too, not dead-snake ones. What if the nearest garage doesn't have a tire to fit our RV? What if it's too expensive to get a new one put on? What if something's wrong with the whole wheel and it will take months to get fixed?

OMGH Item Number Two is totally working. I won't even have to come up with any more crazy ideas to get myself to Nashville if Bertha is dead in the water—or dead on the asphalt, I suppose.

I start singing—and picture myself arriving at Lacey's dad's furniture store, with Kenzie in tow, just in time to prevent another hand-holding session between Lacey and Jack. A loud tractor trailer rolls by us and then stops.

A scrawny man with a green baseball cap leans out the driver's door and calls, "Y'all need help?"

I leap up and race past Dad to get there first. "Nope! We're all good here." I jerk my thumb toward Dad, who's making his way to the truck. "My dad's an expert mechanic. He'll have the tire on in no time. He's—"

"Thank you for your faith in me, Maya Mae, but I think I could use a little help." Dad places his hands on my shoulders and talks to the truck driver about the tire.

I slink out from under his grasp. Why didn't I talk faster? I could've gotten rid of that guy, and eventually Mom and Dad would've given up on the tire, and then we all could've gone home.

I flop down into the dusty grass next to Bug. Mission so not accomplished.

"He called in on his CB radio," Dad says after the trucker leaves. "He told them exactly what kind of tire we need, and a tow truck will bring it by soon."

And not more than a half hour later, a truck with flashing yellow lights arrives, dashing my dreams of a dramatic furniture-store reunion with Jack—and pretty much everything else I want right now. The tow truck guy gets the tire on the RV in less than fifteen minutes, and we're on our way again.

I guess tires don't cost all that much after all.

It's time to get serious. I bring up the notes app on my phone and put my brain to work on coming up with real ideas to get home.

Operation Maya Goes Home (OMGH)

(In time for Dueling Duets.)

Countdown: T minus 15 days

How to Get Home to Audition with Jack and Win

♪ 85 ♪

His Heart with My Voice and Stellar Personality:

1. ~~Convince Mom and Dad this is the worst idea ever.~~

2. ~~Bertha needs major repairs~~ (tires don't count, I guess).

3. K fakes lots of broken bones & needs me to
   spoon her soup.

4. Walk. Phone mapping app says this will take only
   253 hours. Which is like 10½ days if I don't sleep,
   eat, go to the bathroom, or stop at all.

5. ?

"Wow, look!" Bug's got her nose squashed up against the window later that day. "Mountains!"

In the distance, blue hazy lumps rise out of the earth. We stopped and took the stupid sign photo when we entered Colorado hours ago. So far, Colorado has looked exactly like Kansas—flat with lots of grass.

Until now. And even though I'd never in a million years admit this to Mom or Dad, I'm a little excited. I've never seen real mountains before—I mean, the Smokies and the Ozarks don't really count. Something about these extra-large mountains seems so romantic.

As close as the mountains appear, it takes another hour or so before we can really see them. They loom over the buildings that seem to have come out of nowhere. I peer out the window to get a better look and try to think of songs about the mountains. My phone buzzes, and I peek down.

It's Jack.

Jack!

No. What are you doing in Kansas?

Holy potatoes. He texted me back! Except now I have *no* idea what to say.

As we drive past houses and shopping malls and as I try to come up with something interesting to say to Jack, I spot a person standing on the side of the highway, with . . . something. I squint, and as we get closer, I realize it's a man wearing a huge backpack and holding a cardboard sign. The sign reads, DENVER. The guy's got it in his left hand, and he's sticking his thumb up with his right hand. A hitchhiker.

"I didn't know people really hitchhiked," I say. "Isn't it dangerous—like serial-killer dangerous?"

"Very dangerous," Mom says.

"Not really," Dad says at the same time.

Mom glares at him.

"What?" Dad says. "Don't you remember that time the truck broke down and we—"

Mom makes a slicing motion at her throat.

But it's too late, because I figured out what Dad was trying to say.

"They hitchhiked," I say to Bug.

Her eyes get round, and she starts asking them a million questions. Dad goes on and on about the nice old man who picked them up somewhere in Alabama and got them home to Nashville. Mom is heaving big sighs, like she wishes she could shut him up already.

But I'm thinking about something else entirely.

I have a real idea to get myself home.

Chapter 8

15 days until *Dueling Duets* auditions

Okay, so I can't exactly stick my thumb out for a ride at a rest stop somewhere while Mom and Dad are waiting for me in Bertha. I have to wait for the right moment.

That doesn't stop me from texting both Jack and Kenzie. **Might have a way home soon.**

I just have to figure out the when and the where. Now that I sort of have a plan, I can lean back and enjoy gazing at the mountains as we lumber through Denver and head up the highway.

When we pull into a wooded campsite, Bug and I

practically fly out of the RV, eager to get out of the cramped space. The first thing I hear is a rushing stream.

Bug points toward the woods. "There."

We run through the trees, leaping over rocks and fallen limbs, until we're standing at the edge of a two-foot drop-off.

The stream is more like a raging river. The water rushes by, pouring over boulders, carrying branches and leaves in such a hurry you'd think it was late to something.

"It's the spring melt," Dad says from behind us. "The snow up in the mountains is finally melting, and all that water is flowing down into the rivers and creeks."

"It's June," I tell him. "How can there still be snow?"

"It's colder here," Bug says, as if she knows everything. Which she probably does—at least about nature-y stuff.

Dad nods. "Summer comes late to the mountains. While it's ninety degrees at home right now, it's only seventy here, and it'll drop into the forties or fifties tonight."

I shiver, suddenly thankful (just a tiny little bit) for Bertha the Beast and the pile of blankets on my bunk. Another good reason to go home: It's not freezing at night in June.

"Come on back up," Dad says. "We're going to make Bunyan Burgers on the fire tonight!"

I have a hard time getting overly excited about hamburgers

in aluminum foil, but I follow him back to the campsite. After dinner, it starts to get dark, so I crawl into my bunk between the piles of books and blankets. I send Kenzie a text.

Gonna hitchhike home. Need to lose Mom & Dad. Ideas?

While I wait for her answer, I sing scales to the TTT and try to smooth the wrinkles out of my audition shirt. Mom and Dad are in their room. Dad keeps apologizing for almost starting a forest fire with our campfire tonight. My phone buzzes.

M—don't think you should do that, Kenzie's written.

Annoyance flickers through me. **Why not? Only way to get home. Mom & Dad hitched once.**

I'd worry about you. What if scary person picked you up?

Duh. Won't ride with scary person.

Pls don't do it. We'll think of a diff plan.

I don't text her back. Instead, I warm up my voice some more while contemplating how seamlessly Taylor made the switch from country to pop. But I can only think about that for so long before Kenzie's words start flitting through my brain again. I finally have the perfect way to get home, and it's like my best friend doesn't even want me to come back.

My phone buzzes again.

You be here by Thurs? L says we can use the studio again.

In two seconds flat, I go from excited to hear from Jack to completely weirded out by the fact that he called Lacey "L." But maybe that doesn't mean anything. After all, he still wants to audition with *me*. I hurry up and write back, **Hope so!**

Then I sit up and launch full-out into "Highway Don't Care" so I don't sound too awful once I get back. But what Kenzie said is still bothering me. She's just nervous about me trying to hitchhike home, that's all. But when I get there, she'll be so happy she won't care how I arrived. And Jack will be so thrilled to have his partner back that he'll forget all about Lacey. I project my voice even more as I think about stunning the *Dueling Duets* judges and winning the whole contest. Mom and Dad won't be angry about me leaving once that happens. I hope.

"Maya!" Mom calls. "Enough, please."

I finish the last part of the song before sliding under the covers. I close my eyes and drift off to dreams of singing for millions, and none of them ever ask me to stop.

It's pitch black when I wake up to pounding on the door. I reach over to flip on my light and blink in the sudden brightness. I'm still in my jeans and sweatshirt (which is good because it's completely freezing in the RV), and Hugo is zonked out on my chest. I heft him onto the nearest stack of books and blankets.

Dad trudges through my cubbyholes as I'm climbing down the ladder. Bleary-eyed, he stumbles over some blankets that fell off my bunk and mutters a few curse words.

After tossing the blankets out of the way, I follow him to the front. Bug's curtain is closed. Bertha could roll off a cliff and she'd still be asleep.

Dad pushes the door open and shields his eyes from the flashlight shining in his face. Cold air gusts into the RV. I cross my arms for warmth and peer around Dad to see a tall man in a brown ranger-looking uniform.

"Your fire is still going. You need to put out all the embers before turning in," the man says as if it isn't one o'clock in the morning. "That's how forest fires happen."

I guess no one told him about the ginormous bonfire Dad started earlier.

"Sorry about that," Dad says in his garbled middle-of-the-night voice. "I'll take care of it."

The ranger disappears into the darkness, his flashlight swinging an arc of light back and forth as he walks. Dad shuffles to the bedroom, probably to find a sweatshirt, or maybe a winter coat. I start to shut the door, when the ranger's flashlight catches a glimpse of bright yellow across the way.

I squint. No, it can't be. Closing the door behind me, I step down onto the dirt in the dark. I jog past the picnic table and the glowing embers in our fire pit to the thin line of trees separating our campsite from the next one.

Sure enough, a bright yellow RV with a faded sunshine smiley face on the side sits parked in the site next to ours. Gert. And Shiver.

"This is beautiful," Dad says in the morning when he steps out of Bertha.

I take a deep breath. The air smells way cleaner than home. The mountains are gorgeous in the twinkling sunlight, and the river rushes from behind the trees.

But it's not enough to make me forget my life in Nashville.

"Why don't we stay an extra day?" Mom's standing in the open door, nibbling on her last bit of bagel. "I need to hit the grocery, and I'm sure the girls would enjoy exploring. And maybe we could have dinner again with Gert and her granddaughter."

Dad claps his hands together. "A hike! Who's up for a hike?"

"Me!" Bug leaps through the door, past Mom, and lands

on all fours on the ground. I swear I never did stuff like that when I was nine.

"Maya Mae?" Dad looks at me.

I kick at a piece of the fuzzy-looking sagebrush that's everywhere out here. If Mom's going to the grocery, and Dad and Bug go on a hike, that leaves me alone.

I can put my plan into action.

So I put a hand on my stomach and make a sour face. "I don't feel good. I think I'm going to lie back down."

Mom brushes bagel crumbs off her fingers and lays the back of her hand to my forehead. "You don't feel hot."

"It's my stomach. I don't think my burger was done last night."

"Go lie down. I'll be back in a couple of hours to check on you. Call if you start to feel worse."

I make my way—as pitifully as possible—to my bunk. Lying on my side with a hardcover book digging into my spine, I close my eyes and pretend to go to sleep.

When I no longer hear the truck motor or gravel-crunching sounds, I creep down from my bunk. I stuff clothes and some essential things—to ensure I don't smell, because that's not exactly the impression I want to make on Jack when I see him again—into my backpack, plus my phone charger and earbuds, some mascara, a couple of paper-backs, and my audition shirt. I pop my sparkly purple cowboy hat onto my head. I pick up *Everything Y'all Ever Wanted to Know* and then put it back down. It's way too heavy, and Mom and Dad can ship me everything else once I get home.

In the bathroom, I rake a brush through my hair and do my Heidi braids before putting the hat back on. Kenzie would tell me just to wear a ponytail already. I can't wait to hear her say that in person.

I scribble a note to Mom and Dad so they don't call the police or anything. Although I guess they will anyway, but hopefully I'll be on my way to Nashville by then. I put the note on my bed.

We don't have any cardboard, so I grab a piece of notebook paper to make my sign. Using a black marker, I write *NASHVILLE* as best I can with my shaking fingers. Well, actually it looks more like *NASHVille* because I run out of space. But whatever. As long as people can read it. I slide it into my backpack.

My phone buzzes just as I'm about to put it in my pocket. It's Kenzie. M!!! You're making me worry. Tell me you're not hitching. Ugh, she's making me even more nervous. I decide to text her back once I'm on my way.

I head to the door and don't look at Bug's bunk when I pass it. I know she'll be super disappointed that I'm not here anymore, and that makes my stomach feel all twisty. I can't even think about how Mom and Dad will react. I tried to explain it to Mom—more than once—but she just didn't get it. I'll just have to win *Dueling Duets*, and then we can all be together again.

Outside, with my backpack on and my phone in my pocket, I glance through the trees to the yellow RV. No one in sight. Thankfully.

"See ya, Bertha. Wouldn't want to be ya," I whisper to the Frankendeer and the freaky-eyed doe. I walk quietly past Gert's RV and up the hill to the campground entrance. I look up and down the little road at the entrance. Not a soul. I turn left toward the main road.

The mountains loom in front of me, all green and blue and still snow-capped. It feels like I'm the only person in the world. I almost expect a bird to land on my arm, like in a Disney movie or something. I could live here when I'm grown up and famous, but not now.

A song tickles my mind and I start singing one of Dad's old favorites, "Country Roads" by John Denver. No one's in sight. It's just me and the trees and the mountains. And I'm going home.

When I finally reach the main road, I drop my backpack and stand near the stop sign. There's a convenience store behind me, and I'm tempted to go in and get a drink. But I only have maybe an hour before Mom comes back. I hold up my *NASHVille* sign and stick out my thumb. And try to ignore the kind of sick feeling in my stomach.

Cars pass. Semis pass. An older lady in a truck slows down, stares at me, then rolls down her window. I smile and pick up my backpack. I can't believe this actually worked!

"Honey, where are your parents?" she asks.

"Um . . . not here." I didn't expect anyone to ask that question, but it seems kind of obvious now. "My dad got sick and they flew him to a hospital in Nashville. Mom had to go with him. So I'm trying to get there too."

That is the worst lie ever.

The lady squints at me from behind blue-rimmed glasses. "Why don't you call the police? They'll find you a safe way home."

"I . . . uh . . ." Think, Maya, think.

"Here, I'll pull over and call for you." She starts to roll up the window.

"No, wait! It's okay. That's a good idea. I'll go in the store and call them." I wave at her and start toward the store, praying she'll drive off. Just as I reach the door, she finally leaves.

Whew. That was a close one. I go back to my spot by the stop sign. And wait and wait and wait.

I check my phone. I've been standing here fifteen minutes already. I didn't think it would take this long.

I stick my thumb out again and pull my sweatshirt sleeve over my other chilly fingers.

"Are you crazy?"

Holy potatoes! I whip around so fast I almost drop my sign.

Shiver's behind me, one earbud in and a giant black bag hanging from her shoulder. The sunlight glints off her blue hair, making the light brown underneath stand out.

"Leave me alone." I turn back to the road.

"I didn't realize you were this stupid. Where are you trying to go, anyway?"

"Home. Why do you care?"

Shiver comes to stand next to me. "I don't, not really. Except that I don't want you to get kidnapped."

"I'm not going to get kidnapped. Hitchhiking isn't as dangerous as everyone thinks. My parents did it when they were young."

"And that was the 1950s or something. You know, poodle skirts and 'oh gosh golly gee whiz.'"

I ignore her.

"What kind of hat is that? Are you auditioning for clown college? Because someone went a little crazy with the bedazzler there."

I ignore her. Again.

"What's so great about home?" she asks.

"You like riding around in that ugly yellow RV?" I counter as I squint down the road for possible rides.

Shiver shrugs. "It's not so bad. Look, if you don't come back with me, I'm going to find your parents and tell them what you're doing."

I stare at her. "Why don't you leave me alone?"

"Fine. Have it your way." She starts across the parking lot.

Ugh! I'm so mad at her I could scream. Or pull that annoying blue hair. I yank out my phone. Almost noon. Mom'll be on her way back anytime now.

Stupid Shiver. She messed everything up. Who knows when I'll make another chance to catch a ride. There's no way I'll make it to Nashville before Thursday now. I don't even want to *think* about having to tell Jack it's going to be a few more days.

I hike back toward the campground. Shiver's a few steps ahead of me. I avoid looking at her and fix my eyes on the pine trees that line the sides of the road.

Shiver stops and turns around, hands on her hips. "So now you've wised up?"

"No. I ran out of time, thanks to you." I move past her and keep walking.

"You're a strange kid, you know that?" she says to my back.

I snort. "*Kid.* Like you're way older than me."

"I'm thirteen. You're, what, ten?"

I turn and glare at her. I mean, I know I'm short and have this annoying baby face, but *ten*? That's practically the same age as Bug. "I'm twelve."

"Wouldn't have guessed that. You're kind of a midget. And you wear those braids all the time."

I swivel around and walk as fast as I can. Like I'm going to explain my crazy Simba hair to Shiver. Kenzie can get away with making jokes about my braids, but that's because she's practically a sister. Shiver is anything but.

She trudges along behind me.

"What were you doing up there anyway?" I ask without turning.

"Buying candy bars. Is that a crime?"

I bite my lip to keep from being rude right back to her.

A truck slows down beside us. I'm really hoping it's not that sweet old woman again, wondering where the police are.

Mom's face sticks out the window. "Maya?"

"Hi."

Her forehead wrinkles. "What are you doing here? Why aren't you in bed?"

"Oh . . ." How many lies am I going to have to make up today? "I felt better, so Shiver and I decided to go for a walk."

Shiver gives me a sideways glance.

I send her ESP signals to please, please, please not give me away. Although she hates me, so it's probably pointless.

"Ooookay. I'm glad you feel better." Mom looks at Shiver and smiles. "Your mom and I used to go for long walks together before we could drive."

"Guess you didn't have much else to do," Shiver says.

Mom laughs. "Guess not. I have to go pick up Dad and Bug. See you girls back at camp." She drives on down the road, past the campground. Even though I'll probably get back first, I'm glad I left the note to Mom and Dad on my bed, and not somewhere they'd find it right away.

"Thanks," I say to Shiver.

She shrugs. "Whatever."

"Why'd you cover for me?"

"I don't know. Next time I won't bother, okay?" She frowns and plugs in her other earbud.

"Fine, be that way," I say, even though I know she can't hear me. I whip out my phone and text Kenzie as we walk.

I need a new plan.

Chapter 9

13 days until *Dueling Duets* auditions

The smiling yellow sunshine on Gert's RV glares at me as we drive away the next morning.

"Isn't this fun?" Mom says to Dad. "And just think, we'll probably see them again in Cody."

Dad nods enthusiastically. "Buckle up, girls. We have a long day of driving."

I stare at my phone. I texted Jack to let him know plans had changed, and he hasn't written back yet. Can texts get lost, like mail does? Maybe he never even got it. Maybe I should text him again. But what if he did? Then it would look weird if I texted him the same thing two times in a row. But if he did get it, why hasn't he texted me back yet?

Ugh. Why are boys so difficult?

Bug breaks out a new book called *Wildlife of Yellowstone*. When Mom brought it back for Bug yesterday, Bug tried to give away one of her other five books. Mom told her to keep it since I'd brought ten thousand books.

Which is a total overestimate. There are probably only a hundred stuffed into my cubbyholes. Or maybe two hundred.

So while Bug reads, I open my notes app and update OMGH.

Operation Maya Goes Home (OMGH)

(In time for Dueling Duets.)

Countdown: T minus 13 days

How to Get Home to Audition with Jack and Win

His Heart with My Voice and Stellar Personality:

1. ~~Convince Mom and Dad this is the worst idea ever.~~

2. ~~Bertha needs major repairs~~ (tires don't count, I guess).

3. ~~K fakes lots of broken bones & needs me to spoon her soup.~~ (Not believable.)

4. ~~Walk. Phone mapping app says this will take only~~

~~253 hours. Which is like 10½ days if I don't sleep,~~

~~eat, go to the bathroom, or stop at all.~~ (I don't

even like Dad's 2-mile hikes, so . . .)

5. ~~Hitchhike!~~ (Shiver. Ugh. Also, scary.)

6. ?

My phone dings. I flip it to silent and read Kenzie's text.
**So glad you didn't hitch. Brad told me about this kid from
Memphis who did & no one ever saw him again.**

So, yeah. No more hitchhiking. Although I'd never admit
to Shiver that she was right.

Maybe I can catch a train or a bus? I write back.

No bus. Scary ppl.

Seriously, are there scary people on every form of trans-
portation in this country? **How much is train, you think?**

IDK. Have $20 from allowance I can send you.

That won't work. She'd have to send it to the mail for-
warding service, and then Mom and Dad would see it and
want to know what Kenzie sent me. Not to mention that it
would take forever to get to us.

This coming-up-with-ideas thing is really hard.

About an hour later (after I pester Kenzie for more
updates on the Twizzlers situation, grill her about whether

I should text Jack again, and try to convince her to show up at the commercial's filming), we stop at the WELCOME TO WYOMING sign for the required picture. The rest of the morning drags on. I listen to music, I sing until Mom gives me a Look, I text Kenzie, Bug quotes me weird facts about buffalo and mule deer, and Mom and Dad talk about their first visit to Yellowstone a million years ago.

When I look out the window, all I see is miles and miles of . . . nothing. Waving grass, hills, rocks, a few cattle. And these funny-looking antelope-like animals with horns. Pronghorns, according to Bug and her book.

Around noon, Dad pulls Bertha over to a "natural wonder" called Hell's Half Acre. Which totally sounds like something Shiver would love.

Ugh, why am I thinking about Shiver?

"It looks completely abandoned," Mom says.

We pour out of Bertha, blinking in the sun. This is the most depressing place I've ever seen. Weeds poke up here and there in the dirt where a building used to be. A falling-down chain-link fence separates the road and parking area from . . . whatever's behind it.

And at a place called Hell's Half Acre, I don't think I want to know what's behind the fence.

So of course, Bug races up and presses her face against it. "Wow! Come look at this."

Dad joins her, and I finally decide that whatever's over there can't be too awful.

"Wow," Dad says.

It is pretty neat. Below us, through the metal diamonds of the fence, are all these rock formations. Mostly tall, pointy spires, but some blob-looking rocks, and some arches. They're striped in brown, tan, white, and red. I've never seen anything like it, but I'm not in the mood to admit I'm impressed.

While Bug tries to figure out how to get behind the fence so she can climb through the pointy rocks, I park myself on the dusty ground and rack my brain for OMGH ideas. My phone buzzes. Jack! His text reads, ok.

What does that *mean*?! Maybe it just means I need to come up with a new idea, fast. I'm still thinking as we pull into the Cody campground (Yeehaw Cowboy Times Campground—I am so not kidding) around sunset. And as I go to sleep that night. I dream about riding home on a pronghorn through a bunch of pointy striped rocks while Bug runs alongside me and quotes statistics about pronghorn attacks.

So much for helpful dreams.

* * *

The next morning, I'm sitting in a chair outside with Mom and Bug while Dad empties the waste (*eww*) from Bertha. It's early and quiet. The campground is way off on the far side of town, overlooking some mountains shrouded in white haze.

Mom's face is scrunched up into that "I'm so stressed" look. She's typing away furiously on the keyboard. It seems really unfair that she's the only one making money to pay for our groceries and gas and campsite fees. If only she'd realize that me trying out for *Dueling Duets* could be the answer to everything. Except she and Dad have zero faith in me, so I don't think that's going to happen any time soon.

Several other RVs are in the park, but no bright yellow one yet. Knowing I won't see Shiver today puts me in a good mood. Or as good a mood as possible without having another plan for OMGH.

Wait . . .

If there are other RVs, then there are other people traveling all over the country. At least one of them has to be headed toward Tennessee.

Maybe they'd give a nice girl in Heidi braids and a purple cowboy hat a ride home.

I smile as I text Kenzie, who's headed to the pool and promises to keep an eye on Jack. I decide not to let him know I'm on my way home until I'm actually on my way home this time. Now I just have to find an excuse to go around and talk to everyone until I find the right person. It would be a lot safer than hitchhiking. After all, Mom and Dad are always going on and on about how friendly other RVers are. And there's no way I'd take a ride with people whose RV is all dirty or full of weird things that scream serial killer, like decapitated doll heads or petrified rodents in jars.

Once Dad finishes the waste dump (ugh), we take off to do touristy stuff. Dad's way too enthusiastic about a bunch of old buildings lined up to resemble a fake Old West town. Bug finds some woman in a store (that sells a weird combination of saddles and paintings of wistful-looking cowboys) who talks to her for an hour about Yellowstone. I daydream about finding the perfect family to give me a ride home.

Bug's practically skipping down the sidewalk as we walk to dinner that evening. "Did you know that thousands of bison live in Yellowstone? They used to be almost extinct. Isn't that crazy?"

"Crazy," I repeat as I read Kenzie's Twizzlers report.

At pool today: Lacey was all giggly like 2 yr old. Jack kept looking at her with dopey smile.

My stomach churns.

"And there are two kinds of bears. Black bears and grizzlies. I hope we see both," Bug goes on.

"From a safe distance," Mom adds.

BTW, I found out something big, Kenzie texts.

What???? I type as I skirt around a bench on the sidewalk.

"Do we have bear spray?" Bug asks Mom and Dad. "And we need a whistle. And maybe some pots and pans to hit together. You're supposed to make a lot of noise to scare bears away while you're hiking."

"We'll get some spray," Dad says. "And whistles."

"I think we'll leave the pots and pans in the RV," Mom says.

Lacey's def trying out for DD. No partner.

My stomach is practically down to my feet right now. I kinda guessed she wouldn't let the opportunity pass her by, but hearing Kenzie confirm it is so not good.

Did she tell you?

Nope. She was telling J. Kinda hinting at the no partner thing.

Really, really, *really* not good.

Can you tell J how much I've been practicing the song? And that you know for sure I'll be home real soon.

You got it. BTW, commercial filming is tomorrow. Will tell him am planning on career in movies & make him invite me to it.

You're the best.

NO MORE TWIZZLERS!

I want to hug her through the phone. I miss her so badly it makes my throat close up just thinking about it.

"Here we are," Dad says.

I look up from my phone. We're standing in front of a large, old building. *IRMA HOTEL* is written across the top of the first story. We climb the steps of a huge covered porch and go inside.

"Is this where we're eating?" I ask.

"Yup." Dad rubs his stomach. "Chow time! Wrangle up those stomachs!"

"If he starts talking like a cowboy, I'm eating by myself," I tell Mom.

"You'll be mighty lonesome, pardner," Mom says.

"I don't know you people." I lag behind them as they keep coming up with more and more ridiculous cowboy talk. Even Bug moves off to the side and pretends to be interested in a painting on the wall.

"How many?" the hostess asks.

"Round 'em up, we got four hungry dogies," Dad says.

I want to die right next to the PLEASE WAIT TO BE SEATED sign. The hostess doesn't even bat an eye. I guess lots of people's dads come in and say stupid stuff like that.

"Look, there are Gert and Shiver." Mom points across the restaurant.

No. No, no, no, no, no. If anyone can completely mess up OMGH—again—it's Shiver.

Gert looks up and waves us over. "Join us. We can scoot that table over and make one big table."

Dad and one of the waiters push the tables together, and before I can say anything, I'm stuck eating next to Shiver.

She eyes the steak that I order. "That's a dead cow, you know. Shot up with antibiotics and hormones."

"Adalie," Gert says in a sharp voice. "That's enough."

Shiver/Adalie ignores her. "That's before they stuffed him into a dirty pen with a hundred other cows and killed them all with no concern for their humanity."

"Don't you mean 'cow-manity'?" Bug says to Shiver.

"What?" Shiver gives my sister a blank look.

"You said 'humanity.' But they're cows. So it would be 'cow-manity.'" Bug is dead serious.

Dad laughs, and Gert does too. Even Mom cracks a smile.

"It's not funny," Shiver says.

I totally agree, since I don't feel like eating steak now. Stupid Shiver. Adalie. Whatever her name is.

Gert pats Shiver's arm. "Lighten up, honey."

Shiver jerks her arm away and stuffs her earbuds in.

At least she won't talk to me if she's listening to music. What has she got on there anyway? If you nickname yourself Shiver, you're not listening to anything fun. It's probably that clangy, noisy rock that Kenzie's brother Brad listens to, with some tattooed guy shrieking about pain and destruction.

After dinner—which for me is just mashed potatoes and green beans, thanks to Shiver—Dad's all excited about the pretend gunfight outside the hotel. Chairs are lined up in front of the porch. The whole street's blocked off, and a bunch of fakey-looking wooden buildings the size of sheds are positioned here and there. I look around at all of it and wonder if Kenzie's managed to get herself invited to the furniture store filming tomorrow.

Dad makes us sit in the front row. I end up stuck next to Shiver. Great. She'll probably go off on how cowboys were mistreated or something completely ridiculous. I text Kenzie for an update.

Mom touches my arm. "Maya, it would mean a lot to your dad if you put your phone away for a while. Kenzie can wait."

It takes all my self-control not to roll my eyes, but I stuff the phone into my pocket. I slouch in my chair, cross my arms, and try to think of a good excuse to go knocking on the doors of strangers' RVs. Gert pulls Shiver's earbuds out when the show begins.

It doesn't take long for the fake gunshots to start ringing out. I glance down the row at Dad, who's grinning his face off like he's at Disney World. He looks so happy. It's kind of cute in a way. He never looked like that when he worked at the insurance company back home. It makes my heart melt just a little bit, and that Worst Daughter in the World feeling creeps back into my brain. What if I win *Dueling Duets* and get a huge record deal and we have enough money for a new house? Would Dad find another job? Will he be this happy?

I've just turned back to watch the show when there's a thunk from somewhere on the other side of me, and I feel Shiver move.

"Gran? Help!" Shiver yells.

I whip around. Shiver's huddled over something on the ground.

Gert.

I leap out of my chair as the people behind us stand and lean over to see what's going on. The fake gunshots stop, and a couple of the actors jog over to us.

Gert's lying on the ground, her eyes closed.

"Gran, Gran, Gran," Shiver says as she shakes Gert's arm.

"Someone call 911!" Dad yells as he cradles Gert's head in his arms and Mom feels for her pulse.

One of the actor-cowboys pulls a phone from his jeans pocket and punches the buttons. He starts talking, phone in one hand and gun in the other.

Shiver's rocking back and forth, still holding Gert's arm. "What's wrong with her? Why isn't she waking up?"

I grab Bug's hand and squeeze. *Please let Gert wake up. I'll take back every mean thing I've ever thought about Shiver.* Gert's just lying there, her long white hair flowing out from under Dad's arms.

"Does she have any medical problems?" Mom asks Shiver.

"I don't know." Shiver's voice rises into a wail. Tears run down her cheeks, streaking black mascara everywhere. Her earbuds dangle, grazing Gert's arm, which suddenly jerks.

"Gran?"

"Ad . . . a . . . lie?" Gert's voice is faint.

"Gert, don't move," Mom says. "An ambulance is on its way."

Gert pats Shiver's hand and closes her eyes.

In no time flat, the ambulance pulls up next to the shed-building marked SALOON. A woman in a red old-timey dress tells the EMTs what happened. They try to ask Shiver questions, but she can't answer them. I stand back with Bug, wishing there was something I could do.

"It looks like a stroke," a tall, skinny EMT says. "We need to move." They don't waste any time loading Gert onto a stretcher and into the ambulance.

"Wait, I have to go with her!" Shiver reaches up to pull herself inside.

The skinny EMT holds a hand out. "It's better if you follow," he says. "We need the space to help her."

Shiver stares after them as the ambulance peels away from the show.

"We'll drive you to the hospital, Adalie," Mom says.

Shiver wipes her face with the back of her hand, smearing mascara everywhere. "It's Shiver."

Mom gives her an awkward one-armed hug while one of the actors tells Dad how to get to the only hospital in town. We make our way to the truck as the actors try to pick up the gunfight where they left off.

I want to say something nice to Shiver, but I can't think of anything. So I stare out the window and hope Gert is okay.

Chapter 10

11 days until *Dueling Duets* auditions

We're back at the hospital to visit Gert in the morning. The doctors didn't say much last night, except that she had a stroke. Shiver refused to leave the hospital, so Mom slept on chairs in the waiting room while the rest of us went back to Bertha. Kenzie texted to let me know that Jack told her she could go to the filming. I haven't written back yet. It feels weird and selfish to be thinking about whether Jack likes Lacey right now.

Now the doctors say that Gert can't go home for several weeks. By "home," they mean her house, not her RV. She has to stay in the hospital, and then go to a nursing home for a while. And they can't tell yet if she'll be the same as she was before.

This makes Shiver cry even more. Even though she's been horrible to me, my heart hurts every time I look at her. And Gert was such a fun person, with her crazy long white hair and faded yellow RV, and now she barely even looks like herself. Half of her face seems like all the muscles stopped working.

One of Gert's eyes flutters as Mom sits in the chair next to her bed.

"Adalie," Gert says in a slurred voice.

Shiver looks up. "I'm here, Gran."

"Shelly . . . California . . . take her?"

"You want us to get Adalie to her mother's?" Mom asks.

Gert's head moves, just barely. Mom called her old friend Shelly last night to let her know what was going on. I only heard one end of the conversation, but I could tell Mom was annoyed that Shelly was going to stay put in San Francisco. If it was Grandma who'd had a stroke, Mom would've been on a plane to Louisville in no time flat—especially if Bug and I were with her in a hospital and totally traumatized by what had happened.

"I'm not going anywhere." Shiver grabs Gert's left

hand—the one the doctors said she was having trouble moving because of the stroke. "I'm staying here until you get better."

"No," Gert says. "Here . . . too long . . . home."

Mom reaches for Shiver's hand. "She doesn't want you stuck here in the hospital. She'd rather you be with your mom, and then she'll get better and come home."

Shiver lays her blue head down on her grandmother and cries some more.

"We'll take her home. I'll call Shelly again," Mom says to Gert. "Don't you worry."

A ghost of a smile flickers over half of Gert's face. Shiver holds even tighter to her. I want to be angry that Shiver's moving into our RV, but I can't. Not right now. I can't even be angry at Mom and Dad for moving *us* into Bertha right now.

"Come on," Mom says to me and Bug. "Let's give them some space."

I put a hand on Shiver's shoulder. "I'm sorry," I say, because it's all I can think of.

"Thanks," she says, so quiet I can barely hear it.

I slip out of the room behind Mom and Bug. At least Gert is okay. Or she will be okay. I just hope Shiver will be too.

We stay for two days to make sure Gert is stable. Then we all load into Bertha to head to Yellowstone. Me, Bug, and Shiver are all stuffed onto what used to be the Dirt Den Couch, because that's where the only seat belts are. I've tried to talk to Shiver about Gert, but she clams up every time. In fact, she barely even acknowledges my existence. So now I'm back to working on my own problem.

T minus 9 days. That means I absolutely, positively have to find a ride tonight, or I'm going to be cutting it really close to get back in time for auditions. Not to mention that every minute that passes means Jack might be asking Lacey to take my place.

Since Shiver's here 24/7, I haven't been able to sing anywhere except for the bathhouse at the campground (which actually has really good acoustics), or to even page through *Everything Y'all Ever Wanted to Know*, because it seems like she's always looking over my shoulder and I'm not really sure about sharing the most important thing in my life with her. I even keep my cubbyhole curtain closed so she won't see the TTT.

Back in Cody, Mom called Shelly and asked about getting Shiver on a plane home. Shelly complained about airfare money, and talked about how she'd have to wait until she got paid again. Mom told her she completely understood about financial troubles, and offered to drive Shiver to San Francisco. It's strange, really, because Shelly hasn't talked to Mom in, like, twenty years, but I could practically hear her "YES" through the phone. I mean, what if her former best friend is now a kidnapper or something?

Then, to make the whole thing even weirder, Shelly told Mom that she didn't want to mess up our plans, so we should take our time getting Shiver home. Mom kind of frowned at the phone, and said, "Okay," as if she wasn't really sure it was okay.

So we're going to spend a week or so in Yellowstone and Grand Teton on our way to California. Shiver seems more than okay with hanging out in some national parks with us before getting back to San Francisco. Maybe she's just so concerned about Gert that she's not really thinking straight. Because who in their right mind would want to spend more time in Bertha than they had to?

Since all the beds are taken, she's sleeping on the couch. Which she complains is hard and lumpy and doesn't give her any room to turn over or have any privacy. Like anyone has privacy in Bertha.

"There's a whole free bed," she said this morning when she walked through my cubbyholes to the bathroom. "Full of junk. And I get the couch."

I pulled the covers over my head and propped my feet on a stack of books. And texted Kenzie, who's been really sympathetic. She told me that Jack asked again about when I'll be back. Which just made it feel like ants were crawling in my belly, because I haven't had a chance to look for a ride since everything happened with Gert.

Now that we're officially in Yellowstone, Bug's nose is permanently glued to the window as she searches for animals.

"Maya, you should look out the other side," she says.

I don't really feel like peering past every tree for a critter, but anything's better than watching Shiver listen to whatever it is she has on those earbuds and ignore us all. Plus, if I spot something, Bug will be over-the-moon happy. So I stare out the window across the way and watch the trees go by.

Five minutes pass.

Fifteen minutes.

A half hour.

My eyes are practically crossing. I look away and blink. "There's nothing out there."

"Even if we can't see them, they're probably watching us," Dad says as we approach a sharp curve.

"You just have to keep looking," Bug says. She hasn't moved an inch this whole time.

"When Dad and I were here before, there were animals all over the— Stop, stop, stop, stop!" Mom's hand shoots out toward Dad.

Dad slams on the brakes. The upper half of my body jerks forward and back like a puppet. The tires make this horrible squealing sound, things thunk heavily from my bunks to the floor, and there's a crazy rattling from where the truck is hooked up to the RV.

When everything stops moving, Bug's leaning back into Shiver's lap and my phone is tossed up somewhere near Mom and Dad.

"Everyone all right?" Mom asks in a shaky voice.

"Yeah." I unbuckle with shaking fingers and try to stand up. But I end up sitting back down because my legs can't hold me.

Shiver pulls out an earbud. "Can't your dad drive?" she whispers to me.

I ignore her. "What happened?"

"Look." Dad points ahead through the windshield.

I lean forward. Right in front of Bertha is a buffalo. A huge brown, shaggy, bearded buffalo. Just standing there, staring at us with his dark glassy eyes.

"Bug, you have to see this," I whisper, like it's going to hear me and run away. "It's a buffalo."

"Bison," she corrects me. But then she squeals a little when she sees it.

Shiver rolls her eyes and plugs back into her music.

"Look, there're more," Mom says. Dad's snapping pictures as fast as he can.

After a while, all the bison wander off into a nearby field, and we move forward again.

"That was amazing," Bug says. "He was so close!"

"It was pretty neat," I admit. Not enough to make me want to give up OMGH, though. I wonder how fast a bison can go. Can you ride one like a horse? If I can't find a way home in someone's RV, maybe I could ride a bison home. Now, *that* would make Lacey's eyes pop out.

Shiver just sits there with her eyes closed, like seeing all those bison was the most boring thing on the planet. I go back to texting Kenzie, detailing my new plan to get home. Until the signal disappears.

"Mom, my phone is completely useless. Why isn't there

a signal?" I shake the phone as if that'll magically make the signal come back.

"Oh, we switched phone companies," Mom says, like this is no big deal at all. "This new one is a lot cheaper, but the coverage is spotty."

Spotty? Try entirely nonexistent.

When we pull into the campground, I ask Mom and Dad if I can take a walk and get to know the place. I've already got my hand on the doorknob, ready to leap out and find that one RV that will take me home. Mom looks at me as if she has no idea who I am, while Dad grins and says, "Of course, Maya Mae!"

His grin stirs up something uncomfortable that's climbing through my insides. I ignore it. After all, he and Mom ignored *my* dream.

The gravel crunching under my feet is just a little louder than my pounding heart. What if I can't find anyone who will take me home? Even worse, what if I do and they turn out to be crazy?

No one's around at the RV next to ours. The next one has a campfire going. Three little boys chase each other, and their mom screams at them to sit down and eat dinner.

I pause, and decide against it. If I can't find anyone else, maybe I'll come back to them. The next two campsites have tents instead of RVs. I cross my sweatshirt-covered arms and try to rub the goose bumps away, thinking of how freezing those people must be. It's only six o'clock, and it's already getting cold.

An older couple sits at the picnic table of the next campsite. They're drinking coffee from travel mugs and chatting quietly. The woman is wearing a pink sweatshirt that proclaims *I Love Santa Monica*. It's totally something Grandma would buy and wear proudly. The man has on a hat with a gazillion pins.

I glance at their RV. It looks normal. They have a little map on the back of it, with the states they've been to colored in red. Tennessee isn't colored in. Hmm . . . There's also no scary tire cover, and I'd bet a hundred dollars their TV inside was made in the last ten years.

They're the perfect people to ask. If I can get the courage, that is.

I wish Kenzie was here. She wouldn't be all palm-sweaty nervous about asking a nice-looking elderly couple to drive us home. I *have* to do this for the only thing I've ever really wanted with all my heart.

I dig my fingernails into my hands and take a deep breath

of the chilly, campfire-tinged air. "Um, hi? Excuse me?"

"Why, hello," the man says in a booming voice. "How are you this fine evening?"

Onstage. Pretend I'm onstage, singing for all I'm worth while TV cameras film me from all angles, and I can do this. "I'm good, but, well . . . my name is Maya, and I'm wondering if you might be able to take me home."

The woman tilts her head. "Home? Do you mean to your campsite?"

"I actually kind of live in Nashville?" I don't know why I say it like it's a question.

"Ah, so you can't find your campsite. You get lost on the way back from the bathhouse? All these gravel loops look alike, don't they?" the man says.

"No, not exactly. I have to get back home, to—oof!" Something huge plows into me.

"There you are!" Shiver. Ugh, who else?

I shrug her off and give her what I hope is a meaningful look.

And she completely ignores me. Instead, she goes on and on to the old couple. "My little sister gets lost a lot. She has the worst sense of direction. Come on now, Maya. It's time for dinner."

She tugs my arm and practically pulls me down. I trip over my toes on the gravel and barely have time to wave good-bye to the couple before she's pulled me past their campsite.

"Let me go!" I finally yank my arm from her grasp. "What is *wrong* with you? Why are you always messing up my plans?"

She laughs and crosses her arms. The setting sun glints off the stud in her nose. "Wow, Shiver, thanks for saving my life. *Again*," she says in this high-pitched voice.

Seriously, I don't talk like that. "I was fine. Why do you keep butting in? I need to get home."

"What's so great about Nashville anyway? You're here with parents who actually care about you, and all you want to do is ditch them as fast as you can."

I cross my arms too. "It's none of your business why I want to go home. But I have something huge planned. Something that'll change my whole life. And a best friend who misses me. We're so close, we could be sisters. Not that you'd understand that." Okay, maybe that's not the nicest thing to say, but she's just ruined my best plan yet.

Her forehead crinkles as she hikes up that black bag she carries around everywhere. "What does that mean?"

"Nothing. Never mind. Just leave me alone, okay? Unless you have a better idea on how I can get home." I stride past her toward our campsite.

"Are you mad because you're stuck with me?" Her voice grates on my nerves, as if it's a fork scraping across my teeth.

I count to ten like I have to with Bug sometimes. I think about Gert. I think about how I would feel if that had happened to Grandma.

And I don't say anything.

When I get back, Shiver trailing behind me, Mom, Dad, and Bug are sitting at the bus seat table, eating mac and cheese and the veggie burgers Mom bought just for Shiver.

"There you are." Mom pops a cooked veggie burger between the two halves of a bun and passes it to me. Then she takes a steaming cup of hot chocolate from the microwave. "I thought you'd be cold after your walk." She hands me the mug.

I wrap my hands around it, thank Mom, and do battle with the guilt that's clawing up my throat.

"Thank you for going after Maya, Shiver," Mom says.

Shiver just kind of shrugs and takes the plate Mom hands her. She eats her veggie burger as if she's starving to death, and then Mom promises to let her use the barely there wi-fi coming from the lodge to call Gert on Mom's laptop. Because—of course—there's still no cell signal here, and my phone can't pick up the wi-fi. It's like the Cell Phone God knows I need to talk to Kenzie more than anything in the world right now and is just being mean. And there's no way I'm Skyping her on Mom's laptop where everyone can hear us. I can text her, but it won't send until we come back in range of a signal.

As the sun sets, it gets colder and colder. Dad finally convinces Mom to let him light a fire outside after he promises not to burn the park down. Just as the flames start to crackle, the people belonging to the RV next to us drive up in a little car. They climb out with layers of clothes and enormous backpacks with sleeping bags rolled up underneath.

Hmm. I wonder if they're planning to leave tomorrow. Of course, now that Shiver knows what I'm up to, she'll probably ruin it before I can even ask them.

"Howdy," Dad calls, his new cowboy hat on (which Mom let him get only because it was on clearance).

I slide down in my camp chair and pretend not to know him.

"Go for a hike?" he asks the people.

"We did the Slough Creek Trail," the man says. "Seven miles in, seven back out. Took two days to finish."

"They went hiking for two days straight?" I whisper to Bug.

"It's called backpacking," Shiver says out of nowhere.

"That sounds like the best thing ever," Bug says.

"But where would you go to the bathroom?" I ask Bug. "There aren't any toilets in the middle of the woods."

"You dig a cathole," the backpacker woman says with a smile.

"A what?" I ask.

"You dig a hole six inches deep, do your business, and then fill it in."

"Ugh."

The man laughs. "It's not for everyone. We'll see you folks later." They disappear into their RV. So they might be crazy for taking that kind of hike, but they don't seem psycho crazy. Definitely a potential ride home. If only I can figure out how to talk to them without Shiver seeing.

Dad stares into the fire, then looks at Mom. "Just think of that."

"I have, and no," Mom says as she heads toward our RV. "I'm turning in."

Thank you, Mom. I was starting to imagine this horror movie with Dad dragging us all down some fifty-mile trail for a month, making us pee in holes, and probably getting everyone eaten by bears. Everyone but me, that is, since I'll be on my way to Nashville—somehow.

Just as the wind picks up and I'm about to go inside too, Mom yells from Bertha.

"Maya Mae Casselberry. Get in here this minute!"

Shiver whistles. "Someone's in trouble."

Chapter 11

9 days until *Dueling Duets* auditions

As I move toward Mom's shadowy figure, I wonder what in the world I've done. Did she find out I tried to get a ride home? But how could that happen when Shiver's the only one who knows and she was sitting right next to me?

Mom doesn't say anything when I reach the door. She points toward the back of the RV.

"What . . . ," I start to say, but Mom just keeps pointing.

I walk through the rooms and step up into my cubbyholes. My toe catches on something, and before I know it, I'm sprawled out on my stomach over a mess of stuff. Hugo blinks at me from where he's curled up on a pile of shoes in one of the closets.

Books, blankets, stuffed cats, shoes, clothes. Practically everything that was loose is lying in a heap on the floor. I push some books out of the way and stand up, surrounded by my life.

"This isn't how I left it. It must have fallen off when Dad braked really hard for that buffalo."

Mom takes a couple of steps backward into the kitchen. She opens one of the cupboards, then hands me a box of trash bags. "I think it's time to do something about it."

I stare in horror at the box of Hefty in my hands. I drop them like they're full of Hugo's used litter. "I'll clean it up. Right now." I scoop up an armload of stuffed cats and blankets, and toss them onto the extra bunk.

Mom gives me a sad smile. "We're going to have to donate some of this. Shiver's riding with us now, and there's no reason for her to sleep on the couch when we have a perfectly good bed. I'll help you, and we'll store the bags in the truck until we get to a town."

Tears prick my eyes. "You're not being fair. This is my life. Mine, not yours!"

Mom tries to hug me, but I push her away. She grips the

doorframe as if she needs it to hold her up. "I know how hard this is, but try to think of it like this. It's just things, Maya," she says. "It's not your life."

"Not my life?" I echo. Every single thing here is a memory, a reminder of something good and happy. Something that existed before my parents messed it all up.

"Honey, we have to share this space, and it's not very big. I wish I could let you keep everything. I tried to for as long as possible, but now we need this bed for someone to sleep in."

"For *Shiver*. She's not even part of our family." The second the words are out of my mouth, I feel bad for saying them.

"Compassion, Maya, please." Mom closes her eyes and puts her hand to her forehead. When she opens them, she says, "Let me help you. It won't take long if we work on it together."

"I don't need your help." I put as much ice into my voice as possible. It's hard to be entirely mad at Shiver—it's not her fault that Gert got sick and her mom won't come get her. But Mom? I can definitely be mad at her. I glare at her until she says, "I'll be right back here if you change your mind." Mom steps through my stuff to get to the bathroom.

I want to hurl the box of trash bags against the wall, but

that would only bring her in here again. Why can't she realize she's pulling out pieces of my heart?

What I do know is that I need to get out of here, like, yesterday. I whip out my phone.

Mom making me get rid of my stuff!!!! The text doesn't go through. The faint wi-fi from the lodge is pretty much nonexistent right now.

Mom comes out of the bathroom, and I shove my phone back into my pocket. "Are you sure you don't want help?"

"No!" Like I'd ever let Mom help me decide what to throw away.

She bites her lip, and for a moment, I think she's going to cry. I don't know what she has to cry about. I'm the one who's losing everything. "All right. I'm headed to bed," she says. Then she disappears into the back of the RV.

I plop down on the floor and take a deep breath. Mom said we'd store the bags in the truck until we found a Goodwill or something. That buys me some time, since I really doubt there are any thrift shops in the middle of Yellowstone. Once I'm back in Nashville, my parents can ship my things home. I can keep them in Kenzie's basement.

I feel a little better, but it doesn't stop me from thinking about every little thing as I put it into a bag. The horse book series I was obsessed with in fourth grade. The program from the fifth-grade musical I starred in. Ticket stubs from my favorite concerts. And the blankets Dad bought when an ice storm came through and knocked out our power at home for a week. We all had to huddle together on the couch to stay warm, and Mom told ghost stories to take our minds off how freezing it was, until we gave up and checked into a hotel.

How can Mom expect me to give up these memories?

I put it all into the garbage bags and vow not to let any of it go.

T minus 9 days. Or eight days, really, as I watch the time on my phone change to 12:00. I yank out my earbuds and listen. It's completely silent inside Bertha. Well, silent except for Dad's snores.

Time for drastic measures, as Kenzie would say. Right after I got into bed tonight, I updated OMGH with my best plan yet. And now it's time to put it into action.

I heft Hugo off my stomach and resettle him in a nest of blankets. Then I slide the little curtain away from my bunk. Shiver's curtain is closed. Very, very, very carefully, I climb down my ladder. The ladder squeaks and I stop, frozen halfway between the bed and the floor.

When my heart finally slows down, I finish the climb and step silently onto the floor. I'm like a jewel thief from some *Mission Impossible*–type movie, moving without a sound toward the living area. Well, one that wears an oversized T-shirt from Carrie Underwood's *Blown Away* tour (put on in the safety of my cubbyhole so Shiver couldn't see it). Now to find Mom's purse.

Please, please, please don't let it be in the bedroom. I really don't think I could tiptoe in there and lift her wallet while she and Dad are sleeping.

My heart is up in my throat when I spot the lemon-yellow handles peeking over the armrest of the Used-to-Be-Dirt Den Couch. Sitting next to the purse, I rummage through until I find Mom's matching yellow wallet. Inside, four shiny credit cards look back at me. Four! Which one should I pick? Maybe I should use the one with the fuel company logo on it, and earn Mom and Dad some free gallons of gas with my sneaky purchase.

I half expect Shiver to come flying out of her bunk and rip the card out of my hand. But she doesn't. Bertha and everyone inside are completely silent.

I rifle through Mom's purse until I find a pen and a notepad. Then I squint at the card. It's really hard to read credit card numbers in the dark. After tilting it this way and that, I jot down the numbers and the expiration date.

I wipe my sweaty palms on the couch cushions and put everything back as I found it. I clutch the scrap of paper in my hand as I tiptoe through the freezing RV to my cubbyhole.

Once I'm tucked under the warm blankets and Hugo's snuggled on my legs, I peer at it with the light from my phone. One time at school, Lacey bragged about "borrowing" her dad's credit card to buy a pair of jeans online. It sounded so wrong to me—like stealing. Except here I am, doing the same thing. I don't feel any better about it now . . . but this isn't like a pair of jeans. It's my whole life. It's the only dream I've ever had. I wouldn't be doing this for something as silly as a pair of jeans. I would never do something like this if it wasn't *super* important.

Somehow that still doesn't make me feel all that great. But I slide the piece of paper between the back of my phone and its hard plastic case anyway.

Phase One of the newest plan of OMGH is complete.

I shove down the guilt feelings as I send texts that won't actually send to Kenzie and Jack, telling them I'll be home soon. Then I fold my audition shirt and put it right where I can see it, plug in my earbuds, and fall asleep to "Highway Don't Care."

Chapter 12

8 days until *Dueling Duets* auditions

The morning air is cold and full of pine and this horrible rotten egg smell that Dad calls sulfur. I hug my arms to my chest and wish I'd put on a thicker sweatshirt as I peer into the hot spring.

According to Bug, hot springs are just really pretty geysers that are also hotter than boiling water. She's definitely right about the really pretty part. The hot spring is the most perfect blue I've ever seen. Even Shiver looks interested. Which makes sense since it almost matches her hair. I pull out my phone with freezing fingers and snap a picture to send to Kenzie. I'll send it when I get close enough to the Old Faithful Inn to pick up the wi-fi again. I check for the hundredth time that the slip of paper with Mom's credit card number is still tucked in behind the phone.

I can't believe I'm sightseeing with Shiver. But she was the only other one who thought the ranger program on insects in Yellowstone sounded boring and kind of icky. So we're looking at the geysers while Mom, Dad, and Bug are at the program.

Also, I kind of don't want to be around Mom since she's still bent on making me give everything away. I need to get Phase Two of my newest OMGH plan into action tonight, before we leave the park and end up back in thrift-shop-ridden civilization.

I lean farther over the fence to get a better picture. I really want to capture the puffy light-blue cloud-looking things floating in the turquoise water.

"Don't drop that. You'll ruin the spring," a guy's voice says from behind me.

It's so unexpected that I do almost drop my phone. Shiver and I flip around to face a tall, skinny guy with curly brown hair who looks about our age, wearing jeans and a Yosemite National Park T-shirt.

"Who are you?" Shiver whirls her earbuds around like a lasso as she studies the boy.

"Remy."

"And what makes you the boss of the world, Remy?" she asks.

I cover my mouth so I don't laugh. Shiver can be really funny—sometimes.

He holds up his hands. "I'm just sick of tourists doing stupid stuff. That's all."

"Ha. That's hilarious, coming from another tourist." I turn and start walking toward the next geyser on the concrete trail. Shiver falls in next to me. It's weird—almost like we're friends.

"I'm not a tourist," Mr. Remy Bossypants says from behind us. "My parents are park rangers in Grand Teton."

"Then go order people around there," Shiver says over her shoulder.

Remy runs in front of us and turns around so he's walking backward in order to face us. "Look, I'm sorry. I didn't mean it in a bad way. Have you guys seen Old Faithful go off yet?"

Shiver raises her eyebrows, like she can't believe he's still existing in her space, much less talking to her.

I decide to give him a second chance. He is awfully cute, after all. And it'd be nice to tell Kenzie about *something* good from this whole trip. "Not yet. I think it's due around eleven, right?"

A smile lights up Remy's face. "Yup. You'll love it."

I'm wondering how I can snap a picture of him to text to Kenzie without weirding him out, when he stops suddenly in front of us.

Shiver nearly runs into him. "What's your problem?"

His tan face shades red. "Sorry, I just thought of something. I know the best place to see Old Faithful, but it's a little hike. Want to go?"

"In your dreams," Shiver says at the same time I say, "Sure."

Shiver glares at me, and just like that, whatever friendly moment we just had is gone.

"Come on, it'll be fun," I say to her.

She frowns. I probably should've said it'd be full of black, depressing moments. Then maybe she'd be more into it. She grabs my arm and pulls me away from Remy. "You can't go off by yourself with some guy you just met. Seriously, have you got some kind of death wish?" she says in a loud whisper.

Anger prickles through me. She's talking to me like I'm

some dumb kid. "Remy hardly looks like a murderer. He's the same age as us," I hiss at her. "And look at all the people. This isn't exactly an ideal kidnapping situation."

Shiver shakes her head. "I'm going too, then. If he tries anything, spray him with that and we'll run like nobody's business." She flicks a finger against the can of bear spray dangling from my backpack. Mom bought a can for each of us back in Cody and makes us carry it everywhere.

I glance at Remy. He's got his hands stuffed in his pockets and is kicking a pebble across the paved walkway. I'd rather hike without Shiver hanging over us like a dark rain cloud. But I know Mom would never let me hear the end of it if we separated. The only way she agreed to let us check out the geysers on our own was if we promised to stick together.

"So where is this place?" I ask Remy.

He points at the hill rising behind Old Faithful. "Up there. It's the best. Just a handful of people, so you don't have to fight for a good spot, and you can see the whole area."

He leads us down the walkway and past the benches that ring the front half of Old Faithful. It's a gorgeous day with a soft blue sky, and it's actually getting warmer. I pull my sweatshirt off and tie it around my waist.

"You should've been here last year," Remy says as he

watches me tie my sleeves. "There was still four feet of snow on the other side of the park. Dad and I pitched a tent at the Canyon campground, and one night it snowed another couple of inches. When I unzipped the tent in the morning, snow blew in all over our sleeping bags."

"You slept in a tent in the snow?" Shiver asks. "That's dumb."

I glare at her and say to Remy, "That sounds awful. Why didn't you check into a hotel?"

"It was an adventure," he says as we cross a bridge over a rushing blue river and start up a path into the woods that cover the hill.

We pass a few people as we make our way up the trail—Remy, me, and then Shiver, lagging behind, earbuds in.

"Wait." Remy stops in the middle of the path.

He holds a finger to his lips and then points to a rock. On top is a furry brown lump of a thing, fast asleep. It looks like a beaver without the paddle-shaped tail, all round and cute like it's straight out of one of those Japanese cartoons.

"What is that?" I ask in a whisper.

"Marmot," Remy whispers back.

I wish Bug was here. She'd love this little roly-poly guy. I sneak my phone up and get a picture for her. Then I act like I'm taking another picture of the marmot, but really I'm snapping one of Remy to send to Kenzie. She'd never forgive me if I didn't send her evidence of my hike with the cutest guy I've seen since . . . well, since Jack.

"What are you doing?" Shiver asks in a regular tone of voice. The marmot jolts upright and scurries off the other side of the rock and into the trees.

"I *was* taking a picture of the marmot, but you scared it off." I shove my phone back into my pocket.

"Nuh-uh. You were totally taking a picture of him." She points at Remy, her lips curled as if she just ate a lemon.

"No, I wasn't. Come on, let's keep going." I lead the way uphill. I can't even look at Remy, I'm so embarrassed. Thanks a lot, Shiver.

We climb and climb and climb. Shiver's breath is coming in little wisps.

Now that I think about it, I'm out of breath too. This hiking stuff is hard. Of course, I'm not going to tell Remy that. He's breathing just fine and totally looks like the outdoorsy hiking type. He'd think I was a total wimp.

We keep moving uphill. Just when I'm sure I'm going to need to sit down and die in the middle of the trail, the trees to our right open up.

"Wow," I gasp. My legs are burning, but the view up here is something else.

"There's Old Faithful." Remy points to the cone shape way, way down below that's constantly pushing out steam.

"Duh." Shiver's sitting on a huge rock behind us.

I ignore her and turn to survey the landscape in front of me. All around Old Faithful, hundreds of people are gathered in a fat semicircle. Off to the right, more geysers steam. The whole place looks like it's on fire, except there is no fire. And way off in the distance, open fields and mountains make it all seem like a painting.

"It's perfect," I say in whisper, almost afraid I'll disturb the whole scene.

And then Old Faithful erupts.

The people behind us ooh and aah, and cameras snap like a chorus. I grab my phone and join in.

I've never seen anything like it. Water shoots straight up into the air, and falls back down as spray. Steam billows even higher. Even up here, I hear the *whoosh* of the water as it's forced out of the ground. Dad'll be really disappointed that he missed this. It's a hundred times better than a stinky ball of twine. But I don't know that it would beat singing with Jack.

It goes on and on. When it's finally over, I keep staring at the cone, waiting for it to happen again.

"What did you think?" Remy asks.

I don't have any words.

"It wasn't bad," Shiver admits. "But we could've watched it down there with everyone else."

Remy smiles at me, and I know he's thinking the same thing I am. Up here, with so few people, it felt like the geyser went off just for us.

"Want to walk the rest of the trail? It goes around to some other geysers." He pushes some curls behind his ear and all I want to do is sigh and grin. What is wrong with me? I like Jack, not this know-it-all guy. Obviously.

"We have to get back. We're supposed to meet her parents at noon," Shiver says like the most boring person on the planet. "I'm calling Gran after lunch, remember?" she says to me. And I feel kind of bad for not remembering that.

"Sorry," I say to Remy.

"So how long are you here?" Remy asks as we start back down the trail. Once again, Shiver's lagging behind us. Probably with her earbuds in. Which is fine with me because that lets me talk to Remy without her butting in with something completely rude.

"I think we're leaving tomorrow. We're going to Grand Teton, and then California to drop off Shiver, and then . . . I don't know." Except I'm really going back to Nashville tomorrow, but I can't say that and risk Shiver overhearing it.

"Aren't you going back home?" He holds a tree branch back so it doesn't smack me in the face. I wonder if Jack would've done the same thing. Not that I can really picture him hiking.

"I wish. My parents are living some insane dream. They thought it would be fun to move into an RV and drive all over the place. They actually sold our house."

Remy's eyes widen. "Wow, that sounds great."

I laugh. "To you, maybe. I just want to go home. I hate Bertha."

"Bertha?"

"The RV. It's like being stuffed into a tiny ugly can with your entire family . . . and her." I jerk a finger back toward Shiver.

"I used to hate being dragged out here every summer. Every May, Mom leaves for the Tetons. And the day after school ends, Dad and I drive to Yellowstone, stay a week, and then join Mom. For the whole summer. I always get back the week before school starts. I miss out on everything that happens back home."

"Every year?" I can't imagine not having all my summers full of fun with Kenzie.

"Yup. I hated it. Like, so much that I'd beg to go back home and stay with my cousins. One time, I even thought I'd bike home, by myself. All the way to Denver. Crazy, right?"

I nod and make some kind of noise in agreement, except . . . it's not that crazy at all, considering how many ways I've already tried to get home.

"But after a while, I got used to it, and now I wouldn't trade it for anything," Remy goes on. "While everyone else is swimming in a concrete pool, I'm swimming under waterfalls."

When I look over at him, he's smiling, as if leaving everyone makes him super happy. "Huh" is all I can manage to say. I really like swimming in a concrete pool with Kenzie. Although watching Old Faithful was nothing short of amazing. And I love the mountains. But it's not Nashville, and I belong in Nashville.

As we wander down the trail, he talks about his parents. His mom helps visitors with things to do, while his dad does nature talks and leads guided hikes. Something I could totally picture Bug doing when she's grown up.

Before I'm ready, we're back in front of the lodge. From here, I can't see the area with the big rocks and great view high on the hill, even though I know that if anyone is still up there, they can see us.

"I should go find my dad," Remy says.

"Thanks for the hike." I want to smile at him, but for some reason, I feel shy all of a sudden.

"Maybe I'll see you guys in Grand Teton," he says. "We could hike again."

I go warm all over as he waves good-bye.

"I hope not," Shiver says as soon as he's out of earshot.

"Why are you so mean?" I ask. "He was really nice."

"He's full of himself," she says as she runs her fingers through her blue hair.

"You didn't hear most of what he said. You were busy listening to Death Thrash or whatever you've got on that thing." I point to her phone with the earbud wires snaking out.

"Yes, that's exactly what I'm listening to. You know everything, Maya." She stuffs the earbuds back in and we wait in silence for my parents and Bug. I wonder how many secret hiking trails Remy knows about, if he likes country music at all, and if he has any friends here.

I don't know why I'm thinking about him. I *should* be

thinking about how much I'm going to need to practice once I get back home.

When my family arrives, Bug's full of energy and facts about disgusting creepy-crawlies, and Dad's got a handful of brochures and a book called *Your First Backpacking Trip*.

I eye the book. "Mom?"

She sighs. "Your dad's talked me into letting him try backpacking overnight by himself. One of the rangers told him about some easy trails in Grand Teton that go around the lakes."

"I'm going to test it out, and then we can all go!" Dad says.

Mom looks at me and shakes her head just slightly.

"I want to take an overnight hike," Bug says.

"Maybe next time, Bugby." Dad pats her on the shoulder.

"Why just one night? You could go for longer," Shiver says out of nowhere.

Dad smiles at her like she's suggested the best thing ever. "That would be great, except we need to get you home."

Shiver shrugs. "I'm not in any hurry."

As we walk toward the truck, I fall back with Mom. "Is it safe to let him go by himself? I mean, who's going to keep him from getting eaten by a bear or falling into a lake?"

Mom sighs. "We're going to have to trust that he'll be

okay. I'm thinking I might go a couple miles in with him, just to make sure."

Okay, this makes me feel just a little nervous about putting the next step of OMGH into action. What if Dad goes out hiking and does something stupid, and I'm not here to help?

My phone picks up the inn's wi-fi and buzzes with a text from Kenzie just as we reach the truck.

M—911! J asked L to be his DD partner!

I grip the door handle. I can't even breathe. I *knew* this was going to happen. I should've been there already to stop it. And Jack didn't even have the decency to text me! I'm half angry at him and half at myself for not getting home faster.

But I *will* be home in time for the audition. And once I'm there, Jack will have to try out with me. After all, he asked me first, not Lacey.

He just *has* to.

Chapter 13

7 days until *Dueling Duets* auditions

Midnight again. It's just barely T minus 7 days. I shove those tummy-rumbling feelings of guilt about leaving Dad and his scary hiking idea behind by reading Kenzie's text again. I couldn't get any more information from her, because the second I got into the truck, the wi-fi disappeared.

I make a wish to the TTT, touch my audition shirt for luck, and sneak down my ladder for the second night in a row. Mom's laptop is on the table. I unplug it and carry it to the passenger seat in the front, which is probably the best place to make the least noise. Bug is right above me, but of course, she'll sleep right through this.

I settle into the worn brown seat. When I open the laptop, it makes that chime that practically screams, "Hey, wake up! Someone's on your computer!" I cringe and wait to hear footsteps.

Okay, guess that wasn't as loud as I thought. Time to get to work.

I pull up the internet browser, which is crazy slow since we can barely get a wi-fi signal from the lodge. My phone can't pick it up at all. When Google finally pops up, I type, *fly home.*

Ninety gazillion matches. I click the first one and wait and wait and wait. When it loads, I plug in all the information. It tells me the nearest airport is in Bozeman, Montana. Wherever that is.

Whatever. I'll figure that out later. I hit the submit button. After what feels like an hour, the results pop up.

$460?! Seriously? Mom is going to kill me when she sees that on her bill.

But desperate times call for desperate measures, right? At least, that's what Kenzie would say. Making it onto national TV to jump-start my career (and save Jack from Lacey) is totally worth $460. And I *did* try to talk to Mom and tell her how much I needed to go home, so it's not as if I jumped right away to doing something as crazy as this.

I select the one-way flight to Nashville and fill in the boxes. Then I pull the folded piece of notebook paper from behind my phone and smooth it flat on the laptop.

Mom's Visa number. Something twinges in my stomach as I type it in. $460 is a lot of money. I don't know how much Mom makes with her job. It's enough to keep gas in Bertha and food in the fridge, but is it enough to pay for a really expensive flight home? What if I charge this on her card and then she and Dad can't afford to buy groceries? She has that worried look on her face when she works sometimes. I'm not sure if it's because of work or money.

I type the numbers in and stare at them.

It's an emergency, right? I mean, it's a once-in-a-lifetime opportunity.

I type in the expiration date. The next blank asks for a CSC.

What the what is a CSC?

I click on the little blue question mark next to the blank. *CSC is the three-digit code on the back of your credit card*, the little pop-up box tells me.

I groan. I didn't even know that existed, so obviously I didn't write it down when I copied the card number and expiration date last night. I could give up, or I could look for Mom's purse.

"Maya?" a sleepy voice says from behind me.

Holy potatoes! A little shriek leaps from my mouth, and the laptop slides off my knees as I jump up.

"What are you doing with Mom's computer?" Dad's standing behind me, rubbing the sleep from his eyes.

I bend down to get the laptop. The screen glows extra bright, tattling on me.

"What's going on?" Mom appears behind Dad. "Why do you have my laptop?" She steps around him and pulls it from my hands before I have time to close the airplane ticket window.

I brace myself for yelling or at least a guilt trip for almost charging $460 to her credit card and being a horrible daughter, but all Mom does is sigh.

She clicks the laptop shut and says, "Come back to the table and sit down."

It's like I'm walking to my own death—or maybe the dentist—when I follow her and Dad to the kitchen table. I slide into the bus seat on the opposite side from them.

Dad flips on the little battery-powered light on the wall. It makes their faces look sort of bluish. I sit on my hands and wonder if I should say something first.

"Dad and I had a little talk earlier," Mom says.

This does not sound good at all.

"We know this has been harder on you than any of the rest of us," Dad says with very un-Dad-like seriousness. "And you've been such a trouper about the whole thing. I want you to know how much that means to me. And to your mom."

Okay, there's no way they know about the hitchhiking plan or about me trying to find a ride with another RV. I relax just a tiny bit.

"So we were talking tonight, and while we wish we could afford to let you fly home for that TV show, we can't." Just hearing Dad say that makes me feel awful about almost spending so much money. And that sad look on Mom's face doesn't help either.

I look at my hands. "I'm really sorry. It's just . . . I promised Jack I'd be there."

"But you've already told him you can't do it, right?" Mom asks.

I nod, even though it's not entirely the truth.

"I'm sure he can find another partner. No shortage of girls wanting to be country music stars in Nashville!" Dad smiles as he says this. Little does he know how true it is.

They don't get my passion for music. At all. I don't even want to talk about it, because I know it won't change anything.

"It's Kenzie, too, isn't it?" Mom says softly. "You miss her."

I nod, because I do miss Kenzie. That's not exactly why I'm so desperate to get home, but it is one of the reasons.

"What if we made sure you had time to Skype with her?" Dad says.

"We can go up to the lodge in the morning," Mom adds.

They both have this hopeful, "please love us" look on their faces. Skyping is so not the same as seeing Kenzie in person, but it's not a horrible idea.

"Okay," I say anyway. "Thanks!" I force a smile. Then I stretch my arms out and yawn before they can ground me or anything. "I think I'll go back to bed."

"Aren't you forgetting something?" Mom holds out her hand.

I drop the handwritten credit card number into it, even though it feels like I'm giving up my last chance to get home. Not that I could've used it anyway without feeling awful for the rest of my life.

"I'm sorry I almost did that. So, um, good night?" I slide

out of the seat and take a step away from the table.

"Not so fast," Mom says.

I should've known there was no escaping this part. I turn around just in time to see Mom nudge Dad. If I didn't know what was coming next, I'd think it was funny that Mom has to remind Dad to be the bad guy every once in a while.

He holds out his hand. I'd complain about giving up my phone, but it's kind of hard to when I know exactly how guilty I am.

"So . . . when can I have it back?" I don't know how I can live without talking to Kenzie. And what if Jack comes to his senses and finally texts me?

"Tomor—" Dad starts, but Mom interrupts him.

"In a few days," she says. "This will give you plenty of time to think about what you did. And what you would have done to our family if you had gone through with it."

My face goes warm. I'm super glad I didn't buy that ticket. "Okay," I say in a teeny, tiny voice.

"We expect you never to do anything like that again," Dad says.

I know it's serious when Dad's using his Stern Father voice. "I'm sorry," I whisper as I clutch my hands behind my back and wish I could escape to my cubbyhole.

"Maya." Mom touches my arm as she and Dad get up from the table. "We love you. And I promise this will get easier as time goes on. You have your whole life ahead of you to audition for as many singing shows as you want. Now, get some sleep."

They disappear into the back of the RV. I trail behind them, and once I'm tucked in under my blankets and stuffed animals and Hugo and my shimmery silver shirt, I imagine the OMGH list in my head. *This* is the only opportunity for *Dueling Duets* (and Jack—even though I'm kind of mad at him right now). There's no way life in Bertha will ever get easier.

Chapter 14

7 days until _Dueling Duets_ auditions

The ride through Yellowstone and into Grand Teton National Park gives me lots of time to think. Mostly because I don't have a phone. I think about OMGH, of course. But also about my duet. I've barely been able to practice since Shiver arrived. I need to find a place where she can't hear me, or else I'll be completely out of tune by the time I get home.

Because I am definitely going home.

Somehow.

Bug smiles at me and passes me a purring Hugo. Sometimes sisters know exactly what you need.

When we pull into the campsite, I race through my setting-up-camp chores. Then I give Hugo a kiss on the head, grab my backpack, and go in search of a non-Shiver-populated place to work on my song.

Behind Bertha is a path through the trees. The painted deer glare at my back as I step onto the little trail and Dad yells, "Happy exploring!"

I glance behind me, just to make sure Shiver isn't following.

The path isn't too long, and before I know it, I'm standing on a ledge overlooking an enormous blue lake with mountains soaring on the far side. The peaks are so high, they're hidden by puffy white clouds.

Okay. Even I can admit this is kind of amazing. Like, take-your-breath-away amazing. But I'd trade all the gorgeous snow-capped mountains in the world to be back at our house in Nashville, hanging out with Kenzie, seeing Dad go to work, and preparing for my audition (and still having a partner!) without having to hide out.

I forgot to grab a camp chair, so I plop down right on top of the flattened pine needles and sand. My feet dangle over the side of the ledge, which would make Mom crazy if she saw. She has a thing about heights. I drop my backpack and wonder if I'm far enough away from Bertha. I'll have to chance it, though. I need the practice. Besides, Shiver probably has her earbuds firmly planted in her ears.

I do some vocal warm-ups. It feels good to finally let my voice out. It always clears my head and makes it easier to think. A kayaker glides through the water below, and the boats moored there bob in the waves whenever the wind blows. Every once in a while, footsteps sound on the path behind me. I check to make sure the footsteps aren't Shiver's, and then I go back to warming up. And thinking.

Anything that costs more than one hundred dollars to get home is out. So what does that leave? Not much. At least, nothing that I haven't already tried.

I stand (Marianne Phelps says that your voice is always more powerful when you stand because you can breathe more deeply) and launch into the song, singing straight up to the mountains. It doesn't sound too bad, considering I've barely practiced. When I finish, I run through it one more time, paying careful attention to the emotion I put behind the words.

The sun sinks lower, until it's hidden behind the sharp-topped mountains across the lake. The sky goes all pink and gold just as I finish the last of the song.

All of this practice has *got* to lead to something. What can I do?

Kenzie couldn't come up with any good ideas. At least, not ones that don't involve faking broken bones. I sit down again and hum the chorus of the song.

Wait! Maybe I've been asking the wrong person. I need someone who's been in this situation. Who's probably thought through all the possibilities. I need Remy! But how am I going to find him? It's not like I got his number or anything. Just the thought of seeing him again makes me feel as if I've run for miles.

Campfire smoke and the scent of cooking meat waft through the trees and distract me from daydreams of running into Remy on a trail, in a restaurant, on top of a mountain. . . . My stomach growls. Something sharp pokes me on the cheek.

What the . . . ?

I slap my face harder than I mean to. A squished brown dot with legs comes away on my hand. Eww. I wipe the dead mosquito off on a nearby tree trunk. Another one stings my neck, and suddenly there are three on my arm.

"Aggh!" Some animalistic sound erupts from my throat. I grab my backpack and run for the campsite.

"Maya?" Mom's dancing around like a disjointed puppet, slapping her arms.

"What's with these mosquitoes?" I jog in place as I wave my hands in front of my face. The tiny vampires hover just beyond my hands, waiting for an opportunity to feed on any patch of skin they can find.

"This is insane! Dad's looking for the bug spray." Mom waves an arm at the RV.

Dad flies out the door, aiming the canister at Bug, who's examining the welts on her hand. He dances around her, spritzing here and there.

"Shiver?" he asks when he finishes with Bug.

Shiver holds out her hands, and he sprays into them. As she wipes the spray on her face and rubs it into her hands, I realize that's all she needs. She's wearing tight black jeans and a long-sleeved T-shirt with the name of some band I've never heard of on it. And her huge black boots probably crush a million mosquitoes each time she takes a step.

"Hold still, Maya Mae." Dad aims the canister at me.

"I can't! They're eating me up." I hop up and down as he shoots me with bug spray.

Even when we're all covered, the mosquitoes buzz in our faces, looking for a way in.

Mom studies the hands flying all over as we keep smacking various parts of our bodies. "Who wants PB and J in the RV tonight?"

Dad beats everyone inside.

"Are you sure you still want to do this?" Mom asks Dad the next afternoon, as we wait in line at the visitors center. "What about the killer mosquitoes?"

"They only seem to come out in the evening. I'll hide in my tent and read."

"That won't help with bears."

Dad waves his hand like bears aren't any scarier than Hugo.

While Mom goes through a litany of bad nature stuff and Dad shrugs it all off, I check out a display of framed photos on the wall. Maybe I should send a postcard to Kenzie. I should send one to Jack, too, just to remind him that he *already* has a partner. Except by the time the postcards arrive, I'll already be there. If I can find Remy, anyway.

"What's that?" Shiver pokes my backpack.

"What?" I slide it off my shoulder.

"It looks like that huge book."

A corner of *Everything Y'all Ever Wanted to Know* sticks

out of my bag. I yank the zipper shut. "Nothing. Just a book. Why, what's in *your* backpack?"

Probably a book on how to ruin people's very important life plans.

"None of your business." She wanders across the small room and studies a map tacked to the far wall.

The couple in front of Mom and Dad turn to leave. As they walk through the door, Mom points to the ginormous bags on their backs with stuff dangling from the sides and bottom. "But you don't have *any* of that," she says to Dad.

"Can I help you?" the woman at the desk asks. Her long curly brown hair cascades out from under her ranger hat. If my hair did that, I wouldn't be stuck with Heidi braids all the time.

Dad gives her a huge grin. "I'd like to go backpacking!"

The ranger bites her lip. I'm pretty sure she's trying not to crack up at Dad's enthusiasm. "All right. How many of you, how many nights, and which trail?"

"Just me. I'm not sure which trail. Maybe a week?"

"One night," Mom corrects him.

"Have you backpacked before?" the ranger asks Dad.

"No, but I'm ready to start." He pulls out his *Your First Backpacking Trip* book.

"Well, we advise you to go with at least one other person, especially if you're new at this. For safety reasons."

Bug practically leaps toward Mom and Dad and places her hands palms down on the counter. "I'll go with him! I'm a Girl Scout, and I know all about trail safety."

"No," Mom says before Dad can even open his mouth.

Bug's face falls. I squeeze her arm. As annoying as she can be sometimes, I hate seeing her disappointed.

Mom studies the map taped to the counter. "What's an easy trail to start out with?"

"Challenging," Dad says. "I'd like a *challenging* trail."

Behind the ranger, a door labeled OFFICE opens and another curly brown head pops out.

I blink. I can't believe my luck!

Chapter 15

6 days until *Dueling Duets* auditions

"No way," I whisper as I stare at Remy. It's got to be divine intervention or something.

Like a shadow, Shiver appears behind me. "What's *he* doing here?" She doesn't whisper.

Everyone looks up at her, including Remy.

"This is my son," the ranger says. "He's just waiting for his dad to pick him up."

Remy's face breaks into a grin. "Hi, Maya."

My face goes all warm. Is it possible for someone to get even cuter in two days? I wave at him.

Mom's glancing back and forth between us, while

Dad and the ranger lady just look confused.

"Shiver and I met Remy at Yellowstone," I supply.

"Are you guys going on a backcountry hike?" Remy asks.

Shiver snorts.

"Just me, son," Dad says as if he's ninety years old. I guess that when you have two daughters, you call boys you just met "son."

Remy's mom, who I realize now looks just like him, gets back to the trail options and what Dad will need. Remy listens in and nods as if he's some kind of park ranger in training. Every once in a while, he says something like "That one's near some moose habitat" or "Didn't part of that trail wash out last month?" While they talk, I try to figure out a way to meet up with him again without looking desperate.

Although I am desperate. Desperate to get home. And spending more time with Remy is definitely a nice plus.

Finally, Dad settles on a trail and has a list of stuff he needs, courtesy of Remy.

"Thank you for your help," Mom says. "Maybe when your husband gets back, you all can come on over to our campsite for some dinner."

Say yes, say yes, say yes. I throw what I hope are ESP signals toward Remy's mom.

She waves a hand. "It's my job, but dinner would be lovely. Especially since it seems our kids are already friends."

Yes! Now I just have to get Remy alone. And keep Dad from catching the entire park on fire while Remy and his parents nibble hot dogs.

"See you around," Remy says to me. He drops his voice to a whisper. "I kind of have the run of this place. And I know some secret trails here, too."

I could not smile any more than I am as I follow my family out of the visitors center. I can't believe this is happening. Not only do I have a cute outdoorsy guy just dying to show me around Grand Teton National Park, he might also help me figure out how to get to Nashville.

OMG he's here! I type to Kenzie. Of course, she can't read it. The text goes to the back of the line where all my texts to Kenzie are waiting to be sent. There's no cell signal here in the campground—plus, my phone was sitting inside a drawer in Bertha for two days. Mom finally took pity on me and gave it back, but not before grilling me on whether I'd learned the consequences of my actions.

I stuff the phone into my jeans pocket and try to look

cool. Which is almost impossible because Remy is here. To see me!

"Did you swallow a mosquito?" Shiver asks. She's slouched in a camp chair, earbuds dangling around her neck, being the least helpful person on the planet. As usual.

I don't answer her. Instead, I make myself busy by lighting the mosquito-repellent candles Mom picked up at the park general store. I'm wearing my super-cute red sandals, even though the mosquitoes are trying to eat my feet.

"Welcome!" Dad waves his barbeque tongs in greeting. "Grub's almost ready."

Remy's dad, who's tall and thin and bald, sets a plastic container on the picnic table and joins Dad at the grill.

Bug sneaks a peek into the container. "Chocolate chip cookies!"

While Mom makes a fuss over the cookies to Remy's mother, I give him a smile.

"Hey," he says as he shoves his hands into the pockets of his cargo pants. I could swear he looks embarrassed.

"Hey yourself." Ugh. Why did I say *that*? I sound like Dad. All I need to do now is call him by some obnoxious nickname. Remy-Bemy or something.

"So this is home?" He gestures at the RV.

"Bertha, live and in person." I wish—so, so, so hard—that Remy was coming over to my house in Nashville. There was nothing weird or embarrassing about my house there.

"Why does it say 'Gloria' on the back? Over the deer?"

"Yeah . . . that's what my dad calls this thing. I don't think it looks much like a Gloria. Which is why I renamed it Bertha."

"No, it's definitely a Bertha. You should paint a cow over the deer. Really bring out the Bertha-ness of the whole thing." He pushes some curls behind his ear and tugs on his plain gray T-shirt.

And my heart melts.

But what I'm thinking is that he saw the freaky-eyed doe and Frankendeer and he didn't run away screaming. He saw *Groovy Travels with Gloria*, and he doesn't seem to expect some whackadoo singing '70s TV family.

In other words, Bertha and my crazy family have not scared him away. I try to remember how Jack reacted to Bertha, but I can't right now. It's hard to remember what Jack even looks like with Remy standing right here.

"So, um . . . you want a tour?" I ask. I can't believe I just offered that. But if the outside of Bertha didn't weird him out, the inside won't.

He nods, and I yank open the door and lead the way inside. He laughs at our ancient, tiny TV and says how cute Bug's cubbyhole is.

"Do you have a dog or a cat?" He taps Hugo's food bowl with the toe of a worn tennis shoe.

"A cat, Hugo. Mom and Dad got him when I was two, so I don't even remember a time when he wasn't around. He sleeps with me every night." Oh my God. Why am I saying all this to Remy?

"I had a dog who did that. She died a couple of years ago." He gives me a sad smile.

I want to reach out and touch his arm to let him know that I understand. But that would be weird, so I don't. Instead, I tell him I'm sorry about his dog. Then I lead the way back to my cubbyholes.

"This is your bedroom?" he asks.

"Yup." My face goes warm as I realize last night's pajamas are lying on the floor. I snag them with the heel of my sandal and slide them into the open closet. Then I move the door shut, very quietly, as I point across the narrow aisle.

"That's Shiver's side." For the first (and probably only) time, I'm actually thankful that most of my stuffed cats and Barbies and other kid things are in plastic garbage bags in the truck. Shiver doesn't know it, but she helped me save face in front of Remy. I pull open the curtain I always keep shut on my side. "And this is mine."

He picks up one of the few stuffed cats I still have on my bunk. A black-and-white one that Kenzie gave me because it looks like Hugo. "My best friend back home gave me that."

"That's really nice," he says, kind of wistfully. I wonder if he's missing his best friend at home. "I don't have a whole lot of friends here. You know there are kids who live in the park all year long?"

I shake my head. I can't imagine living in the wilderness all the time.

"Yeah, they're all really close. I'm kind of like an outsider to them, since I'm only here for the summer. Then at home, I miss the best part of the year, so it's hard to fit in there, too. And I don't have any brothers or sisters. You're lucky to have two."

I snort. I can't help it, even though my heart hurts at what Remy's just said. Shiver as my sister? No way. "Um, Shiver's not related to us. At all." I tell him the story of Gert and how we're taking Shiver home.

"Your parents are really cool."

"Yeah, I guess." Cool and my parents are two things that don't go together at all. He doesn't say anything else.

Outside, our parents laugh about something. I need to ask for his help, and fast, before someone comes barging in and announces dinner's ready.

I pull my phone from my pocket. "So, um, can I ask for your help with something?"

He puts the Hugo cat onto my bunk—right next to the real, sleeping Hugo—and looks at me, curious. "Sure."

"I have to get home. Like, yesterday. I have an audition in six days, and I promised my duet partner I'd be there." No need to mention that my duet partner has a new partner. Once I let Jack know I'm on my way, he'll *have* to drop Lacey. I hope. "And it's *crucial* to my future career."

He tilts his head, like he has zero idea what I'm talking about.

"As a singer. Country music. The audition's for this *huge* reality show that I just know I can get on, but only if I can actually show up for the audition." I almost mention Jack, but decide not to. It feels weird to talk about Jack with Remy.

I open my OMGH list, scroll past the embarrassing part about Jack, and pass the phone to him. "I've been trying for days, and nothing's worked out. I have a hundred dollars in birthday money, but that's it. And I was wondering if maybe . . . I mean, since you tried to get home too, a long time ago, you might have an idea?"

I stand there and twist a braid around my finger as he reads the list.

"You were going to *walk* to Tennessee?" he asks as he hands the phone back with a grin. I must look super anxious, because he drops the smile right away. "You're really serious about this, aren't you?"

"Um, yeah. Weren't you when you tried to bike home?" I don't add that I only thought about walking for, like, ten seconds. "Singing is my whole life."

He's quiet for a minute as he stares through the doorway toward the kitchen. I almost literally have to bite my tongue to keep from going, *So? Are you going to help me or not?*

"I don't know . . . I mean, I *want* to help you. But isn't this kind of extreme for a TV show?"

"It's not just *any* TV show. It's called *Dueling Duets* and . . . I'm really good, I promise. I know I can make it. Listen, I'll sing for you, and then you can decide." I open my mouth, about to belt out a song and not even caring if Shiver hears when Remy holds up a hand.

"It's okay, you don't have to prove it or anything." He

turns a little red. "I mean, I don't mind if you sing. I'm sure you're really good or you wouldn't be trying so hard to get home. But, um, you can sing, if you want?" He shifts his feet and looks everywhere but right at me.

Awkward. I close my mouth. "Um, maybe later, then?"

He's quiet for a moment, and I'm pretty sure he's going to say no. Instead, he takes off his hat and runs a hand through his hair. "Can I think about it?"

"Sure. It's just . . . I don't have a lot of time."

"Can you meet me tomorrow and I'll let you know?"

I turn around to close my curtain so I don't have to look him in the eye. I don't know why I thought this would work. I barely even know the guy. "Yeah, sure." Maybe he'll change his mind. In any case, spending more time with him isn't a bad thing at all. Just thinking that makes me feel all warm again.

Outside, we round the back of Bertha and Remy admires the spare tire cover again. "You know, I kinda like those deer."

Chapter 16

5 days until *Dueling Duets* auditions

Early the next morning, Mom and Dad take us up to the top of Signal Mountain. Which is totally appropriate, because up there I finally get a cell signal. I don't know how Remy lives without a reliable cell signal. Or maybe his parents actually pay for halfway decent phone service. All my stored-up texts to Kenzie send, one-by-one.

A message immediately comes back from her. **OMG!!! Can't wait to see you. Tell nature hottie thx. M's got a boyfriend! ;)**

My face goes red, right on top of that mountain. I barely even know Remy, but the idea of him being my boyfriend isn't a bad one at all. And it's sort of hard to keep crushing on Jack when I haven't seen him in so long—and considering how fast he dropped me as his partner. I'm definitely going to miss Remy when I leave. I wish there was a way I could still hang out with him and go home at the same time. At least I'll have that sneaky picture I took when I first met him.

I think about sending Jack a text for two seconds, but don't. I'll do it when I'm actually on my way home.

That afternoon, I find myself on a nature hike with Bug and Shiver, waiting for Remy.

"Now, this is an aspen," Remy's dad says to the tour group. He knocks on a tree overlooking the lake.

I glance down at my phone. 12:10. Where is Remy? Right before he left our cookout last night, he said he'd be here with his dad's guided hiking group at noon. The longer it takes, the more knotted up my stomach gets. Maybe he's decided no but is too chicken to actually tell me.

"You can tell this is an aspen because the bark is white and the leaves are heart-shaped. When the wind picks up, you can hear the leaves rustle and see them flutter, which is why some people call them quaking aspens." Remy's dad cups a hand around his ear, as if he's listening to the tree.

Bug steps next to him and puts her ear right up to the tree's trunk.

"What are they going to do next, hug the tree?" Shiver mumbles next to me, one earbud dangling against her shoulder.

Laughter rises in my throat. I try to stuff it down, but it gurgles out as some kind of strangled sound.

"You okay?" she asks.

I nod. There's no way I'm letting her know I almost laughed at her joke.

"Aren't you going to listen to the tree?" a voice says from behind me.

Finally! I turn around and smile. Remy, his hair curling out from under a tan hat with a brim all around, leans against another tree.

An irritated sigh escapes Shiver, and she plugs in her other earbud.

Fine by me. I don't want her listening in anyway. "So?" I ask in a stage whisper.

He nods, and I about leap toward him to smother him with a hug. But I don't, because the whole idea makes me blush just thinking about it, and also because he'd probably go running off. "And?" is all I say, like I didn't just think about hugging him.

He nods again toward all the people. We're going to have

to wait until we can get away to talk without Shiver or Bug or his dad overhearing.

"So do they really look like they're quaking? The trees?" I ask him.

His smile takes over his whole face. "Sure, when the breeze blows. Did you know that groups of aspens are connected underground? That's why you usually see a lot of them all together."

Sure enough, there are about six or seven aspens around the one where Bug's still listening. "That's really interesting," I tell Remy.

Shiver rolls her eyes for the thousandth time.

"Where are your parents?" Remy asks as we follow the group along the path through the trees. Sunlight glints off the lake beyond, and the mountains tower over everything.

"Back at the lodge." I jerk my thumb over my shoulder. "Mom needed the wi-fi to get some work done. And she ordered Dad to read more about backpacking before tomorrow. She wants to make sure he won't eat poison ivy or get bit by a rattlesnake." The crowd stops, and I let my fingers trail over the bark of another aspen while we listen to Remy's dad talk about how you can eat the petals of bluebells if you get hungry while hiking.

So gross. Who would eat some random dirty plant that bugs have been crawling all over? Besides my little sister, I mean.

"I wish I could go on a backcountry hike by myself," Remy says once we start moving again. Shiver's right in front of us, too close for us to talk about plans to get me home. I don't trust that those earbuds are turned up loud enough. "Mom and Dad are making me wait until I'm sixteen."

"Why?" I ask. "I mean, not why do you have to wait, but why do you want to go?"

"It's so peaceful out there, especially when you get up into the mountains. Hardly any people, just you and the wilderness."

"Sounds . . . scary."

Remy laughs. "Yeah, I guess it could be. One time Dad and I were way up in Death Canyon on the trail—"

"Death Canyon? Shiver would like that one," I say, just to see if she can hear me. She doesn't look back, but I still don't want to take any chances.

"It's not as hard as the name makes it sound," he says. "But we came around a corner, and there was a bear right there, just chowing down on a plant. She looked up and stared at us. Then she wandered off into the woods. It was amazing."

If my eyes were any wider, they'd fall right out of my head. "That's insane. You could've died!"

He shrugs. "Bear attacks are pretty rare."

"But they happen! What if that bear was extra hungry and thought you looked like dinner?"

"Then I guess I wouldn't be here right now." He pushes a curl back under his hat. "With you."

That last part makes me go warm all over. I suddenly wish I'd taken the extra time to put mascara on this morning. But that's kind of hard to do when Bug's pushing her way into the bathroom to brush her teeth and Mom keeps reaching in to clean something.

"Over here," Remy says in a quiet voice. He takes a couple of steps off the trail onto a small lookout over the lake. The group slowly passes by us as we act as if we're admiring the view.

I follow his lead and put my hand over my eyes to get a better view of the mountains. It's like we're in some kind of spy movie, exchanging nuclear codes or something while trying not to look as if we know each other. Which is good, because I can't stop thinking about the way he said *with you* and the way it's making my heart beat super fast.

"You know how I told you about how I hated it here at

first?" he says out of nowhere. "After a while, I found out that I feel more at home here than at our house in Denver."

"Oookay . . ." How can you feel at home without your actual house?

Remy smiles. "You think I'm crazy, right?"

"Kinda. So what's your idea?"

He sighs a little, and I feel like I've disappointed him or something. In the distance, Remy's dad's voice echoes through the trees, but other than that, it's silent at our little overlook.

"Do you have a bike?" he asks.

I nod.

"You could ride that—"

"All the way home? That's only a little less crazy than my walking home idea. And didn't you try that once?"

"You didn't let me finish."

"Oh. Right. Sorry."

"Okay, so you ride your bike, but only to the nearest bus station," he says.

When I texted Kenzie about taking a bus home, she told me it would be full of scary people. Except that now I don't really have a choice. I've run through every other possible option. "How far is the bus?" I ask.

"Not sure. We'll have to look it up. Can you meet me at the lodge tomorrow?"

"Sure." I really, really, really wish today was tomorrow.

"Hey, check out the mountains."

I follow his finger. Clouds have lowered themselves over the tops of the tallest peaks, letting just the tip-tops of the mountains peek out.

"It looks like they're wearing scarves," I say.

"I never thought of it that way." Remy gazes at the mountains. We're completely, totally alone.

So of course I start wondering if Remy's going to try to hold my hand.

I kind of hope he does, but now that's all I can think about.

As the clouds shift, it looks as if the mountains' scarves are blowing in the wind. I wonder if Mom and Dad are seeing this from their spot in the lodge's lobby. I feel like singing, but Remy might think that's weird. So instead, I dig my phone out of my pocket and snap a picture to text to Kenzie whenever I get a signal again. "There's something a little magical about those mountains, isn't there?" I finally say.

Remy's eyes light up. "This is what I think heaven is like."

And I know exactly what he means. Except my idea of

heaven also includes Kenzie, Hugo, a real house, a pool, and a fabulous music career. And Bug, if she isn't being too annoying. And Mom and Dad, acting like their old normal selves. No Shiver, obviously. But the mountains can be there, beckoning from across the lake and wrapped in clouds. I really could stare at them all day, especially with Remy right beside me.

I don't realize I'm humming until I catch Remy glancing at me.

"Sorry," I say.

"It's okay. Don't you owe me a song anyway?" He's smiling, so I'm going to guess that he's serious. I smile back and break out into the Band Perry's "Don't Let Me Be Lonely."

When I finish, he's looking at me like he's never seen me before. Then he says, "That was really good. You're going to win that audition, you know."

Okay, normally I love attention when I'm singing, but now I just feel all warm and weird. I can't look at Remy. So I lean forward and look at the mountains and pretend I'm not thinking about how much I like him.

His hand just barely brushes mine, and I pull in all the available air.

It's actually, really happening! Eek! This nice, cute, funny guy is going to hold my hand. Wait, what am I supposed to do? I wish I could hit pause right now so I could discuss the whole situation with Kenzie.

"There you are," Shiver says from behind us.

Remy yanks his hand away and uses it to adjust his hat.

"Come on, the talk's almost over and we're supposed to meet your parents. And you completely ignored your sister for the entire hike." Shiver's standing at the bend in the trail, her hands on her hips. She sounds like Mom.

I glare at her. Seriously, she's determined to ruin every single good thing that happens to me.

There is absolutely no way she'll mess with my new plan. I don't care if I have to lock her in Bertha's bathroom to make it happen.

As we move along the trail, I update OMGH:

Operation Maya Goes Home (OMGH)
(In time for Dueling Duets.)
Countdown: T minus 5 days
How to Get Home to Audition with Jack
and Win His Heart with My Voice and Stellar
Personality:
1. ~~Convince Mom and Dad this is the worst idea~~
   ~~ever.~~

2. ~~Bertha needs major repairs~~ (tires don't count, I guess).

3. ~~K fakes lots of broken bones & needs me to spoon her soup.~~ (Not believable.)

4. ~~Walk. Phone mapping app says this will take only 253 hours. Which is like 10½ days if I don't sleep, eat, go to the bathroom, or stop at all.~~ (I don't even like Dad's 2-mile hikes, so . . .)

5. ~~Hitchhike!~~ (Shiver. Ugh. Also, scary.)

6. ~~Find ride with another RV family.~~ (Shiver. Again.)

7. ~~Buy plane ticket with Mom's credit card.~~ (Busted. And guilty.)

8. Bike to the bus . . . somewhere!

Chapter 17

4 days until *Dueling Duets* auditions

A wi-fi signal is the best thing ever. Like having a giant glass of water after running. Or that perfect pair of comfy, worn boots (which I just so happen to be wearing right now). Or winning *Dueling Duets*.

My stomach is full of pasta from dinner, and I'm lounging on a couch in the lobby of Jackson Lake Lodge. My family (and Shiver) are all sprawled out on chairs and couches, soaking up the wi-fi like it's long-lost gold. Even Bug, who's curled up with Dad reading about horrible things that can happen on backcountry hikes on some website he pulled up on his phone. Through the giant picture window (and it is one *serious* picture window, reaching from the floor all the way up to the ceiling), the sun sets behind the mountains. It's kind of perfect, actually.

Especially because Remy's next to me on the couch. Not next-to-me next to me—more like sitting close enough that I could reach out and hold his hand. If I were brave enough to do that, which I'm not. We've both got our phones on, and we're pretending to text or whatever while we whisper to each other. Dad made me paddle-boat and hike up to some canyon earlier, while Remy spent the day helping his dad.

"So where is the bus?" I ask him once I'm sure no one's listening. Especially Shiver, who's not-so-conveniently sitting right across from us.

"Cody. I looked it up earlier. But that's all I had a chance to check on," Remy whispers.

"What are you two whispering about?" Mom asks, without even looking up from her laptop.

"Uh . . ." Remy's apparently not so good at the lying-to-parents thing.

"Nothing." Wow, Maya, that was genius.

Mom finally looks up and smiles at us. Then she goes back to work. Great. Now she thinks we're whispering . . . I don't know, whatever people who like each other whisper.

I can almost feel the red creeping up my neck when Remy talks again. "I'll look up how far it is, and you check on the ticket prices."

"Remy, what are these flowers?" Dad calls as we're punching searches into our phones. He holds up a picture in his backpacking book, showing us some gorgeous purple blooms. Bug's madly scrolling through something on his phone, probably trying to find the answer first.

"Showy fleabane," Remy says.

"Know-it-all," Shiver mutters from her seat across from us.

I really can't wait to get away from her, scary bus people or not. I've tried to be patient and understanding, because I know she's still sad about Gert, but really—there's only so much grumpiness I can take.

I finish typing in the info for a one-way ticket from Cody to Nashville. "Ugh, two hundred and fifty dollars."

Remy leans over my shoulder. "Hey, not if you get the kids' rate. That's only one hundred and fifty."

"I'm *not* a kid, thank you very much. It says here that ages twelve and up are adult rate." Really, adults can be short. Not everyone ends up at supermodel height.

"But they don't know that, and you can pass for younger." Remy looks all pleased with himself.

I don't want to pass for younger is what I want to say, but I don't. I get what he's saying. I either pretend I'm ten, or I can't afford to go home. "Okay, fine. But how exactly am I going to get a ticket? No way will they sell me one." Across from us, Shiver narrows her eyes at me, but doesn't say anything.

When she goes back to her phone, Remy whispers, "This part I have figured out. We'll get you one online."

"But we'd need a credit card. I already tried that with a plane ticket and got in huge trouble. And if we can somehow figure out how to use cash, I only have a hundred dollars." I chew on my lip in frustration. "This isn't going to work after all. Everything I try seems to backfire. I'm too young, I don't have enough money, Shiver gets in the way, serial killers."

"Serial killers?" Remy pushes a curl behind his ear and scrunches up his mouth, like he's trying to figure out what in the world I'm talking about.

"Never mind. I feel like I've tried everything. Maybe I should just give up. Forget *Dueling Duets*, like Mom and Dad want, and try to forget my dreams until I'm grown up. Pretend Jack never asked me to sing with him, and get used to not having an actual home in an actual place with friends and school and—" I stop, realizing I just mentioned Jack to

Remy. But either he didn't notice or he doesn't care. "I mean, just forget about having a normal life."

"Normal life is way overrated," Remy says.

Okay, I like him, but that's just crazy. "I want to go home."

He glances at me, and I could swear he looks a little sad. I pat my Heidi braids, feeling slightly self-conscious.

"Well, then let's do this," he finally says. "We'll get someone—an adult—to buy your ticket at the bus station. And . . ." He fishes through a pocket and shows me the tip of a single bill. "My grandparents sent me this for my birthday. You can have it."

I glance at it. A hundred dollars! But he can't give me his birthday money. Maybe if it was twenty bucks, but a hundred? "Remy, thanks, but I can't take that."

"It's okay. I don't have anything I want all that bad, and you need to get home."

"So *if* I take it, then who would . . . Oh!" My brain lights up with an idea. "We'll pay them! Like, if the ticket costs a hundred and fifty dollars, I can pay them fifty dollars to buy it for me." I'm almost afraid to hope for it, but this just might actually work, since together we have two hundred dollars. "Okay, so how far do I have to bike to get there?"

"It's, um . . . a little over thirteen hours to ride a bike from here to Cody. I'm sorry, Maya. I didn't realize it would take that long." Remy shows me the little blue line on his phone that shows the route from Signal Mountain Campground, where Bertha's parked, to the bus station in Cody.

I trace it with my finger. "Thirteen hours. That's a whole day. I can do it."

"You can?" Remy lifts his eyebrows. "It gives you plenty of daylight if you don't stop too much, but that's a seriously long bike ride. Have you ever done one like that before?"

I think for a second. The farthest I ever rode my bike was with Kenzie. We went from her house to this amazing street fair one time. It took maybe an hour to get there. "Kind of? Not really. But if I do this, I can get home. And I want that more than anything in the world. I'll sleep on the bus."

"Then I'm going with you," Remy says.

"To Nashville?"

"To Cody. I've got a bike."

"You'd really ride that far with me?" I think my jaw might actually be hanging open.

"Sure. Why not? It'd be an adventure." Remy smiles,

probably dreaming of running into a herd of buffalo and being chased by coyotes. "And besides, it's more fun to have someone along, right?"

He looks right at me then, and I'm pretty sure I'm going to melt into my seat.

Bug laughs, and I glance over, hit with a pile of guilt as big as Bertha that I'm planning to leave my family. Dad's telling Bug how he plans to catch fish in the lake to eat for dinner on his big hike, while Mom's frowning at her computer. And Shiver's watching us—again.

I *have* to do this. In fact, what I'm doing will actually help Mom. If I can win *Dueling Duets*, she can come back home. And then she won't have to look so stressed out every time she opens her laptop.

"Plus," Remy goes on, "that road between the park and Cody can be really windy and narrow. You need someone with you." He clicks off his phone and sets it on the couch.

"Thank you," I say. I'm relieved—and really, really happy at the thought of spending all this time with Remy. Riding all the way back through Yellowstone seems kind of scary, and I'm glad I don't have to do it by myself. "But how will you get home?"

He shrugs. "I'll call my parents."

I smile at him with probably the biggest smile I've had since leaving home.

"What are you two morons gossiping about? You've been whispering since Remy got up here." Shiver slides into the empty armchair next to me.

"Nothing." I shove my phone into my backpack.

She gives me this look, like she's dying to know more. As if I'd ever tell her my plans. She'd come up with ninety reasons they wouldn't work, and then would do something annoying to stop us.

"Your parents asked if we all want to get ice cream. You too." She jerks her blue head at Remy.

Mom and Dad are standing up, waiting for us, and Bug's motioning her arms at us like she's flagging down an airplane. "Of course," I say. Who turns down ice cream?

Remy and I get up and join the rest of my family, Shiver trailing along behind.

"Hey, nitwit," she says just as we all step into the diner. When Remy and I both turn around, she says, "Him, not you. You left your phone. Here." She hands him his cell and gives us both an extra-glarish glare.

"Thanks," Remy says, not paying any attention to Shiver's look. "Okay, so you guys have to try the Mount Owen. It's ice cream and chocolate chip cookies and huge. Bet you can't eat a whole one."

I smile. No one challenges my ability to eat ice cream. "You're on," I say.

Shiver rolls her eyes. She probably hates ice cream.

Dad's alarm goes off at five the next morning. It's backpacking day. And Maya Goes Home Day, but he doesn't know that, of course.

"I don't like leaving you all alone," Mom says after breakfast in the dark. Dad's outside, hefting his giant backpack into the bed of the truck, next to my garbage bags of stuff. Mom insisted on hiking in the first few miles with him to make sure he doesn't tumble down a mountain or anything.

"We'll be fine, really!" I'm itching to grab my own backpack and get moving.

"Maybe you should stay up at the lodge? Take in some ranger talks? Use the wi-fi?"

I can't be separated from my bike, so this is a Big Fat No. I put on a good pout. "But you promised we could stay here and watch TV and act normal for a change."

Mom pushes her lips together, and I can almost see the wheels in her head turning. "All right. But stick close to the RV—that means you, Bug." She looks over my shoulder at Bug, who's eating trail mix for breakfast. "Don't talk to strangers. Don't open the door to strangers. Don't cook anything with the oven. Don't—"

"We won't drown, set the RV on fire, cut off any fingers, get kidnapped, or let wild animals attack us, okay?" Now, please go. . . .

Mom smiles. "I forget how grown up you are sometimes, Maya."

And *that* makes me feel super guilty. As in, how can I run off and leave her and Dad and Bug here in Bertha? Not only will they worry about me, it also seems kind of . . . selfish. And maybe it is. But I'm desperate. I'll miss the biggest opportunity of my life if I don't leave now. One that's about to be handed over to *Lacey*, of all people.

"I'll be back sometime after lunch," Mom says. "As long as Dad doesn't fall into a lake or anything. Wish me luck."

"Luck," I tell her as she gives me and Bug and even Shiver one last hug.

"If I'm not here by three o'clock, call out the search party." With that, she waves and is out the door. I have a weird, achy feeling in my chest, but I ignore it. I have a mission to complete.

Shiver rummages in the fridge for more food, I guess, while Bug sits at the bus seat table and opens a book. I try to look like I'm doing something totally normal as I make my way back to my cubbyhole for my backpack. I do one last-minute check to make sure I have everything I need. I yank hard at the zipper to get it closed again. Then I unfold the note I wrote last night and spread it out on top of my bunk, with a small stuffed cat on each corner to hold it in place.

Dear Mom, Dad, Bug (and Shiver),

By the time you read this, I'll be on my way to Nashville to try out for Dueling Duets. I really miss home. I hope you all do too. When I win, I'll get us a new house. I'll call you when I get there. Please don't donate my stuff but send it as soon as you can, and take care of Hugo for me.

Love,
Maya

P.S. I hope Dad didn't get eaten by a bear on his hike.
P.P.S. I'll miss you.

I give Hugo one last snuggle. He yawns and swats at my braids. "See you soon, big guy," I whisper to him. Then I pop my purple hat onto my head, climb down the ladder, and head to the door.

"I'm going down to the cliff," I announce.

Bug leaps up from the bus seat. "I want to come!"

Duh, Maya. Of course she'd want to come. "Um, you can't," I say.

Bug gives me a confused look, while Shiver does that eye-narrowing thing again. She pulls out an earbud.

I look at Bug. "I mean, you can, but give me a few minutes first. I have to take a shower, and then I'll go to the cliff."

"You took a shower last night," Shiver says.

"So what? I want another shower. I like being clean." I push open the door.

"Why are you taking your backpack?" she asks.

"Because I have stuff in it. Shower stuff."

"Hurry up," Bug says. "I want to see if there are any animal tracks down there before people stomp all over them."

I slide out and close the door behind me. The sun is just beginning to light the sky. "See ya, Bertha." I pat the dirty RV on the side before making my way around back to get my bike.

Our bikes are lined up in a row and chained to a tree

behind Bertha. I fish the keys from a pocket in my backpack and pop the lock. It's a good thing that Bug's bike was the one Dad demolished back in Texas. After pulling mine out, I redo the lock, and roll my bike around the side of Bertha.

Where Shiver and Bug are waiting for me.

Chapter 18

3 days until *Dueling Duets* auditions

"Uh, hi." I can't think of anything else to say. What are they doing out here? And how in the world am I going to get rid of them? I'm supposed to meet Remy near Jackson Lake Lodge in thirty minutes.

"Hi yourself," Shiver says, her arms crossed.

Bug has her arms crossed too, and frowns at me. Like a mini Shiver, with different hair. It's really sort of creepy, actually.

"So . . . what are y'all doing out here?" I stand over my bike, ready to go, and exchange my hat for the helmet in my stuffed backpack.

"We know what you're up to," Shiver says.

"Uh-huh," Bug adds.

I wrap my hands around the handlebars. "And what exactly do you know?"

"Oh, give it up, Maya," Shiver says. "You and Remy aren't that good at conspiring. I heard you talking last night, and then I saw that map on his phone. You're biking to Cody to try to get home."

This is so not good. But I can't let them stop me. This is probably my last chance to get home, unless I somehow win my very own private airplane to swoop in and pick me up. "So what if I am?"

"You know she's been doing this your whole trip," Shiver says to Bug.

"Why, Maya?" Bug asks. "Won't you miss us?"

Bug knows how to make my heart hurt. "Of course," I say. "But I had plans to try out for the show, and then Mom and Dad hatched *this* plan, and now I'm a gazillion miles from home. I have to get back. This audition is my whole life."

"What show?" Shiver asks.

"*Duel*—" Bug starts, but I jump in before she can out me to Shiver.

"It's nothing. I mean, not nothing, but it's a reality show."

"Seriously? You're running away to try out for a *reality show*?" Shiver curls her lip as she looks at me.

"You don't get to judge my dreams, okay?" And that's all I have to say to her. I turn back to Bug. "Plus I miss Kenzie, and she misses me." I don't mention Jack. Shiver would never let that drop. Not to mention that it's weird to think about Jack when Remy's just down the road, waiting for me.

Bug bites her lip. She likes Kenzie because Kenzie's always been super interested in whatever odd little fact Bug's told her.

"And what exactly are you going to do once you get to town?" Shiver asks. "If you make it, that is."

I hop onto my bike and ride in a little circle. "I'm going to take a bus home. I have the money," I say before she can accuse me of sneaking on or anything.

"A bus?" Shiver looks as if I just suggested that we all eat mud. "Yuck. Do you know how many weirdos ride cross-country buses?"

"I don't have to talk to anyone."

"Don't worry about that. They'll talk to you anyway."

I brake and put a foot down. "How do you know? Have you ridden a bus?"

Shiver huffs. "No, but I read. And I watch movies. Plenty of creepers on buses, trust me."

"I'll take my chances, thanks. Look, I have to go now. Love you, Bug. Tell Mom and Dad I'll call them soon."

Shiver jumps in front of my tire.

"What are you doing?" I ask. Although it's pretty obvious. She's trying to ruin my plans—again.

"You're really going to do this?" she asks. "Bike all day and then ride a scary bus all night?"

"No, I just made all that up." Really, if I don't move now, Remy's going to think I've chickened out. I hate the thought of him waiting up there by himself, thinking I'm not going to show up.

"Leave your parents and your little sister here for some reality show? That's so selfish, you know."

Like I needed to be reminded about that. Bug gives me the same look she does when she finds out I've eaten the last chocolate chip cookie.

"I wasn't going forever," I lie. "Just until after the audition, and then I'd come back. Unless I have to leave again for filming or something."

Shiver tilts her head as she looks at me. I'd say it seems like she's thinking, except I can't really tell anything about

Shiver. Nothing that's on the inside, anyway. "Hmm. Then I'm going too."

"To Nashville?" Why in the world would she want to go to Nashville with me?

"No, stupid. I'm riding with you to Cody. So if you get trampled by a buffalo—"

"Bison," Bug corrects her.

"Whatever. If you get hurt, then I can get your sorry butt rescued. I kind of owe your parents, in case you haven't noticed."

Nooooo. Like the ride isn't long enough without Shiver there. "Remy's going with me."

She rolls her eyes. "Ha. Like that kid'll be any help."

Is she serious? No way does Shiver outrank Remy in the Scary Nature Stuff Rescue Department.

"I'm going too," Bug pipes up.

"What? No. It's, like, a whole day just to ride to the bus station. You can't go. And you don't have a bike," I tell her.

Bug takes two steps and puts her face right in front of mine. "I am too. You're not the boss of me, Sister-Abandoner. And Shiver and I can ride Mom and Dad's bikes."

Shiver smiles like some weird kind of proud parent.

"Fine. Y'all go inside and get your stuff. I'll wait here." I put my backpack on the ground to show that yes, I will wait. "And I'm not abandoning you, by the way," I say to Bug.

Bug doesn't say anything, just stands there in that Shiver-like pose with her arms crossed.

"Nice try," Shiver says. "All I need is my backpack. Bug, can you grab that for me while I wait here?"

Ugh.

Bug races inside and emerges from Bertha three minutes later, Shiver's black backpack in one hand, and her own green one, covered in Save-the-Whatever buttons and national park pins, already on her shoulders. She's got her helmet and Mom's, too.

"I left a note for Mom," Bug says as Shiver takes the keys from me and unlocks the bikes from the tree.

"Good." Shiver rolls Mom's bike to Bug. "It's nice that some people actually care about parents who love them."

"Right," I say as soon as Bug's on the bike. "I'm going now." I pedal out, Bug right behind me, and Shiver hurrying to get Dad's bike unchained.

"We should wait for her," Bug says when we reach the campground entrance.

"If we have to." Of course Shiver would be the one holding me up. Bug and I wait next to the huge bulletin board that has campground rules and ranger talk schedules and bear warnings tacked to it. I guess I should be thankful that the plan is still on, even though I'm dragging along my sister and the most annoying person on the planet.

Shiver finally pedals up. "Gee, thanks for waiting," she says.

"You're welcome," I say in the most curt tone possible. "Let's go before Remy gives up on me actually showing."

It's so early, there are barely any cars on the road. We ride in single-file silence, except for the obnoxious yawns from Shiver in the back. I pedal hard on purpose, hoping to make her change her mind. It's freezing, like usual. And every once in a while, patches of the low fog that covers the lakes and hides the mountains creep onto the road. It feels like riding through clouds. Or maybe riding through the set of a horror movie.

It doesn't take long to reach the turnoff to Jackson Lake Lodge. I roll my bike to a stop when I spot Remy relaxing against a tree, his bike lying on the damp ground next to him. Even with Bug and Shiver behind me, my face instantly goes all smiley when I see him.

"We have a party," he says when he spies Bug and Shiver.

Party. Ha ha. "Shiver figured it out, and then they both insisted on coming," I tell him.

Remy stands and starts folding the rain poncho he was

sitting on. "You guys realize this is over a hundred-mile bike ride?"

Bug's eyes light up, like she can't imagine anything better than riding a bike all day long.

"I saw your map," Shiver says. "Bug and I are coming to make sure she doesn't do anything else stupid."

The "she" is obviously me. "I'm not my dad," I say to Shiver. "I can ride my bike without starting an avalanche."

Shiver sweeps her eyes over me, as if she's assessing whether I'm fit enough to ride my bike over a hundred miles. I'm not, really, but who put her in charge?

"We have to go if we want to get there before dark," Remy says.

As we roll back onto the empty road, Remy coasts next to me. "Thanks for coming," I tell him.

"I wouldn't miss this for anything," he says.

Wait, is he talking about the bike ride? Or me? I fumble for something to say. "Hey, the mountains are gone." I gesture at where they should be, through the trees. It looks strange, as if they've been erased or painted over in flat gray.

"Yeah, they disappear in the rain and the fog sometimes," he says. He smiles a little, like he has good memories of mountains gone missing.

That smile almost makes me wish I could audition here instead of in Nashville. Almost.

"I'm going to stay in back, in case anyone runs into trouble," he says.

Such a Remy thing to do. I'm glad he's looking out for my little sister (and Shiver, I guess), but I'm a little annoyed that he can't ride next to me. Bug drifts back to ride with him, probably to grill him with questions about bear poop and tree fungus.

As we ride, the bright morning sun starts to burn away the fog. But it's still not warm enough for me to take off any of the three layers I put on this morning. Or my gloves. If I weren't wearing a helmet, I'd have a fluffy hat pulled down over my ears. I'm bundled up like it's almost Christmas.

Yet another reason I'm ready to get home. Hello, shorts and flip-flops! I'm so excited for normal summer clothes that I shoved a pair of flip-flops into my backpack. I'll put them on as soon we get somewhere warm.

I'm daydreaming of lying poolside in a cute new swimsuit when I hear a siren.

Chapter 19

3 days until *Dueling Duets* auditions

It's not a siren, really, but more of a *WHOOP!* sound. I peer over my shoulder, past everyone else, and spot a white SUV with a green stripe and the National Park Service logo on the side. The ranger inside is waving us off the road.

So. Not. Good.

I brake, and everyone else falls in behind me.

"That didn't take long," Shiver says. She's breathing heavily, and I know this is exactly what she wanted. She's probably imagining lounging on Bertha's couch to watch whatever we can get on our ancient TV.

The ranger steps out of the car before I've decided on a

good lie. I can't believe I didn't think this through ahead of time. He's assessing us and is about to say something, when Remy unbuckles his helmet.

"Remy?" the ranger says. "A bit early for a bike ride, isn't it?"

"It is," Remy says, looking every inch the good camper, "but my friends wanted to hike the Polecat Creek trail up around Flagg Ranch. This is Maya, Adalie, and Emmeline. Mr. Hicks." Remy waves his hand in introduction.

If looks could kill, Remy would be dead from the stares Shiver and Bug are both throwing at him for using their given names.

"They're staying at Signal Mountain," Remy adds. The ranger's about to open his mouth again, but Remy plows on. "Any sign of bear activity up by Flagg Ranch? I told them we might get up there and have to turn around."

I bite my lip to keep from smiling. Remy's somehow turned into a much better liar. Maybe it's just lying to parents that bothers him. Or maybe this is his element.

Ranger Hicks leans against the side of his SUV. "Not since last week. You should be okay up there. Now, back down around Two Ocean and Emma Matilda Lakes, that's a different story."

Remy nods. "Yeah, my mom said they were thinking of closing the trails there for a little while."

"Probably have to. Don't really care to add to the death toll."

They chuckle like this is some weird park ranger inside joke. Bug's eyes are completely round, and she's probably adding "hike around Two Ocean and Emma Matilda Lakes" to her mental to-do list.

Ranger Hicks moves around to the driver's side of his car. "Hey, you kids want a ride up to Flagg Ranch? That's a long way to ride a bike."

Remy and I look at each other. He shrugs, but I mouth, *Yes!* I mean, my legs are already a little achy and we still have a gazillion more miles to go. And he knows Ranger Hicks, so it's not like taking a ride from a stranger. Although I already tried to do that . . . twice.

"Sure, thanks," Remy says.

Ranger Hicks loads our bikes onto the bike rack on the back of his SUV. Then we all climb in and . . . wow. I never in a million years thought I'd be thankful for soft seats in a car. I lay my head back and relax as the trees fly by outside. Every mile gets me a little closer to *Dueling Duets*. In fact, I'm so, so, so comfortable and happy, I could fall asleep.

"Here we are."

I open my eyes to see the ranger pulling over. There's a sign near a perimeter of trees that announces the trailhead. When we stop, Ranger Hicks unloads our bikes. We make a show of wheeling them over to a post near the trailhead, and Remy stretches a chain around them.

"Well, you be careful now." Ranger Hicks climbs back into his car.

"Always." Remy waves, and the ranger drives off.

"How . . . ?" Shiver's watching the car disappear down the road.

"Perks of being me," Remy says.

"Huh." Shiver turns back and looks him up and down, as if she's seeing him for the first time. And for once, it seems she's at a loss for a snarky comment.

"We need to wait a few minutes before we move on," Remy says. "His patrol ends at the park border, so he'll be turning around and heading south again really soon."

He leads us onto the trail, just a few feet in. Then we sit and wait.

"Thanks for getting us out of that one," I tell him.

"No problem. This trail is a really good one. Lots of wild-flowers and a pretty creek. You know, if this doesn't work out and you guys come back through here," he says, almost as if he's hoping I flame out at the auditions.

And I admit—once I get past Remy wishing I'd mess up—it sounds kind of good. Strolling hand in hand with him along a trail, flowers of every color bobbing in the breeze, sunlight sparkling on the water, birds chirping.

I kind of wish I could have both—music career and my family, Remy and Kenzie, and Nashville and the mountains. But I can't. I have to choose, and really, there's no choice. I have to follow my dreams. And sometimes I get so homesick it feels like all the lonely and the sad have filled up the place where my heart used to be.

"Maybe another time," I tell him with a smile.

His face falls just a little, but he recovers fast and starts quizzing Bug on the plants growing around us. It's quiet here, with only the sounds of birds and the breeze through the trees. There are a few other cars parked in the lot across the road.

I'm about to ask Remy if we can leave yet, when the brush rustles behind me.

I freeze. "What is that?"

We're all silent as we peer into the tall pines. More rustling, and something large and brown moves slowly through the trees.

"It's a bear," Shiver whispers, panic in her voice. She jumps up, and I can't help it—I'm right there with her.

Remy holds up a hand. "It's not a bear." He squints into the trees.

The thing moves again, and now Bug backs down the trail toward our bikes.

A large oblong head bobs into view between a break in the pines. It's chewing slowly and not even looking at us.

"What *is* that?" Shiver asks through her teeth.

"Moose," Remy answers.

"It doesn't have antlers," I say. Every moose I've seen in pictures has looked like Bullwinkle—with giant, scary-looking, person-killing antlers on its head.

"That's because it's a female," Bug says. "We should go. They can get really aggressive."

"Especially if she has a baby around," Remy says, almost completing Bug's sentence.

Quiet as librarians, we shuffle back to the trailhead, where Remy unlocks our bikes. Keeping one eye on the trail in case of sudden moose charge, I climb onto my bike. When everyone's ready, Remy leads the way past the Flagg Ranch lodge to the main road.

The sun shines over the trees as we start riding on. And

on and on and on. Until my rear end feels like it's fused to the bike seat and my legs start to burn. I've definitely gone farther than I did that day with Kenzie last year.

I slow so that I can pedal next to Remy. "I thought you said we were close to Yellowstone."

"We are," he says.

Okay, so his idea of close and my idea of close are two totally different things. "Like, how many miles close?"

Remy juts out a lip as he thinks. "Maybe a couple more miles?"

I can survive a couple more miles. If I can breathe, that is. I pedal harder and take up the lead again.

Until I run out of air and have to fall back.

"We've barely even started and Wilderness Chick here is already worn out," Shiver says as she coasts past me.

Whatever. I can totally hear her trying to catch her breath up there. I wish Kenzie was here. We could lean against each other and complain about the whole thing. Except I'm partly doing this to get back to Kenzie, so that doesn't really make sense. Maybe Mom, then. She'd be panting and sweating right beside me, and we'd exchange looks and "are we there yet" complaints from behind everyone else. Except that makes me feel guilty for leaving all over again.

Guess I'm alone in my whole death-by-bicycle thing. Except for Shiver.

"Don't go too fast," Bug says from right behind me. "You might get altitude sickness."

Right.

Yellowstone, Yellowstone, Yellowstone. The word rolls around in my head. We're almost there. We have to be. I just have to keep pedaling. Which is not easy, considering that my legs hurt and my back hurts, and I think even my toes hurt.

Not more than fifteen minutes later, we roll up to cars parked at a pull-off. A whole bunch of tourists are snapping pictures of themselves and their families in front of the Yellowstone sign.

"Break?" Remy asks.

"God, yes," Shiver says.

"Sure," I say. What I really want to do is dive off my bike into some grass and sleep for the rest of the day. Instead, I roll onto the pull-off like a normal biking person, climb off, and try not to plop down too fast against the short post holding up a wooden railing near the sign. Last thing I want is Bug and Remy thinking I have attitude sickness or whatever it's called.

Shiver collapses next to me and lies down, eyes closed, while Bug inspects a pretty yellow flower growing nearby. I gulp some water and eat a granola bar from my backpack in two bites.

"How much farther?" Shiver asks from the ground.

Remy's not even sitting. Instead, he chews trail mix while he watches tourists mug for the camera. "Oh, I don't know. Still over a hundred miles. Next landmark is Lewis Lake."

Shiver peers at him with one eye open. "And where exactly is Lewis Lake?"

"In Yellowstone," Bug answers. "Don't you remember driving by it on the way down here?"

"I *know* it's in Yellowstone." Shiver closes her eyes again. She's probably rolling them under her lids.

"We can't stay here long," Remy says. He closes his bag of trail mix and stuffs it into his backpack.

"Wait," I say. "We need a picture."

"Really?" Shiver asks. "You're just like your parents."

"Am not. I just want to remember this, that's all." Am I really like Mom and Dad? I can't be, right? I mean, I'd never pluck my kids out of their normal lives and dream auditions and plop them into a hideous motor home and visit creepy abandoned places like Hell's Half Acre and offer to drive obnoxious girls named Shiver home to California. Instead, I'm Completely Sensible Maya—the only Casselberry who has her head on straight.

Remy and Bug pose on either side of the sign. Shiver heaves a sigh and joins them like I'm asking her to walk the plank or something.

"Smile!" I yell. Remy grins, Bug gives herself bunny ears, and Shiver rolls her eyes.

Perfect.

We pedal away, up the road toward Lewis Lake, which Remy says is about ten miles away. I start daydreaming about Kenzie's reaction when I step off the bus in Nashville. I'm wondering if I should let Jack know I'm coming for sure or surprise him mid-rehearsal with Lacey, when I hear Remy and Bug talking behind me.

"You'd be great at it," Remy's saying.

"Really?" Even without looking at her, I can tell Bug is in awe.

"Yeah, you should talk to my parents when we get back. They can tell you everything you need to know."

"Need to know about what?" I ask over my shoulder.

"About being a park ranger!" Bug says.

"You'd be really good at that, Bugby," I tell her. She'd be

the perfect park ranger. She already knows everything about every place we stop. They probably wouldn't even have to teach her anything.

After this, we're quiet. I don't know about everyone else, but just keeping my feet pushing the pedals is taking all of my energy. Plus, the road is really narrow through here and the traffic has definitely picked up.

I'm dying to ask how much farther to the lake. But every time I almost let it slip from my mouth, I force it back down. Partly because I'm afraid it'll still be forever away, but mostly because I don't want Remy to know how exhausted I am yet.

I peek back at him. He's turning his head left and right, taking in the scenery. Which is pine trees. Lots and lots of pine trees. He barely looks as if he's breathing hard, and he definitely doesn't look like his toes hurt. He's hardly even broken a sweat, while I pulled off my sweatshirt back at the Yellowstone sign and tied it around my waist. Also, my backpack is creating a massive sweaty spot on the back of my two shirts now. Which will make me look super cute when we stop again, I'm sure.

Then I realize I've been staring at him for who knows how long. I yank my eyes away before he can notice.

Shiver's still rolling along, but looking more droopy than

Remy. About as droopy as I feel, actually. Why hasn't she turned around yet? I mean, she's only coming to keep an eye on me. That can't possibly be a good enough reason to put yourself through this bike-riding torture.

The trees finally thin out some, and I feel like I can breathe again. Mostly. Now there are rolling hills and a river that sometimes flows close to the road. Remy points out some mule deer grazing nearby, and I finally have to ask.

"So, um . . . how much farther to the lake?"

"I don't know, maybe about five miles? Or it could be closer to seven."

So not helpful. Somehow I thought Remy would know the exact mileage. Like, 4.2 miles and then turn left. Kind of like the GPS Mom had in her car back at home.

I wonder what time it is. It's *got* to be three or four in the afternoon by now. Although that wouldn't be good, because Mom would be back, and I really need to be a lot closer to Cody by the time that happens. I'm trying to figure out how I can reach around, open my backpack, and snag my phone and a granola bar, when Remy speaks up.

"There's the sign!"

I squint ahead. Sure enough, a little brown sign announces Lewis Lake with little pictures of a picnic table, a campground, and something that looks like a boat. Up in front, Shiver waits for a car to go by, then makes the left into the turn-off. We roll down a short pine-lined road that opens up into a parking lot with picnic tables set back in the trees—pine trees, of course. I don't think any other kind of tree grows here. Shiver tosses Dad's bike into the grass and promptly sprawls out on one of the benches of the closest picnic table. I try not to think about how Dad would've never thrown his bike aside like that.

I park my bike gently, and almost have to peel myself off the seat. Every single muscle in my body is on fire. I hobble over to the other side of the picnic table like I'm a hundred years old. Bug leaps off Mom's bike and stretches, while Remy gets off his as if riding a bazillion miles is a normal, everyday thing for him.

Which it might be. I don't know.

I pull out my phone. 9:36 a.m. Seriously? Oh well, I suppose that means we're making good time. It would be soooo nice if another ranger came by and gave us a ride again.

"Can we eat?" Bug asks. "I'm starving."

Remy opens his backpack and brings out trail mix, peanut butter sandwiches, beef jerky, and a pouch of tuna.

I gape at it for a second. Then I pull out my food.

"Got enough granola bars?" Remy asks with a smile.

"Maybe." I pretty much dumped all the boxes of granola bars into my backpack. "Um . . . trade you a couple for one of those sandwiches."

Remy slides me over a baggie with a peanut butter sandwich and accepts two chocolate chip granola bars.

"Food's in your backpack," Bug says to Shiver.

Shiver opens an eye. "You opened my backpack?"

"Just to throw in some food. So we wouldn't starve." Bug shrugs, totally ignorant of the fact that Shiver looks ready to explode into some huge, raging fit.

What *does* she have in that backpack?

"I can get it out." Bug takes a step toward Shiver.

Shiver bolts upright and yanks her bag toward her. "I'll find it." She barely unzips the backpack and thrusts a hand inside.

And pulls out a can of green beans.

"There wasn't a lot to choose from." Bug's already flipping open the can opener gadget on her Swiss Army knife. "Dad and Maya took all the hiking food."

Shiver unzips her bag farther. Four small boxes of cereal, a jar of peanut butter, a bag of wasabi peas (Mom's favorite), and a can of cat food join the green beans on the table. Shiver picks up the cat food and raises her eyebrows at Bug.

"That's not to eat. That's to distract bears."

Shiver doesn't even question this. Instead, she surveys everything else on the table. "Why was all of this in *my* bag?" she asks Bug.

"Because I have maps, a guidebook, a compass, a first aid kit, a—"

"Okay, okay. I get it. Here, peanut butter?" Shiver holds the jar out to Bug.

But Bug's already opening the can of green beans. Only my little sister would pick cold green beans over peanut butter straight from the jar.

Shiver tosses the cereal, the wasabi peas, and the can of Tastee Time Salmon and Anchovy Dinner back into her bag. "Anyone got a spoon?" she asks.

Bug pops the lid from the green beans. Flipping the Swiss Army knife this way and that, she unfolds a spoon and passes it to Shiver.

Of course. She really would make an awesome park ranger.

"How far have we gone?" I ask Remy through bites of heavenly peanut butter and wheat bread.

"About thirty-five or so miles from Jackson Lake Lodge. So, a little farther for you guys."

I round that up to a nice forty miles and report that in a text to Kenzie. Which doesn't go through. I'm chewing on the last of yet another granola bar and rebraiding my hair, when Remy disappears under the picnic table.

Chapter 20

3 days until *Dueling Duets* auditions

"What are you doing?" Shiver asks Remy in the loudest voice possible.

"Shh! Act like I'm not here. They might recognize me," he hisses around a stick of beef jerky. He's shoved a hat on his head too.

"What?" she says.

I kick her from across the table and nod at the ranger's car that has just pulled in. Shiver glances at it and then sits up straight.

"I should go over there and tell them exactly what's going on," she says as she scoops out another hunk of peanut butter.

Bug frowns at her. "You'd ruin the whole adventure."

"Adventure? Seriously? My whole body hurts and we're probably going to get run down by a herd of buffalo." Shiver shoves the spoon into her mouth.

"Bison," Bug says as she watches the ranger get out of her car and make her way to the first picnic table.

"You didn't say anything to Ranger Hicks," I say to Shiver. "So I really doubt you would now." I hope. I loop the ponytail holder around the end of my braid and flip my hair over my shoulder.

"How do you know?" Shiver screws the lid back onto the peanut butter jar.

"Don't you dare! You've ruined every other plan I've had."

"Because they were all stupid plans!"

"They were not! That old couple was really nice."

"Really nice murderers, you mean."

I kick her again. She kicks back.

"Ow!" Under the table, Remy's got a hand to his cheek. Ugh, I can't believe I just kicked the guy I kind of, maybe, sort of like.

"Sorry," I say. Then I sit up and glare at Shiver.

"Just act *normal*!" Remy hisses from down around our feet.

"Looks like she's stopping at every table," Bug says.

"Then how are we going to explain a boy hiding under ours?" Shiver asks.

"She's coming," Bug says through closed lips.

"Don't say anything!" I whisper to Shiver. She just shrugs and acts like she hasn't made up her mind.

"Good morning!" the ranger calls. She's smiling, and has long blond hair pulled back into a ponytail under her Smokey the Bear hat. She's like a grown-up Bug.

"Hi!" Bug says all chirpily.

"I'm just making sure everyone is aware that we've had bear activity around here lately. So we need to make sure that all trash goes into the locked bins over there, and that nothing is left out on the tables." She points across the parking lot to some big brown bins, which are everywhere around here. They're practically impossible to open. You have to push a latch and pull up at the same time, usually with an armload of something gross that's spilling all over you.

"Great, thanks!" I say, just as chirpy as my sister.

"Is he okay?" The smiling ranger points at Remy, who she can totally see under the picnic table.

"Oh, yeah, fine! Just looking for . . . a . . . um . . . contact lens I dropped," Remy says. Then he starts feeling around the cement like a blind person.

"Need some help?" The ranger squats down but Remy waves behind him.

"No, no thanks! I'll find it."

I dive under the table too. "I'll help him, but thank you!" I shout up to the ranger as I pretend to look for a contact lens. It's a good thing I'm freaked out that she might not buy our story, or I'd be even more extra freaked out that I'm right next to Remy.

The ranger waves and walks back toward her car.

"That was close," I say to Remy.

"Yup, and I know her too. She was in Grand Teton last summer."

The ranger gets to her car, stops, and looks back at us.

"Uh-oh." Remy flips around so fast his hat knocks forward over his curls. "Is she coming back?" he whispers.

"I don't know." Please no, please no, please no. Except she definitely is. And we were *so* close. She must've recognized Remy right before he turned around.

"Hey, guys!" she shouts. "Where are your parents?"

Launching the boat? Running to the store? Taking a jog? Grooming a dog? On a hike in Grand Teton, with no idea where we are? No, Maya, think!

"We're staying up at the next campground. You should

see our RV. It's probably the ugliest thing ever," Shiver says out of nowhere. "Mom and Dad said we could picnic and bike back, as long as we come home by eleven."

The ranger squints down the road into the sun, almost as if she can see that campground from here. "That's got to be, what, eight miles?"

"Yeah, that's why they dropped us off. They wouldn't let us bike here and back. Because, you know, sixteen miles would be a *really* long way."

I'd give anything to see Shiver's face right now, but I have to pretend to help Remy find his nonexistent contact lens. I pat the ground and peer into the grooves in the concrete.

"All right. Well, be careful. Watch out for animals and speeders. And make sure you ride single file." Out of the corner of my eye, I see the ranger give Shiver and Bug another wave before she slides into her car and takes off.

I scramble out from under the table. "What was that?" I stand with my hands on my hips, waiting for an answer from Shiver.

"What?" She shrugs as she puts the peanut butter back into her bag. "I just saved your whole dumb plan. Thought you'd be okay with that."

I am, actually. I'm just really, really confused. "But I thought you were going to turn us in."

"I changed my mind." With that, she slings her backpack over her shoulders and moves toward the bikes.

I gather up my trash, shove it into my bag, and follow, with Remy and Bug right behind me.

"But why?" I ask. My muscles are pretty much screaming at me when I get on my bike again. But I'm too curious about Shiver to care.

Shiver pauses for a moment, almost like she has to think about her answer. Then she glances back at Bug, who's pedaling behind us next to Remy. "I didn't want to disappoint her. She was excited about going along."

"Really?"

"Well, I definitely didn't do it for you. You know, Maya, if you took three seconds and realized what you actually have here, you wouldn't be so into leaving it all behind." Shiver checks for traffic and then coasts onto the main road.

"Right. Crazy parents, a kid sister who's more into insects than anything else, and a podunk RV. I hit the lottery or something."

"All of them love you and actually want to spend time with you. Some people don't get any of that." Shiver's back is to me, so I can't see her face. But I'm pretty sure that "some people" means her.

"I didn't mean it like that," I say softly. "I just want my old life back."

"Your new life is a pretty good one," she says.

I bite my lip and don't say anything else. Whatever comes out of my mouth isn't going to convince her that me going home for *Dueling Duets* is a good thing.

I think back to when we first ran into Shiver, with Gert, in Texas. Gert said something about a divorce and getting Shiver away from "all that." But even if her parents are divorcing, that doesn't mean they don't love her. There are plenty of people in my class at school whose parents are divorced, and they get along fine with both their parents. Even Sonya's dad, who moved to Chicago, calls her all the time, and she's always flying up there to visit.

But I'm not sure Shiver has the same situation as Sonya. I don't know what situation she has, but now I'm thinking it isn't so great. And maybe this is why she hasn't really been in much of a hurry to get home and seems so down on me leaving my parents. But that still doesn't explain why she decided to help me get to Cody.

"Oh no!" Bug's voice interrupts my thoughts about Shiver.

I brake and twist around. "What's wrong?"

Bug's peering down over her handlebars. "I have a flat."

Remy pulls up alongside her. "That's not too bad. We just need a patch kit and an air pump. Have you got one?"

"No," Bug says in a small voice.

Okay, this is history being made—the first time my little sister hasn't been prepared for the worst-case scenario.

Remy looks to me.

"I don't have anything like that."

Bug chews her lip and looks like she wants to cry. "I can't ride on a flat tire. You'll have to keep going without me."

I lean over and hug her. "Bugby, I'm sorry." I definitely didn't realize how much she wanted to do this. Though I really shouldn't have been surprised. Bug lives for outdoor stuff, and a bajillion-mile bike ride through two national parks is probably a dream come true for her.

"I can walk with Bug to the next lodge," Remy offers. His face looks a little pained, and I know he'd much rather be riding to Cody.

With me. Which makes me feel so warm I wish I'd worn a short-sleeved shirt.

"That won't work," I say, pushing my sleeves up. "I need you to help me get to Cody. Shiver can walk with Bug."

"Excuse me? I said I was going with you, period." Shiver crosses her arms.

"No one has to come with me," Bug says in a little voice. "I'll walk by myself and hang out at the lodge until later. Then I'll have someone call Mom and Dad to come get me."

I feel awful for her. And then underneath everything, there's this itty-bitty nagging feeling that she's afraid I'm leaving her—for good. I put my arm around her, shove my guilt down, and level my gaze at Shiver. "Don't be silly," I tell Bug. "You're not going by yourself."

"You don't get to tell me what to do, Maya," Shiver says. "I said I'm going with you, and I am."

"What are you talking about?" I practically yell. "You just said you only lied to that ranger because you didn't want to disappoint Bug, and now Bug can't go any farther. Besides, this is *my* idea. Mine and Remy's. The whole point is to get *me* to the bus station so I can go home already! I don't need *you* to do that."

"Well, too bad, because I'm not going anywhere." The sun glints off that stud in her nose, making her look ten times cooler than I'll ever be. I don't get her at all. I mean, Cody is hardly San Francisco, so why does she want to go there so badly? Though it doesn't seem like she really wants to go to

San Francisco, either. In fact, I'm not sure where Shiver really wants to be at all.

"I'll draw you a map, and you can go on with Shiver," Remy says. "It'll be like I'm there, even if I'm not."

"I have a map." Bug flips her bag around, unzips it, and pulls out a folded-up map of Yellowstone.

Of course she has a map. I wish she had a patch kit and a pump instead, though. The long ride would be a lot more fun with my little sister pointing all out the good stuff to see and making me laugh with her weird insect facts. The same way she made life in the RV a whole lot better.

On the side of the road, Remy kneels in the sagebrush and purple wildflowers and spreads the map out on the gravel. "Okay, we're here."

I sit cross-legged next to him, half on the gravel and half in the sagebrush. I wait for Shiver to join us, but she just stands there next to a pine tree, glaring at everyone.

Okay. Looks like it's up to me to get us to Cody and not take a wrong turn into a bear den or something.

"I think I have a highlighter." Remy reaches for his backpack just as Shiver starts kicking at the tree. "Leave the tree alone," Remy says as he rummages around in his bag.

Bug looks over at him like he's the God of the Forest

or something. At least I'll feel better knowing Bug is with Remy. I'll just have to think of that when I start wishing he was with me.

"Whatever," Shiver says, but she stops kicking the tree. "Just get us the directions, Map Boy." She pulls out a bottle of nail polish and starts touching up her thumbnail.

Who paints their nails in the middle of a bike trip?

Remy finds his highlighter. "Okay, so up and around the lake, out of the park, through the canyon along the river, past the dam, and there—Cody." He marks the whole route in yellow highlighter, stopping at the *C* in "Cody."

"Great. Can we go now?" Shiver shoves the bottle of nail polish into her backpack and drums her wet nails on the handlebars of her bike.

"Thanks again for all your help," I say to Remy as I fold up the map and add it my backpack.

"No problem. Wish I could go with you." He takes his helmet off, ruffles his curls, and pulls his tan hat out of his bag. Then he gives me the rest of his peanut butter sandwiches, jerky, tuna, and trail mix.

"Thanks," I say, because I can't think of what else to say. Except maybe, *Hey, I really like you, and I wish you lived in Nashville.*

"No problem. Text me when you can and let me know how it's going."

Oh my God, he wants me to text him. "Um . . . I don't have your number."

I don't even have to look at Shiver to know she's rolling her eyes.

He rattles off a string of numbers, and I plug them into my phone. And maybe I put a little heart after his name. Maybe.

"Ready to walk?" he asks Bug.

"I guess," she says. "Have fun, Maya. Maybe take some pictures and send them to Remy so I can see, okay?"

I wrap my arms around her. "I'll miss you, Bugby. But I'll see you really soon. I promise."

"I'll miss you too," she says, her voice muffled. "Come back to Gloria soon. I'll let Hugo sleep with me while you're gone."

I can't say anything else because my throat is too tight. I climb on my bike and start to pedal after Shiver, turning back to wave at Remy and Bug.

Now it's me and Shiver versus the road. And the bears. And the weird steam that comes up out of the ground every once in a while, like off to the right behind a bunch of naked pine tree trunks that Bug would tell me had been burned in an old forest fire.

Me and Shiver versus the road, the bears, the scary steam vents, and . . . the buffalo?

"Um. Wow." Shiver brakes to a stop.

"Holy potatoes," I add.

Chapter 21

3 days until *Dueling Duets* auditions

"Shoo!" Shiver says, getting off her bike and waving her arms at the bison.

"Um, I don't think that's going to work." I take the opportunity to check my phone. No signal, of course. When I look back up, the bison is just standing there and staring at us as he chews something.

"Come on, get!" Shiver yells at him.

He snuffs and I almost jump a mile up in the air. "Bug said these things can be really dangerous. Maybe we should just be quiet and wait."

"Hey, Mr. Buffalo," Shiver says, totally ignoring me.

"How about you go over there and let us by, hmm? I'll get you some buffalo treats at the store, okay?"

I snort, but then something really crazy happens.

The bison blinks and slowly, slowly (super slowly) trudges off the road and into the trees.

"How . . . ?" I start to ask, but Shiver looks just as stunned as me. Then she shakes it off and hops right back onto her bike. I kind of can't help but look at her with a little bit of admiration. I mean, how did she do that?

"How much farther to the lodge?" she asks as we pedal on.

"I don't know." I let go of my pedals and let the bike coast down the small hill we've crested. "Remy said it was only a few miles."

"'A few' meaning how many, exactly? Pull out the map and see." Shiver's trying to steer her bike and pick another song on her phone at the same time. She keeps wobbling back and forth in front of me.

"It's a piece of paper, not a GPS. I have no idea where we are right now. Do you?"

"Hmm." She doesn't look up from her phone. I guess that's her way of acknowledging that I'm actually right.

Then she plugs in both earbuds. For a second, I thought

that maybe—just maybe—she was okay. And now she's back to typical Shiver.

At some point in math, we learned how many feet were in a mile. What was it, 5280, or maybe 5820? Whatever, I'll just call it 5500. So if it takes about 5500 steps to walk one mile, and say maybe one push of my pedals covers three feet, that's . . . um . . .

I pull out my phone from my pocket and use the calculator. I figure out that it'll take something like 9167 pushes of my pedals to get to the next lodge.

One. Two. Three. Four. Five.

Oh. My. God. This is going to take forever. Like, I think my legs will actually fall off and my spine will snap before I reach 9167. Not to mention that I can't even feel my butt anymore.

One. Two. Three. Four. Five. Six . . .

I'm somewhere in the 2000s when Shiver finally says something and makes me lose count. But it doesn't matter, because what she's saying is, "Sign! Look, a sign for Grant Village!"

"That was the best ice cream ever." I swallow the last of my cone and lean back against the wall of the lodge.

"Mmm-hmm." Shiver ate hers in about three seconds flat.

I know I shouldn't spend money, since I need every cent I have for a bus ticket and for at least a few meals along the road. But I was starving, and that ice cream looked about ten times yummier than the granola bars or trail mix in my backpack.

"We should look up better directions to Cody," Shiver says without opening her eyes.

I pull out my phone, and voilà! Wi-fi signal! All my texts send, including the one with the ice cream cone picture I just took for Bug. Maybe Remy will buy her one once they finally make it up here on their walk.

As I pull up a map, I sit and enjoy the cool of the concrete underneath me and the most amazing feeling of *not* being on a bike. Once the map pops up, I look up directions to the bus stop in Cody and check how many more miles we have to bike to get there.

101 miles. Just under nine hours.

I want to cry. Instead, I let out some kind of strangling noise that makes Shiver open one eye.

"What?" she asks.

I don't say anything. Just show her the map.

"I *really* didn't need to know it was still that far away." She throws an arm over her face.

"I wish I hadn't looked it up." I stuff my phone into my

backpack and stand up. Stretching feels like I'm pulling off my limbs, one by one. And then as much as I hate to say it, I tell Shiver, "We should get going."

"Five more minutes," Shiver says, her arm still over her eyes.

"You don't have to come. I'm the one who needs to be in Cody, not you." I grab my bike from where it's resting against a pole and sling my aching leg over it.

"Five minutes isn't going to change anything," Shiver says.

"Bye." I force my feet to pedal and start moving down the street toward the main road.

"Are you seriously leaving me behind?" Shiver shouts from behind me.

I brake and wait for her to catch up. I take the minute to send another text to Kenzie.

Getting closer. See you soon!

"I told you I'm going the whole way. You don't get to leave me stranded." Shiver glares at me as she rides past.

"I didn't mean to. You just weren't getting up." I pedal hard (or as hard as I can when my whole body hurts) to catch up. Which means every single muscle is on fire by the time we're back on the main road. And I mean *every* muscle. Even my finger muscles. Foot muscles. Knee muscles. Brain muscles. If it has a muscle, it hurts.

Maybe we shouldn't have stopped. This is way worse than it was when we rolled into Grant Village. Or maybe the ice cream did it. I should've stuck to granola bars.

"Shiver?"

"What?" she calls over her shoulder.

Wait. I can't complain to her, because then she'll tell me that she was right. "Nothing." For the zillionth time, I wish Kenzie was here.

I'll just have to suffer in silence. Maybe I should count again. What was the next landmark? I think it was another lodge, alllllllll the way around the other side of the giant blue blob on the map that's Yellowstone Lake.

Sigh.

My right leg cramps. Doubt swells up from my stomach and creeps through my body. My backpack feels heavier than ever, the weight of my shimmery shirt and purple hat and *Everything Y'all Ever Wanted to Know* making the straps dig into my shoulders.

There's no way I'm going to make it another hundredish miles. No way. Not feeling like this. And even if I did, I wouldn't be able to audition—I couldn't even walk onto the stage, never mind wait in line for hours!

Do I really need to try out for *Dueling Duets*? Maybe I

can (somehow) record a demo and (somehow) send it to the right person instead and get discovered that way. And Jack obviously seems to like Lacey now, and Remy is here and maybe it's possible he does actually like me.

Plus, I'm leaving Bug behind. But I'm not—not really. Just for a little while. Although . . . I'm not one hundred percent sure Mom and Dad will come back to Nashville even if I do win the competition. And then what if I try out and don't make it? Then this racing to get home will have been for nothing.

I shake my head. This is so confusing. *Dueling Duets* is the opportunity I've always wanted. I can't miss it.

The road splits ahead. The sign for the right-hand turn-off lists a few places in Yellowstone, and then, at the very bottom: CODY, WYO. 100.

Holy potatoes.

"Wait, did that sign just say Cody is a hundred miles?" I shout to Shiver as we roll past the sign and hang a right.

"I think so," she yells back to me.

"But when we stopped, the map said a hundred and one. There's no way we've gone only one mile since then!" Panic creeps up my throat.

"I think we've gone maybe two or three," she says. "And

they could be counting to a different spot in Cody than we were."

"Only two or three?" That's it, I'm having a genuine, Grade A freak-out right now. "That's *all*?!"

Shiver slows so that we're riding side by side. "Maya, you okay? You're overreacting about a mile or two."

"NO, I'M NOT OKAY! I'm practically dying here. *Dying*. I can't even stop my legs from pedaling even though that's all I want to do right now." I hiccup a sob and then swallow it hard. I'm not crying in front of Shiver. I might be completely losing it, but I'm *not* crying.

"Okay, let's pull off here." She points to a turnoff with a sign that says West Thumb Geyser Basin. "And get it together for a second."

I don't know what she thinks I'm going to get together. My legs? My brain? What I plan on getting together is a phone call to Mom to come get us. And if there's no signal, I'm going to flag down a ranger and admit defeat. The only thing I can hope for is that Mom and Dad see how desperate I am, and agree to get me home right away, somehow.

I am officially the worst former audition partner in the entire world. And the worst best friend. The worst sister and worst daughter, too. The worst everything.

We coast into a parking lot and up to a visitors center. I climb off my bike and let it fall as I collapse onto the pine needle-covered ground. "I'm done," I announce to Shiver. With my eyes closed, because I don't want to see her reaction. I can't believe I'm admitting failure to Shiver. I wait for her to rub it in.

"I'm sorry, what?" Shiver's still straddling her bike on the sidewalk.

"*Done.* I'm not biking any farther. I give up." I open my eyes and stare into the bright blue sky dotted with fast-moving white clouds. Until the sun peeks out from one of those clouds and blinds me. Then I close my eyes again. All I want is my cubbyhole bed and my pillow and Hugo to curl up on my feet. "I hurt. I'm starving. I'm exhausted. I quit."

Shiver steps off Dad's bike and lays it down next to mine. Then she sits right by me. I still don't look at her. I don't want to know what she thinks of me right now.

"You can't. What about your audition? And your partner? Wait, forget that. What about me? I'm supposed to ride all by myself to Cody now?"

I open one eye and turn to look at her. She's biting her lip, almost like she might cry. Which is impossible. I mean,

Shiver, cry over me? "Um, you won't have to ride to Cody if I'm not going, remember?"

"Right," she says. "Whatever. You wouldn't remember anyway since you're so involved with yourself."

"What?" I drag my aching body into a sitting position, and the irritation rises with me. "Why are you so rude?"

"I'm not being rude. Just stating facts."

"What's your problem? No wonder you don't have any friends. You can't be nice for anything." The words fly out of my mouth. I imagine them stabbing her with their mean word power.

And then I feel really, really bad.

Her face twitches and she's quiet for a few minutes. Then she rubs a hand across her eyes and looks at me. "Can we just be nice to each other for three seconds?"

"I'm sorry," I croak out. "I didn't mean that." I wish I could take it back somehow.

She frowns at me for a moment. "Look, Maya, I don't get why you need to be on this show so badly, but I can tell it's something you really want to do. And if it is, you'll never forgive yourself if you don't see it through."

"I know. I just can't do it, though." I try not to think of Kenzie's face when she realizes I'm not coming. Or of Jack and Lacey, singing together. Or of my mom looking permanently stressed out. Or of Dad, getting weirder and weirder. "Why are you being so . . . not mean to me?"

"Maybe I'm trying to be your friend."

I swallow down a whole jumble of feelings that have lodged themselves in my throat.

Shiver looks out over the parking lot. "I wish another ranger would show up and give us a ride."

"Right. Except we don't have Remy to sweet-talk one now."

"Who needs him anyway?" she asks, just as a small bus with a trailer attached to the back pulls up a few feet ahead us, burping and belching the way every bus I've ever seen does. The little accordion doors open, but no one comes or goes.

The side of the bus reads, ADVENTURE SEEKERS!

"Hmm," Shiver says.

"What does that mean?" I ask.

"Follow me."

I sigh as loudly as I can. Because standing up is seriously the last on my list of things I really feel like doing right now. Shiver jumps up, grabs Dad's bike, and rolls it toward the bus.

I peel myself from the ground. I don't even have the

energy to brush off the pine needles that are stuck to my clothes. I drag my bike the few feet it takes to reach Shiver.

"Hey," she says to the man sitting at the wheel of the bus.

He lowers a book. "You girls done for the day?"

Shiver and I look at each other.

I'm totally done for the day.

Chapter 22

3 days until *Dueling Duets* auditions

"Well, come on, then! We got other Adventure Seekers to pick up before we get back to the hotel." The man stands, walks down the steps, and picks up my bike. "Are your parents coming?"

"Um, I think—" I start to say, but Shiver cuts me off.

Shiver laughs—and it sounds really un-Shiver-like. "That's so funny. Only because if you'd seen how happy they were when I offered to take my little sister off their hands for a week."

I'd glare at her if I could stop standing there with my mouth open already. How in the world does she expect this guy to believe she's so much older?

"How far away is the hotel from here?" Shiver goes on. "With all this biking, we lost track."

The man unlocks the trailer, my bike propped against his hip. "'Bout a hundred miles or so."

"Really?" Shiver raises her eyebrows at me.

The man lifts my bike into the trailer, and I'm way too stunned to say anything. What exactly is going on here? I mean, he obviously thinks we're some other people. And somehow, he actually *believes* Shiver.

"So what's going on tonight?" Shiver asks, like this whole thing is no big deal.

"There's the Cody rodeo, and we've got dinner lined up at a Mexican restaurant," he says as he rolls Dad's bike to the trailer and lifts it inside too.

"The rodeo," Shiver says to me, pronouncing the words very carefully, "in Cody. A Mexican restaurant. In Cody."

And then I get it.

"Hop on board!" The man gestures to the door.

So we do.

"Hey." I nod to a messy-haired guy sitting about five rows back, like Shiver and I totally belong here. He's the only other one on the bus.

"Yo," he says. "I don't remember you from this morning.

I'm Stu. My buds call me Sick Stu because, you know, I'm, like, sick on the trails."

I have no idea what this guy is talking about, but I guess Shiver does because she nods and says, "Right on, Sick Stu." And she conveniently doesn't give him our names.

"You guys musta come up yesterday, huh?"

"Um . . . yeah. We did." I bump backward in the seat as the driver takes off. Toward Cody. I can hardly believe my luck!

I can hardly believe that Shiver got us here.

"That's sick, man. Real hard-core adventure, you know?" Sick Stu says.

"Yeah," Shiver says. "Sick."

Then Sick Stu must decide he needs a nap, because he leans back and closes his eyes. Which sounds like a really good idea to me.

I bump Shiver with my elbow. "Thanks," I whisper.

She blinks at me a second and then smiles. "Thank me if we actually get there."

I lay my head on the seat and watch the pine trees fly by, with glimpses of the lake in the background. I stretch out my arms and legs, and before I know it, I'm asleep.

I wake up to a lot of shouting and talking and laughing.

"What's going on? Are we in Cody already?" I ask Shiver.

"No. It's some kind of store." She points out the window at a general store off to my left. "I think they're picking up more people."

I rub the sleep from my eyes and stand up. Sure enough, all the noise is coming from right outside the bus, where there are about six people loading bikes into the trailer.

The driver pokes his head into the bus. "You can get off for a while if you want. We don't leave here till one-thirty."

My legs are all stiff from biking so long and then sitting still. "Come on," I say to Shiver. "Let's go walk around."

"No way." She's already curling into a ball in her seat. "I'm taking a nap."

"Fine. I'm going to look for more ice cream." I figure I'll eat the granola bars and jerky on the bus ride home, so I might as well spend my few extra dollars on some ice cream, right?

I make my way toward the store. Inside, there's a huge freezer full of ice cream. I grab a Drumstick—Bug's favorite— and pay, then check my phone. 1:05. Plenty of time to kill, and I really don't want to get on the bus and have to answer questions about sick trails or yesterday's "adventures." So instead, I unwrap my ice cream and follow a small crowd of people down the pavement past the bus.

I have no idea where they're heading, but I have ice cream, and it's really nice outside now. It's so quiet that I almost miss Shiver's sarcasm.

The group of people in front of me walk to a bridge, and I tag along. As I polish off my ice cream, I shade my eyes from the sun and think about how much Dad would love this. Everything about it, from the clear blue river below to the kids playing in the shallow water. I'm pretty sure we passed through here on our way into Yellowstone, but we didn't get out. He'd be all over this bridge, reading every single sign and probably joining the kids down by the water. Mom would shake her head and laugh. And Bug would be right down there with Dad, probably trying to catch a fish with her bare hands.

A little pang of something—just like I felt when I thought about Bug earlier—hits my heart. Am I actually missing my family? My off-the-wall crazy family?

Well, duh. Of course I am. They *are* my family, after all. And it's not like I won't ever see them again. I will. They can't say no to a new house when I win *Dueling Duets*. And we have the pedestrian bridge in Nashville. Although it's not like you can splash around in the Cumberland River under the bridge. It's probably toxic or something.

I take a picture of the river and put it into a text to Remy for Bug, once I finally get a signal again. I'll send it to Mom and Dad later, when I'm in Nashville.

Nearby, a park ranger is explaining to a family about how even though this bridge is called the Fishing Bridge, no one is allowed to fish from it anymore. His walkie-talkie buzzes with static.

"Sorry, just a minute," he says to the family. He pulls out the radio and listens.

"All personnel, be on the lookout for four missing children. One boy, three girls. Ages thirteen, thirteen, twelve, and nine. All children believed to be riding bicycles. Last seen near Lewis Lake at approximately nine-thirty a.m. Please check incoming text for names and physical description."

Oh no. No, no, no, no!

I duck my head, as if I'm examining the water below. Then I glance up, my heart pounding, but no one's looking at me. So I go.

I don't run, because that would look super suspicious, but I walk really, really fast back to the bus. Shiver's asleep, and I have to shake her to wake her up.

"What the . . . ? Maya, quit it. What's wrong with you?" Shiver bats my hands away.

I hold a finger to my lips and then check around to see if anyone's listening. Sick Stu is passed out in the seat across the aisle, and a couple of the new cyclists are in the very back. In a whisper, I tell her, "Mom must've gotten back early. They're sending out our descriptions to all the rangers and the police and probably the FBI! We have to hide! Or put on disguises. Or something!"

"Calm down," Shiver says, although she looks a little panicked too. Why, I don't know. It's not a big deal at all if she doesn't get to Cody. "Let's just stay on the bus, and no one will see us. And take your hair out of those braids."

For a split second, she sounds just like Kenzie. I undo the braids and then squint at the blue hair peeking out from under her knit hat. "Your hair sticks out a lot more than mine."

She tugs the hat down farther and tries to stuff her hair under it. "Well, not a whole lot I can do about that. Let's just stay low, and we'll get there. Where's the map?" She reaches down to the floor, grabs my backpack, and starts to unzip it. I rip it from her hands.

"Okay. Possessive much?" she asks, looking at her fingers like I burned them.

"No. I just don't like other people digging in my back-pack. Do you?"

She just makes a *hmpf* sound and crosses her arms. Maybe she got us on this bus, but I still feel like she'd find something mean to say about the music I love.

I find the map and spread it out on my knees. I run my finger up the line Remy highlighted until I come to a river that connects to the big lake, with Fishing Bridge labeled nearby. "We're here," I say to Shiver.

She looks over my shoulder. "So we're almost out of the park. That's good."

The other cyclists pass through the aisle, and up front the driver turns the ignition. "Ready to go, Adventure Seekers?" he calls.

"Yeah!" the whole bus echoes back, except for Sick Stu because he's still asleep.

Once the "yeah"s have stopped, the driver pumps up the volume on the radio.

The radio. I grab Shiver's arm. "He can't have that on," I tell her. "What if they broadcast it on the radio? My mom's probably called every police department in the state by now."

"Wow, your mom means business." She raises her eyebrows, almost like she's surprised Mom would call the police when she discovered her kids and tagalong Shiver missing.

But I don't have time to think about that because I have

to figure out how to get the driver to turn off the radio. I channel Kenzie.

"Ohhhh." I slap my arm to my head and dramatically lean back in my seat. "My head! The noise! Make it stop!"

I'm so loud I wake up Sick Stu. "What's wrong, man?" he calls across the aisle.

Shiver catches on. "She gets migraines. Hey, Mr. Bus Driver?"

"Carl," he corrects her.

"Carl, can you turn off the radio?"

"I need my tunes to drive," he says.

"My sister here has a migraine, and if it gets worse, she might puke all over the bus. The noise makes it worse," Shiver tells him.

"Turn it off, man! I can't roll with the vomit!" Sick Stu shouts.

Which, if I really had a migraine, would not help at all.

But it must work, because the music cuts out right away, and the bus goes along in silence. I lean my head against the window to keep up the migraine act. Right outside is the lake, which is so enormous I can't see the other side. Just some dark mountains way off in the distance. Waves lap the shore, and clouds block the sun over half the lake.

It looks almost artistic, so I pick up my phone and grab a picture for Bug.

"What are you doing, Migraine Girl?" Shiver hisses in my ear. "People with splitting headaches don't take pictures."

"Fine," I mutter. I watch the lake until it disappears behind the trunks of burned-out trees.

Not five minutes later, Carl pulls the bus onto the shoulder and shuts off the ignition.

"What's going on?" I ask Shiver.

She shrugs, but there's this worried look on her face.

Carl can't know. I mean, how would he? But then, why are we stopped?

"I can't pull this rig up the road to the lookout, but if any of you want a short adventure with a great view, I'll get your bikes out and you can ride up," Carl announces with a huge grin.

"What?" Shiver asks a little too loudly.

"I know! Sick, right?" Sick Stu says as he leaps out of his seat. He's the first one off the bus.

"I'm going to stay here with my sister," Shiver tells Carl. He nods, and the adults in the back follow him, leaving only me and Shiver on the bus.

After they all ride off, Carl sets up a chair outside and

falls asleep. Shiver moves into Sick Stu's seat and does the same thing. I use the time for some non-migraine-approved reading and some trail mix–eating. If I was hanging out in Bertha, I could've eaten a piece of Mom's leftover lasagna. That tastes about nine hundred times better than some old raisins and peanuts.

I'm through two chapters and half the bag of trail mix before I realize no one's come back yet. What time is it? It feels like they've been gone forever. I check my phone. 2:37. Huh.

When the numbers on the phone show 2:45, I start to get worried. What if the group ran into a bear?

At 3:14, I'm getting really, really annoyed. We need to get to Cody before the last bus leaves at eight o'clock.

At 3:27, when I'm about to march up that hill and drag them down, fake migraine or not, the group pedals across the road. I poke Shiver in the leg, leap back into my seat, and pretend to be fighting off the worst headache in the history of headaches. Everyone loads onto the bus, chattering about the ride to the overlook.

Shiver falls into the seat next to me when Sick Stu arrives.

"Hey, man, you missed a sick ride!" he says.

"Maybe next time, if this one feels better." Shiver jerks her thumb toward me.

I raise my hand weakly, like I'm just in too much pain to say anything.

Trees flash by outside the window as the bus finally pulls out. I'm not Bug, so looking at trees gets really boring after a while. I'm dying to read my book, or check my phone for a signal, or start singing (I can almost feel the notes tickling my throat), but none of those are migraine approved, and Shiver would have a field day if she heard me sing.

Instead, I lean against the window and think about how, with every minute, I'm getting closer to home.

Until we stop again, that is.

"Oh my God. If this is another bike ride . . . ," Shiver grumbles under her breath.

I'm totally with her. If we keep doing this, I'll miss the bus home for sure. And I have to get on one tonight if I want to make it in time for the audition.

Not to mention, the fact that I *know* how worried Mom is right now is eating away at me. If I can just get on the bus, then I can send her a text and let her know I'm okay. Plus, once Bug and Remy call to get picked up, they'll probably have to confess everything that happened, so I'll be found out tonight anyway. I only have to be on my way to Nashville, and everything can go as planned.

Which is why *this* bus needs to quit stopping already!

Carl hops out to help what looks like a big group. These Adventure Seekers don't have bikes. Instead, they're decked out in hiking gear. Some have huge overnight packs, while others just have hiking poles and CamelBaks. They all clamber on board, filling up the remaining seats. Carl climbs back into the driver's seat and starts the engine.

The bus bumps and rolls along. And then it stops. Again.

"Now what?" Shiver grumbles.

"What's going on, man?" Sick Stu shouts up to Carl.

"Looks like they're stopping everyone at the park gate," Carl replies.

And that's when my heart goes into overdrive. I'm ninety-nine percent sure that they're stopping everyone to look for us.

Chapter 23

3 days until *Dueling Duets* auditions

The bus creeps forward.

"The bathroom," Shiver whispers.

"What?"

"The second they see my hair, they'll know. I'm going to the bathroom. Act like everything's normal." With that, she stands up and stretches. Then she rifles through her backpack. I inch sideways just a tiny bit, but all I can see in there is the food Bug packed. She pulls out a little zipped bag and puts her backpack on the floor again.

She makes a big show of opening her zipped bag and

searching inside. Then she moans and clutches her stomach. "Midgie, have you got any car sickness medicine?"

"Midgie"? Really? What kind of name is that? I almost laugh, but I shake my head instead.

Shiver taps the woman in front of us on the shoulder and asks the same question, looking completely pitiful. She says no, but the woman in the next seat up hands Shiver what she needs.

"Be right back, Midgie," Shiver says. The bathroom door in the rear shuts behind her just as the bus rolls up to the gate.

Carl rolls down the window, has a short conversation with the ranger, and then opens the door. When the ranger climbs aboard, I curl into a ball in my seat.

The ranger takes a few steps down the aisle and scans the faces on the bus. I shut my eyes and pretend to be asleep, though I'm pretty sure my heart is hammering loud enough for everyone to hear.

"All right," the ranger says after what feels like a million years. "Thanks, and sorry for the hold-up."

I open my eyes to see him talking to Carl. Everyone on the bus starts chatting again, so I can't hear what the ranger says next. But it doesn't last long, and then he's gone. The bus lurches forward, and my body goes from tense to feeling so light I could lift right up from the seat and float in the air.

Shiver slides in next to me. She gives me a smile, and I smile back.

I think I'm actually happy to have her along for the ride.

When the bus stops again, it wakes me out of a sound sleep. I wipe drool from my face and am thankful Remy's not here to see me like this.

"Why are we stopping again?" I ask Shiver.

"I don't know." She cranes her neck to see out the front. Parking spaces and a river sparkling in the sun make up the view from my window.

I click on my phone, keeping it low so no one will suspect Migraine Girl doesn't really have a migraine. 5:40.

"We don't really have time to stop," I whisper to Shiver.

"Tell me about it," she says. "Especially not when people are looking for us."

Carl parks the bus across several parking spaces. "Buffalo Bill Dam!" he announces. "Everyone off who wants to take the tour."

All around us, people stand up and stretch and make

their way to the door. Everyone except me, Shiver, and Sick Stu, who's passed out in his seat again.

"You guys coming?" Carl pokes his head back into the bus.

Shiver nudges Sick Stu across the aisle. He sputters and blinks, and says, "What?"

"Tour of the dam," Carl says. "You want to go?"

"I think Midgie still has a migraine," Shiver says.

We can't sit here and wait for them to come back. Who knows how long that tour'll take. It could be way past dark by the time we finally get to Cody, and then it'll be too late for me to get a bus home tonight.

After all we've been through, that can't happen. It just can't.

So I stand up and step over Shiver. "I'm feeling *so* much better. Like, my headache is gone completely, and I'm totally up for some adventure. Aren't you . . . Penelope?" I raise my eyebrows at Shiver.

"Sure, Midgester. Um, dam tour adventure?"

"Nah," I say. "Too lame. I think we should get our bikes and make our own adventure. Maybe go down and check out the river."

"Awesome," Sick Stu says. "That's what I want to do."

I look at Shiver. She shrugs. I guess there's no going back

now. And besides, losing Sick Stu shouldn't be all that hard. He doesn't exactly seem to be with it.

"All right, then. This is the Adventure Seekers, after all," Carl says. "I'm glad you're feeling better, Midgie. Let's get your bikes out."

We follow him off the bus. The other Adventure Seekers are across the parking lot by now, headed for the tour.

"Three bikes," Carl says as he hauls out Sick Stu's bike. (Which is bright green and orange, and has yellow flames. As Sick Stu would say, very sick.) "See the road that goes up behind the building?"

"The one with the gate?" I ask.

Carl waves his hand, as if gates can't possibly stop Adventure Seekers. "If you follow that, it'll take you between the river and the main road tunnel. There's probably a way down to the river from there. Just be back here at six-thirty."

"You got it," Shiver says. "Hey, so does this river go all the way to Cody?"

"You bet," Carl answers as he locks up the trailer.

I force my stiff and sore legs to climb onto my bike, and I plaster a smile on my face. "Let's go get some adventure!"

Shiver and I pedal toward the road that Carl pointed out, Sick Stu right on our tails.

"We can follow this road," I say to Shiver. "As long as it goes with the river, we should be okay."

"And it'll keep us off the main road where anyone can see us," she adds.

Huh. When we're not at each other's throats, we actually make a good team.

After a quick check to be sure no one's looking, we skirt the gate.

"Now, how are we gonna lose Sick Stu?" I ask.

"Maybe we can outpedal him?"

Fat chance. As it turns out, Sick Stu is in way better shape than either me or Shiver, plus he probably hasn't already ridden a gazillion miles today.

"I'm going for a swim when we get down to the water," Sick Stu says. The river below is churning and is probably freezing.

"Um, it looks cold," I say.

"It'll be an adventure!" he replies.

"How about you adventure and we stay warm, okay?" Shiver says.

Sick Stu shrugs and pedals onward. After about fifteen minutes, he slows up and points ahead at a dirt path that leads down the banks from the road. "I think that goes to the river."

Shiver and I exchange glances. Then we put every ounce of energy (which isn't much) into our legs and ride faster, past the dirt path.

"Hey, what's wrong?" Sick Stu asks from behind us.

In no time flat, he's caught up and is riding alongside me. "Didn't you hear me? That was a path down to the river."

It's clear we aren't going to lose Sick Stu any time soon. So I stop.

"Maya! What are you doing?" Shiver brakes and turns around.

"The path's back that way," Sick Stu says, pointing behind us. "Wait, who's Maya?"

"I'm Maya. She's Shiver. Or Adalie, actually, but she calls herself Shiver for some reason," I say.

Shiver gives me a Look. I'm not sure if it's because I called her Adalie or because I'm telling Sick Stu our real names.

"Shiver. That's a sick name. So, what, you guys undercover or something? Are you with the FBI?" Sick Stu actually looks a little nervous. Which makes me wonder why exactly.

"No, we're just two girls trying to get to Cody," Shiver says.

Sick Stu looks back and forth between me and Shiver. "So, I guess you aren't going down to the river?"

I shake my head. "No. We have to get to the bus stop, actually, and we—I—have to be there by eight. So we're not going to the river. We're not Adventure Seekers. We're just . . . on a mission."

Sick Stu looks completely blank. I'm about to repeat what I just said, when his whole face morphs into a huge smile and he says, "Awesome. That's a total adventure. Can I go with you?"

"Um, what?" Sick Stu wants to go to Nashville? Wait, he doesn't even know I'm going to Nashville. So he just wants to ride to Cody for, what . . . the adventure of it?

"No way," Shiver says. "The police are looking for us. We have to stay as inconspicuous as possible."

"I can be incons . . . inconc . . . that. Wait, the police? What did you do?"

"Nothing," I say before Shiver can tell him we robbed a bank or something. "It's just that my parents didn't really want me taking a bus home, you know?"

Sick Stu nods. "I get it, man. They're down on the adventure."

Well, not really. More like Mom and Dad live for adventure and I just want to go home. Adventure. That's what Bug called this whole idea. Thinking of her waiting at a lodge with Remy makes my eyes prickle. I blink fast and push the thought away. After all, I don't have time to sit around and chitchat with Sick Stu on this road by the river.

"We have to go," I say.

Sick Stu jumps on his bike and follows us.

"Really?" Shiver looks at me as we pedal along.

"What? He's okay." Sick Stu's no Remy, but he seems eager to help us out.

"Hmpf" is all she says. I guess I'd be surprised if we agreed on everything.

We move along the empty pavement. Shiver's plugged her earbuds in to listen to . . . whatever it is she listens to. Every once in a while, I can spot the main road up above us to the left. The landscape has changed from pine trees to dry, almost treeless hills that tower over the river and the two roads. I take a picture of the river with the steep hill behind it to send to Kenzie and Remy. And maybe Dad, later.

It's not long before our little road travels up a hill to reconnect with the main road. We stop a little ways up, and I dig through my backpack for the map.

"Looks like we have to get on the main road. This one goes way off track," I say, pointing to the line on the map that shows our narrow road disappearing into nowhere.

Shiver rolls her bike backward in order to see the map. "No way. Someone will spot us for sure."

"Maybe not. I mean, they're looking for three girls and one boy, all thirteen and under. Now it's just two girls and . . . him." I point to Sick Stu.

"Hmm." Shiver studies Sick Stu. The guy could be twenty for all we know, but totally looks about sixteen. "Let me see that." She holds out her hand for the map.

"I told you there's no other way," I say.

"Just let me check." She pulls on the corner and I let it go to keep it from ripping. Even though Bug knows way more about nature stuff than I do, I usually get my way on pretty much everything. Which is part of being the older sister, I guess. So it's kind of annoying to have Shiver act like . . . me.

Sick Stu peers over Shiver's shoulder, and together they study the map. While I just stand there over my bike, waiting. Waiting. Waiting. And trying really hard not to think of Bug and Mom and Dad when I look at the rapids-filled river perfect for rafting.

"Come *on*, y'all. We don't really have that much time." The sun's already beginning to lower itself behind the hills back toward Yellowstone.

"All right, fine. There isn't any other way." Shiver folds

up the map and hands it back to me. "We'll just have to risk it. It isn't that far anyway."

I'm the first one up the hill onto the main road. We've been biking for almost exactly five minutes when a police car passes us.

Chapter 24

3 days until *Dueling Duets* auditions

I stop. This is *not* good. That police officer will probably turn around and come back. "What are we going to do?" A panicky feeling rises in my throat. I have to make it. I'm *so* close.

Shiver looks back down the road where the car disappeared. "Maybe he won't come back."

I shake my head. "He will. And probably really soon."

"All right, man," Sick Stu says. "Here's the plan. You guys go up that hill and down the other side till you pick up the river again, and then follow it. I'll keep biking up here. When he comes back, I'll tell him an Adventure Seekers bus came by, and you got on, but I'm staying out to complete the adventure."

Sick Stu sounds so sure of himself that Shiver and I just stand there and blink at him for a second.

"Did you hear me, man?" he asks.

Shiver finally finds her voice. "What if he doesn't believe you?"

Sick Stu pulls out an Adventure Seekers ID card from his pocket. "If that doesn't work, I'll tell him to drive me back to the hotel in Cody."

"But the Adventure Seekers people won't know who we are," I say.

"Right. Then I can act like you fooled me. And by then, maybe you'll already be on your bus home."

"And we're supposed to, what . . . bike along the river?" Shiver asks.

"All the way into town."

It's not a perfect plan, but it's the only one we have. "Okay, let's do that. And thanks, Sick Stu."

"Good luck," he says. "This was one sick adventure." He high-fives us and takes off.

Shiver and I push our bikes straight up the sandy, rocky hill, through the few bits of sagebrush and scraggly bushes.

"Oh. My. God. How high is this thing?" Shiver pants as she drags along beside her bike.

I can't answer her. My legs are burning, and I can barely breathe. But I can't stop. Not until we're at least on the other side, away from the road.

When we finally make it to the top, Shiver drops to the ground on the far side. I fall next to her, my bike sliding just a little in the loose dirt and gravel. One thing that's good about having Shiver by my side—she's just as winded as I am.

I peek over the top of the hill. I can't see Sick Stu anymore, and who knows if the police car has come back. If it has, then I really, really hope the police officer was looking on the sides of the road and not up the hill.

I check my phone. 6:37. We don't have time to hang around here catching our breath. "Let's keep going. I can hear the river down there." I point straight down the hill, toward the quiet gurgling sound below.

We stumble and slide down the mountainside, fighting to hold on to our bikes. I think for a second about leaving them behind, but we might need them again once we get closer to town. I also kind of wish for my hiking boots, which are sitting in Bertha. I never thought I'd miss those things. I try really hard not to think about what my family would normally be doing right now. Eating dinner, Mom telling me and Bug about Dad's big adventure, Bug filling us in on all the animals she saw today, Mom reminding Bug not to talk with her mouth full. All of us squishing into Bertha's tiny kitchen to wash the dishes.

Wait, am I actually missing Bertha's kitchen? There is something seriously wrong with me.

Close to the bottom of the hill, my right foot slides out from under me. I fall and head straight down on my bottom, my bike beside me.

"You okay?" Shiver asks when she finally makes it down to where I'm lying sprawled out just above the river.

"Uh-huh." It hurts. I hurt all over, actually, and I can't really tell where the new hurt begins and the old hurt ends. I'm just one big ball of hurt. I cannot wait to get on that bus and stretch out and sleep, all the way to Nashville.

Shiver holds out a hand, and I grab it to pull myself up. It's not easy moving along the river, because there's barely a bank. Just a narrow ledge and then a little drop-off to the water below. We have to keep our bikes close to us. Bug would've loved this. And Dad, too. Mom would be complaining the whole way, taking all the grumpy thoughts in my head and voicing them out loud.

"Wait," Shiver says. "How do we know we're going the right way?"

"Sick Stu said the river goes all the way to town."

"Yeah, but how will we know when we get to town?" she asks.

"Um, I guess we'll see cars and buildings and stuff?"

Shiver stops and holds out her hand. Never mind that we're totally running out of time. I yank the map from my backpack and hand it over. Then I stand there and tap my foot while she studies it. Something moves in the brush behind me. I peek over my shoulder. Nothing there. Probably a snake, sitting there, just waiting to jump out and gnaw off my foot. Are there rattlesnakes out here? Bug would know.

I wish she was here.

Shiver turns the map toward me and points to a spot on the river where a road crosses it. "This is where the river meets the town. But it's way past where we need to go. So what we should do is cut over here"—she points at a blank space of nothingness—"and then come out on this road and head to the bus stop. What do you think?"

It sounds okay to me. Who knew Shiver was so good at reading maps? "As long as we get there on time."

She folds up the map and sticks it into her own back-pack this time—which is fine by me. I turn forward and trudge on.

And then the ledge ends. Just like that. There's literally no place to walk because this part of the hill turns into a steep drop-off.

"Now what?" Shiver asks behind me.

The last thing I want to do is look down, but I don't really have a choice. I grab hold of the trunk of a lone pine tree and then peer down.

Okay, that's not so bad. Yeah, sure, there are bone-crushing rapids down there, but it isn't all that far down. Like, I could jump and it would be just like jumping off the low dive at the pool back home.

"Down," I tell Shiver.

She looks over the side. And then back at me. "Are you crazy? You want to walk in the river?"

"Not *in* the river. Along the river." I peek over again and point at the little spot of mud where the water almost meets the canyon wall. Well, maybe it's less a little spot of mud than some shallow water *over* the mud.

"Along the . . ." Shiver widens her eyes. "No. Just, no."

I prop my hands on my hips. "Then what, huh? Should

we just give up, go sit by the road, and wait for someone to find us? Well, you can do that, but I'm going to walk down there." Sure, she's been helpful, but who says I can't do this on my own? I grab hold of the tree again and sit, my legs hanging over the edge.

"Hand me my bike once I'm down there," I tell her.

"Wait," she says. "How about we go to the other side? There's room to walk over there." She points across the river to a nice wide ledge. "We can make a bridge. See that big tree limb?"

Sure enough, there's a huge limb standing upright against the ledge. Where exactly that came from, I have no idea. It's not like there are trees tossing off limbs left and right around here. We drop our backpacks and bikes and go to haul up the limb, which isn't as heavy as it looks.

"I'm not going backward. You'll push me into the river," Shiver says as we heft up opposite ends of the limb.

"Why would I push you into the river?"

She stands there and heaves a huge sigh.

"Fine, whatever. I'll go backward." I stumble over rocks and little bits of sagebrush as I back toward the pine tree.

"How are we getting it across?" Shiver asks.

"We'll have to stand it on end." My voice is all breathy.

I've had more exercise today than I've had in my whole life. "And then let it fall."

Shiver immediately drops her end.

The limb slips out of my hands and lands on my toes. "*Ow!* What did you do that for?"

"Sorry," Shiver says. But she's not very convincing.

"You totally did that on purpose."

"Oh, right. I don't have any friends, so I don't know how to help someone carry a tree limb to a scary river in the middle of Nowhere Mountain." She crosses her arms.

Bug would totally correct her—it's a canyon between the mountains, not an actual mountain. "I said I was sorry. And I meant it. It was a stupid thing to say. I was trying to figure out why you wanted to go to Cody so bad. Which you still haven't told me, by the way."

She doesn't say anything.

"Come on, please? I need your help. We have to get that limb into place so we can go across and get to town already. Then you can call my parents to pick you up." I move around to her end of the limb and start to lift it up.

She finally moves forward. "Sorry I keep bringing it up." She doesn't look at me when she says it, but the words sound so heavy that I know it took a lot for her to say them.

Shiver's got a good three or four inches on me in height, so together we're able to push the limb up straight so it can fall over and across the river. It crashes into the brush when it meets the far side. For a second, I'm scared it will snap in half and we'll have to start all over again. But it holds, and now we have a little bridge.

"Thank you," I say as I wipe my dirty hands on my even dirtier jeans. Seriously, I cannot wait to get to Kenzie's house to take a shower and put on clean clothes. "I guess we'll have to leave the bikes behind. You can tell Mom and Dad where they are once I'm gone. They should be okay here." I gesture at the tree bridge. "You want to go first?"

"No way. What if that thing breaks when I'm halfway across? You go first."

"Wow, thanks." I test the limb with the toe of my shoe. It bounces a little, and my heart drops, kind of like it did whenever Kenzie dragged me onto a roller coaster with her at Dollywood. The limb is just barely wide enough to walk on.

"I'll throw your bag over to you once you're across," Shiver says.

"Here goes nothing." I step onto the limb. It bounces again, so I crouch and hold on with my hands. I scoot forward, gripping the bark so hard I'm sure I'll have tree imprints on my palms. The whole thing wobbles every time I move.

All I really want to do is crawl back off, climb over the hill, and take my chances along the road. But I can't, because then we'll definitely get caught and I can hang up any thought of making it home. I've already come this far. I'm not giving up my dream just because a silly tree limb bounces when I move. And I know Mom's super worried by now. The sooner I get on that bus, the sooner I can let her know I'm okay.

I swallow hard and keep my eyes fixed on the other side. I'm almost there. Just don't look down. Don't look down. Don't look down.

I look down.

Chapter 25

3 days until *Dueling Duets* auditions

"Aghhhhh!" A strangled sound erupts from my throat, and I leap off the limb toward the ledge on the far side of the river. I land hard on my stomach.

I lie there, facedown in the dirt and sage and gravel. But I don't care. I made it! I crossed that river on a teeny, tiny tree limb and I'm still alive!

"Maya? You okay?" Shiver's voice calls across the canyon.

I turn over and jump up. "I'm fine! I'm more than fine. I'm fantastic! Woo-hoo!" My whole body is tingly and ready to go. I spring up and down. "What are you waiting for?"

"You're insane. Here, catch your bag." Shiver winds up

and tosses my backpack across the river. I catch it squarely against my chest. Shiver throws her bag across next, and I pretend that the jar of peanut butter and can of cat food and who knows what else she's got in there don't hurt when they collide with my sternum.

Also, I'm dying to pull the zipper back and peek inside.

"Don't you dare open it!" she yells.

It's like she's reading my mind. I drop her backpack next to mine. "Then get over here already."

She crouches down on the limb and starts scooting across, sideways, like a crab. "Um, Maya. This thing isn't very sturdy." Her voice is a little shaky.

"It'll hold, don't worry. Just keep moving."

She inches one big black boot forward, but stops when the limb wobbles again. "I . . . I don't think I can do this."

I kneel at the edge of the ledge. "Yes, you can. Move your other foot."

She slides her hands down the limb, and very, very slowly, moves her other foot across.

"See?" I say. "That wasn't so hard."

"Yes, it was. This is crazy. Why are we doing this? Why don't we just go back and ride on the road?" Her face is super pale. It makes her hair look even more blue.

"Because we'd be seen! And I'm already across. You're halfway here. Just keep going."

She shifts her weight and the limb bounces again. She freezes.

Now what?

I reach over and drag her backpack across the ground. It's the one thing I know will get her across. "You'd better keep moving, or I'm going to open your bag."

"Don't touch that!"

I grab the zipper and pull just an inch. Not wide enough to see inside at all.

"Maya, you creep! That's my stuff." She reaches out an arm, like she's going to swipe the bag away from me. But she's too far away, and all that does is make the limb bounce even more. "I hate you. I'm going to die up here and all you care about is looking through my things."

"Then you better hurry up and get over here and stop me." I move the zipper just a little bit more.

"You're gonna pay for that!" She scoots sideways on the limb.

"Let's see, what've we got here?" I've got the bag unzipped just far enough to get a couple of fingers in. I snag a wire and pull out her phone and earbuds. "Hey, look! I'm going to read your texts if you don't stop me."

"I swear, you'll regret it if you do." She's practically seething, which is kind of funny since she's clinging on to that skinny piece of tree for dear life. She inches down a little more. She's close enough now that she could reach over and grab on to the ground.

I push the power button on her phone, but all I get is a prompt for a password. I toss it to the side. "Oh well, let's see what else is in this bag." I unzip it just a little more. "Could it be love letters? Dear Secret Hot Guy Shiver Has a Crush On, you make my heart go pitter-patter. I love the way your teeth glisten when you smile. I love—"

Shiver swipes the bag out of my hands as she lurches onto the ground from the tree limb. "Don't *ever* touch my backpack again," she says as she crawls away.

I stand up and give her a hand. She slaps it away and clambers up by herself.

"It got you over here, didn't it?" I scoop up my own backpack and wait for her thanks.

She looks back across the tree limb, like she's just realizing this. "Just don't mess with my stuff. Can we go now?"

With one last look at my bike lying on the far side of the river, I lead the way forward. After a while, I see something completely unexpected on the other side of the river.

A house.

"It's an actual house," Shiver says. "Like a place with bathrooms. Where people live."

We stand there and gape at it for a moment as if we've never seen a house before.

"That probably means we're really close to town!" I say.

It's not too much farther when we run into another house. This one has a little footbridge that stretches across the water, which we use to cross the river again. I take a picture of it too, because it's something Mom and Dad would love.

On the other side, I realize exactly how low the sun has gotten. I pull out my phone. 7:18. And I start walking faster, ignoring my achy legs, right past Shiver.

"Hold up! Why are you walking so fast?"

"Time!" I call back over my shoulder. "It's already seven eighteen."

"But we have to get there by eight!"

"I know." Well, *I* have to be there by eight. I guess she's just really wanting to make sure I get on that bus.

We hurry along until the trees on our right open up.

"This has to be the place where we can cut through into town," I say.

Shiver nods.

I scan the brown rocky dirt and the little bits of green sagebrush that dot the land here and there. There aren't a whole lot of trees up ahead. It's mostly flat, but off to the right is a crease that looks like a giant drop-off. I really hope we don't have to go that way. "So, um . . . how do we know which way to go? Maybe we should just follow the river instead, like Sick Stu said."

Shiver scrunches up her mouth. "Straight," she says. "At least, that's how it looked on the map. If we go by the river, we'll never get there in time."

I motion for her to go first. She shakes her head.

"Fine," I say as I tromp forward. "I'll make sure we don't step on any rattlesnakes. Or tarantulas. Or whatever's lurking out here." I pick my way through the nature-y stuff on the ground as Shiver trails behind me.

We walk and walk and walk, until we can't see the river anymore. I can't see much of anything else, either. Just trees and rocks and endless mounds of sagebrush, all casting long shadows. What happened to the houses, like we saw along the river?

Just as we pass this really cool-looking stack of rocks with yellow flowers growing out from the bottom, Shiver says,

"Hey, slow—agghh!" I turn around just in time to see her fall forward into the brush.

"Shiver?" I ask.

"Owwww . . ." She curls up and pulls her right knee to her chest.

"What happened? What's wrong?" I squat beside her, searching for gushing blood or bones sticking out or horrible twisted limbs.

"Caught my foot in . . . oww!"

"Here, grab my shoulder. See if you can get to these rocks." I take her arm and wrap it around my shoulders. She leans about half her weight onto me, and I stumble sideways just a little.

"Ow!"

"Sorry," I mumble. I drop her, kind of ungracefully, onto the stack of rocks.

Shiver peers down at her ankle. "I think I sprained it."

"So it's not broken?"

"I don't know. Do I look like a doctor?" She prods at her ankle, which is starting to swell up.

"Bug gave me a first aid kit. Maybe there's a wrap in there or something." I rip open my bag and pull out the white plastic box with the little red cross on it. Inside, there are Band-Aids, bug bite ointment, goo to clean out cuts with, and . . . a little space where an Ace bandage used to be. "Um . . . no wrap. I think this is the one we had when Dad tripped over his grill last summer. Sorry."

Shiver sighs. Then she stretches out her leg and opens her backpack.

"So, what, you're going to just sit here?" It comes out ruder than I meant it to.

"Yes. I need to think. And I can't exactly walk right now, in case you haven't noticed."

"But the sun is setting and then you'll be sitting out here in the dark." And no way am I hanging around out here in the dark, creepy nowhereness, especially when there's a bus leaving from Cody really, really soon.

She pulls out a mess of holey white cloth covered in colorful thread.

"What in the world is that?" Except I know exactly what it is, since I spent the better part of my eight-year-old summer with it.

"Cross-stitch. Go ahead and laugh, I don't care." Shiver picks up the tiny silver needle with bright pink thread looped through the end. She stabs the white cloth and pulls the needle through the back.

I let out a single "ha." Not because I'm laughing at her cross-stitch. But because *Shiver is doing cross-stitch.*

Blue-haired, music-addict, grouchy Shiver is cross-stitching. This is what she's been hiding in that backpack. I stare as she pushes the needle through one of the millions of tiny holes in the white cloth to create an x. All the colorful x's on the cloth run together to make a bunch of flowers. I can picture the thing covering a pillow on Grandma's floral sofa. My heart feels weird and warm as I realize that Shiver had a secret too.

"Quit staring already," she grumbles.

"Sorry. It's just that . . . I can't believe you have such a weird hobby." Once the words are out of my mouth, I know they didn't come out like I meant.

She stabs the cloth with her needle and then glares at me. "Do you even know how rude you are?"

"That's not what I—"

But she doesn't give me the chance to explain. "Just go. You think you're so smart, you go the rest of the way by yourself. Keep being stupid and get eaten by wolves for all I care."

I squish my lips shut. No way am I telling her about my country music dreams now.

Shiver stabs away at her x-flowers and doesn't look at me.

I stand there for a few seconds. "So you're going to . . . what? Sit on this rock and sew?"

"Exactly."

"That doesn't make any sense." But in a weird way, it actually does. I always sing when I have to think hard about something. Although this is a really strange time to want to sit and think. Even if you do have a sprained ankle.

"In case you haven't noticed, we're here in the middle of nothingness." Stab, stab. Hot pink thread races through the cloth. "And when you get hurt in the middle of nothingness, you have to think about how to get where you're going with a messed-up ankle." Stab, stab. "Or you'll just hurt yourself worse and never get to the . . . bus station." Stab, stab.

Shiver doesn't say anything else. She just sews, stabbing over and over and over, as the sun sets off to the left.

The sunset. Great.

"Fine," I say. "Stay here. I don't have time to sit and think. I'm going to find my way out of here. I have an audition to get to." I fling my backpack over my shoulder, hoping this will maybe at least make her *try* to walk.

Shiver puts her cross-stitch back inside her bag. She doesn't look up at me as she swipes at her eyes. Is she crying?

"I'm sorry," I say again. I reach into my backpack and pull

out half of the remaining granola bars and all of the jerky and trail mix Remy gave me. "Here," I say as I add them to her bag. She doesn't yell at me for opening it this time. "In case you get hungry."

"What are you doing? You can't leave me here."

"I have to. That bus will leave without me. I promise I'll call Mom or the police or someone once I'm on the bus. I'll tell them exactly where you are. You won't be here very long." I zip up her backpack and put it next to the stack of rocks she's sitting on.

"I said *no*." Shiver pushes herself up, takes one step forward, and catches her breath.

I chew on my lip as I try not to smile. I knew this plan would work—no way would she let me leave her behind, even if she'd broken her leg.

"I have to get to town before eight o'clock," she says as she balances against the rocks.

Okay, I totally missed something. "No, *I* have to get there by eight. Unless you want to go to Nashville with me."

"How are you so clueless?"

All right. That's it. She's been hinting at something since early this morning, and it's starting to drive me crazy.

I put my hands on my hips and face her. "Will you just

tell me already? I'm kind of getting sick of the 'oh, I need to go to Cody but won't tell you why' thing."

She rolls her eyes and plops back down on the rocks. "I need to get to the hospital there, before it's closed to visitors at eight. I didn't think my grandmother would be that easy for you to forget."

Ohhhhhh.

"Then again," she goes on, "you're so wrapped up in your own woe-is-me drama, I shouldn't be surprised."

"Hey!" But even as I say it, I know she's right. I've barely thought about Gert since we left her in the hospital. And that makes me feel like the worst person on earth.

"All you care about is getting away from your family as fast as you can for some reality show. My only family almost died, and I want to go see her. And nothing is going to stop me."

"But . . . you can barely walk." It's the only thing I can think of to say.

"I *know* that." She lets out a frustrated sound and then props her chin in her hands. "I can walk, it just hurts a whole lot. If your sad little first aid kit had that bandage in it, I could probably make it."

"Then maybe we need . . ." I look all around, but all I see

are trees and bushes and dirt. "We just need something that acts like a wrap, you know?" If we were near Bertha, there'd be tons of stuff I could use—a kitchen towel, one of Dad's socks, a scarf. Bertha's full of really useful things like that.

"Like what?" Shiver pulls out her cross-stitch again and flattens it against her leg. "This is too small."

As she stuffs the fabric back into her bag, I remember her talking to Bug, right on Bug's level. Looking out for me when she thought Remy was a weirdo. Keeping me from doing what I realize now were really stupid things, like hitchhiking or getting a ride with people I'd never even met before. Lying to the park ranger back at Lewis Lake. Trying to give me a pep talk when I was about to give up—at least, as peppy a pep talk as Shiver can give. Getting us onto the Adventure Seekers bus, and then thinking fast enough to keep us from getting found out. Giving me a hand up when I fell on that hill near the river.

And then I know what I have to do.

"Maybe . . ." I unzip my backpack, pushing aside the remaining food until I see what I'm looking for.

My shimmery silver audition top.

Chapter 26

3 days until *Dueling Duets* auditions

The silver threads in the shirt catch the light of the setting sun, and I heave a little sigh. It's the most beautiful thing I've ever owned, but it isn't something that I *need*. And I can't think about it for too long, or I'll lose my nerve.

"What is *that*?" Shiver's eyes are practically popping out of her head.

"Do you have scissors?"

Shiver nods toward her backpack. I dig through it until I find them. When I pull them out, Shiver slides to the ground and picks up the shirt. She looks at it, then at me.

"This thing is . . . shiny," she says. "Why were you carrying it around?"

I take a deep breath. "It's my audition top, okay?" I look at it again, scissors in my hand.

"What are you auditioning for, some kind of dance thing? This looks like one of those outfits people on that celebrity dancing show wear."

"Do you want your ankle wrapped or not? You better tell me fast before I change my mind."

"Yes, and hey, you made fun of my cross-stitch. The least you can do is tell me what show you're trying out for."

Fine. At least I can stop hiding everything from her. "*Dueling Duets*. It's a country music show. I'm a singer." I look her right in the eye, daring her to laugh.

She doesn't. "You must want it pretty bad."

"It's the *only* thing I want." Well, maybe not the only thing. But it's way, way, way up there.

Shiver hands the shirt back. "So, what, were you going to tie it around my ankle? It doesn't have sleeves."

"No." I can't believe I'm actually going to do this. I open the scissors, take a deep breath, and start cutting. Every snip feels as if I'm snipping apart my dream. But I'm not, not really. I can still audition for the show. I'll borrow something from Kenzie to wear, and I still have my hat.

Shiver doesn't say anything. She just watches as I cut the shirt in a spiral pattern, making one long strip of shiny silver. When I'm done, I wrap it tightly around Shiver's ankle. It looks funny, but it works.

"Couldn't you have picked a better color? Maybe black or, like, a navy blue? I stand out for miles in this," Shiver says as she examines the cut-up shirt wrapped around her ankle.

"That shirt was going to make the judges notice me before I even started singing," I inform her.

"Great. I'm country music fashionable." Shiver tests it out, putting her weight on both feet. "It still hurts, but I think I can do it."

I grab a tree limb lying nearby. "Here, use this too, like a crutch. I'll carry your backpack." If we go now, maybe I can still make the bus.

We start forward, through the nothingness toward where I hope the road is. I'm starting to wonder if this is how Bug feels on a regular basis—all confident and satisfied about figuring things out—when Shiver stops.

"What now?" I ask.

"Nothing," she says. "Just . . . thank you, I guess."

It's so weird to hear Shiver say thank you that I shrug

and keep walking. Except there's something I have to say too. "Look," I say over my shoulder. "I'm sorry I didn't think about Gert being in Cody. I should've figured that out sooner." I turn around, where Shiver's hobbling behind me. "But what did you mean about her being your only family? We were driving you to San Francisco to be with your mom."

Shiver doesn't answer. She doesn't even look at me. It's like she's too busy watching where she steps to talk to me. Or maybe she doesn't want to talk about her mom.

"Okay. Well, let's just get there," I say.

By the time I spy the road, it's almost dark. Cars pass, headlights gleaming, and I've never been so glad to see civilization in my whole life.

And I'm maybe also a little proud of myself for getting here. I'm totally like Wilderness Girl. And a doctor, sort of. I can't wait to tell Remy and Bug all about this. I wish Mom and Dad were here to see me. That little achy feeling twinges again when I think about them.

Shiver and I walk along in the dirt and brush on the side of the road. It's definitely dark, which means we aren't exactly visible to all the cars going by. Which could be scary, but is also really helpful, since probably the whole world is looking for us by now.

Every once in a while, I turn around to check on Shiver. She's slow, but moving. Before I know it, we're *in town* in town. I stop under a streetlight.

"Holy potatoes. We made it. We actually got here." I kind of can't believe it. After all that planning, the epic bike ride, all the problems we ran into, we're in Cody. I've pretty much memorized the directions to the bus stop, and it's only a few blocks away.

Shiver squints up at the street sign. "I have to go that way." She points off to the left.

"And the bus is that way." I point to the right.

"So I guess we split up." She leans on her tree-limb crutch.

"Hey, um, Shiver? Thanks for coming with me." A day ago, those words would've felt all weird coming from my mouth.

She gives me a half smile. "Sure. Thanks for coming with *me*."

That makes me laugh a little.

"So . . . let me know how Gert's doing, okay?"

"And you text me when you get to Nashville," she says.

I turn to walk toward the bus, when I hear a cracking sound. Shiver's still standing behind me, but her tree limb is broken in half and she's gripping the light pole.

She purses her lips as she checks out the two pieces of tree limb in her hands. "I don't care. I've gotten this far, I'll crawl to the hospital if I have to."

I pull out my phone and check the time. 7:50. If I help Shiver get to the hospital, I'll definitely miss the bus. I'll have come all this way for nothing.

And then it's like the sun pops out in the middle of the night. *Not for nothing.* Not if I help Shiver get to the hospital to see Gert before visiting hours are over. All this trouble *will* be worth something. It just won't be something for me.

And right then and there, smack in the middle of Cody, Wyoming, I know I want to sing so badly that I'll find another way. Jack has a partner (ugh), so I won't be letting him down if I don't show up. I feel bad that I won't see Kenzie, though. What Shiver said about Gert being her family is how I feel about Kenzie, even though we're not related. When we left Nashville, it felt like my family was splitting in half. Now that I'm not going back to stay with Kenzie, Bertha is my home. But Nashville and Kenzie also still feel like home. Is it possible to have two homes? I don't know.

But I do know how Mom and Dad will feel if I leave

them to go to Nashville. And if I go now, Shiver will miss seeing her gran for the last time in who knows how long.

I know exactly how it feels to miss seeing someone you really care about.

And when I think of it that way—despite how much it hurts to give up *Dueling Duets* and postpone my dream—there really isn't a choice. I got One Last Big Nashville Blast with Kenzie, so Shiver should have One Last Big Hospital Blast with Gert.

"Lean on me," I tell Shiver. "We'll get to the hospital in time."

She blinks at me. "You'll miss your bus."

"I don't care about the bus. Now, come on or we won't make it there before they close."

Shiver puts an arm around my shoulder. "I don't get it."

I shrug, as best I can with half of Shiver's weight leaning on my shoulders. "There's nothing to get."

"Okay," Shiver says in a slow voice.

I know she wants me to explain why I chose the way I did, but I don't know if I can. I mean, I don't really get it myself. So instead, I change the subject.

"It's freezing out here again. This place is so weird." I shift the backpacks hanging off my other shoulder. "I never thought I'd say this, but I can't wait to be back in Bertha. At least it's warm. And there's a shower and a bed." And Mom and Dad and Bug, but I don't say that out loud.

"I'd rather sleep out here and eat green beans straight out of the can than go home," Shiver says in a low voice as we pass dark, empty office buildings. She's got the collar of her hoodie pulled up over her mouth and nose.

"Why don't you want to go home?" I'm starting to breathe heavily, but at least now I can see the lights of the hospital straight ahead, through some trees. "I mean, since I'm totally giving up getting to Nashville, maybe you can tell me."

Shiver sighs. "You complain about how your parents dragged you out here so you could all have this big adventure together. My mom would never do that."

"Do what? Make you leave home?"

"No," she says. "That's kind of hard when she doesn't really care. I mean, yeah, she's there. But that's all. She barely pays any attention to me. And now all she can think about is her divorce from Stepdad Number Three. It's not like she was in any hurry to get me home."

"Oh," I say. And then wish I could think of something better to say. Mom and Dad sometimes pay way too much attention to me. I've always thought of it as annoying, but

I guess I'd rather have that than what Shiver has.

"I hate it," she says. "I was hoping I could stay with Gran. Maybe go home with her once we'd finished our trip. But I guess I can't do that now."

As I pull the freezing fingers of my free hand into my sweatshirt, an idea hits me. "Why can't you? She'll probably need someone to help her once she gets out of the rehab place."

"I hadn't thought of that. You think she'd want me around?"

"Of course she would!" I say. "I bet she's really sad because you had to cut your vacation short. And I mean, all you can do is ask, right? That won't hurt anything."

Shiver smiles in the streetlight glow. She's not Kenzie, but she's stood by me all the way up here. She's almost like . . . a friend.

"You know, Maya, you're not so bad." She's quiet for a moment as we round a bend in the road.

"You're not so bad either."

"By the way, it's Mozart. What I listen to all the time. So I get your thing about music."

"Mozart? Seriously?"

She nods.

"Huh." And then I have this image of sharing music with Shiver, which is just weird.

Shiver starts to say something else, but stops short as we get to the parking lot in front of the hospital.

Where flashing red and blue lights glint off the hospital building and the parked cars.

Chapter 27

3 days until *Dueling Duets* auditions

"I guess they figured out that we might come here," I say as we stand at the edge of the parking lot.

"But I need to see Gran." There's a twinge of panic in Shiver's voice.

"It's not eight o'clock yet. Let's go." I shift her arm and practically pull her across the lot, between the cars parked here and there.

"We can't get to the door without being seen," she says.

"That doesn't matter. No way have you come this far for them to not let you visit her." I steer her straight toward the hospital entrance and the police cars.

We're maybe halfway there when someone shouts, "Is that them?" A spotlight swings around, completely blinding me. Then it switches off and a whole bunch of people run toward us. Before I can figure out what's going on, there are blankets around Shiver's and my shoulders, someone's pushing a bottle of water into my hands, and Shiver's being carried off toward the hospital entrance.

"Wait!" I yell. I grip the blanket and run through the police officers and hospital employees. I haven't seen Mom or Dad or anyone I recognize yet, but first I have to make sure *something* goes the way we planned.

I reach the group around Shiver and tug the arm of the paramedic carrying her. "WAIT!" My voice carries over the crowd, and they stop. "It's just a sprained ankle. She's okay. Or she will be once she sees her gran. Her name is Gert . . ." I look to Shiver.

"Gertrude Ammons," Shiver says.

"Shiver has to see her, now, okay? It's the whole reason we're here."

"We need to get her checked out first, young lady," the paramedic says.

"No, she's fine! Visiting hours are over at eight, and she—"

A police officer cuts me off. "Don't worry. We'll make sure she sees her grandmother. *After* she gets checked out."

Shiver smiles, and I take a step back. "Okay." I wave as her whole entourage carries her into the hospital.

"Maya!"

I turn around to see a truck pulling up. Mom and Dad jump out and run toward me, with Bug and Remy and Remy's parents in another car, right behind them.

"Maya!" Mom nearly lifts me off the ground in a bone-breaking hug. "Why? How? Never mind." She squishes me in a hug again. And when she's done, Dad takes over.

"Why are you covered in mud?" I ask him as best I can as my lungs are being squashed. "And aren't you supposed to be on an overnight hike?"

"I fell down a muddy hill," he says. "And I *was* on a hike, till a ranger showed up and told me what was happening."

Dad finally lets me go, and Bug grabs me next. "You made it!" she says. "I knew you could do it."

"It would've been better with you," I tell her. And I mean it, one hundred percent. "And I didn't make it, really. Not to the bus anyway. But at least Shiver gets to see her gran. How did the police know we'd come to the hospital?"

"They didn't, for sure," Dad says. "But when Bug told us

that Shiver went with you, we thought she might come here. So they sent officers to the bus station and to the hospital. We were waiting at the bus station when they called us to say you were here." Dad rubs his eyes. "I'm just so glad you're okay, Maya Mae." He hugs me again.

Remy and his parents are hanging back. He grins at me and I smile over Dad's shoulder.

"Maya, what were you thinking?" Mom says as soon as Dad releases me. She puts her hands on her hips, looking at me all stern. Then she hugs me a third time. "You could've been run over by a car, or a herd of buffalo, or attacked by a bear, or . . . or . . . or . . ."

"I just wanted to get home for the audition," I say in a small voice.

"That doesn't make it okay," Mom says.

"I know. I'm sorry I made you worry. Y'all got your dream, and I guess I wanted mine, too. And I missed Kenzie, a lot. I thought *Dueling Duets* was my only chance. And when I won, you could all come home. Then everything would be normal again."

"I'm sorry I didn't take you more seriously, Maya Mae," Dad says, his voice breaking just a little. "I thought maybe you'd get used to our little adventure, and come to think of it as a new normal. And that you understood that your dream isn't dead—just waiting until you grow up."

I swallow the knot in my throat and nod. A new normal. I don't know about that, but I do know that Mom and Dad wouldn't be happy in a house back in Nashville. Bug either. I'm not really sure what home is now, but I think it has to be wherever my family is. And if Kenzie is my family too, then maybe I really can have two homes, at least in my heart.

I guess my dream has to wait. Which makes me want to cry, right here in the parking lot, even though I did willingly give up *Dueling Duets* to help Shiver.

"I was worried about Mom having all the responsibility for making money," I add. "You always look really stressed out when you're on your computer."

"That's because it's a stressful job, honey. Not because I have to worry about making enough money. We're on a budget, yes, but that's because these RVs can have all kinds of maintenance issues. We have to keep up a good savings account for the just-in-case," Mom says.

"Oh." I don't know what else to say.

"You know, if you'd told us what you were planning, we could've let you in on a surprise a little early," Dad says.

"Surprise?" I look back and forth between my parents.

Mom clears her throat. "I looked up this show you were so bent on trying out for, and it turns out that you can send in a video audition. So—"

"We filmed you singing and are going to send it in!" Dad's practically bursting. "And if they like it, they'll invite you to the last set of auditions in Los Angeles."

I blink at him. "Are you saying that . . . ?" I can't even ask the question. I don't want to hear no. "Wait, is it from the talent show? The video?"

Mom grins. "Dad snuck down the trail by the lake at Grand Teton when you were practicing. You remember, back when we first got there? He got some great footage."

I make a sound that's something between a screech and a shout and throw myself at my parents. "Thank you!" Then I pull away. "Um, do I still get to go? If they ask me to come, I mean?"

"Well . . ." Mom trails off, that serious look on her face again. "We haven't sent it in yet. Maya, you scared us to death with this whole thing."

"I know," I say in a quiet voice. "I'm really, really sorry. I hate that I made you worry." I pull on the hem of my dirty shirt. "I kind of figured out, somewhere between all that biking and climbing over a river, that I don't really want to be apart from you all. I missed you." I look up at them. "I promise I'll never do anything like that again. And I mean it. I know it's a lot to ask you to send in that video after what I did."

Mom and Dad look at each other.

"Let's talk some more about it tomorrow," Mom says. "If we're convinced you understand what you did, then we'll send in the video."

If my whole body didn't hurt so much from all the biking and walking, I'd jump up and down in the parking lot. I might still have a chance!

And just at that minute, my phone—which is almost, but not completely, dead—buzzes with a text.

M, you ok???? Your parents called mine!

"It's Kenzie," I tell everyone. I'm ok. Missed the bus. But still might be able to try out.

Really?! Jack & Lacey won't have anything on you. :)

"Maya, are you hurt?" Mom asks, more seriously. "Hungry? Tired?"

"All of the above, but I'm okay." I smile at her. I didn't make it back to Nashville, but I might still be on my way to *Dueling Duets*. And tonight, I'll go back to Bertha—home, or one of them anyway—with my family. "Can we go check on Shiver? I want to make sure they're going to let her visit Gert."

Mom tilts her head, like she's not sure who I am, but she nods. "Of course. And then we're going back to the RV so you can get some rest."

"That sounds great." I smile again. While I'm proud that Shiver and I actually made it here, I'm way too exhausted and achy to think of biking/adventure seeking/river crossing *ever* again in my whole entire life. All I really want to do now is curl up in my cubbyhole bunk and fall asleep under the TTT. I can't believe how much I miss the not–Dirt Den Couch, the teeny bathroom, and even Frankendeer and the freaky-eyed doe.

As we weave through the crowd outside the hospital, Remy catches up to me. I smile way too big when he stops.

Dial it down a notch, Maya.

I smooth my wild hair and brush some of the canyon dirt from my jeans. Which is really kind of pointless since the dirt is practically ground into the fabric.

He reaches over and gives me a quick hug.

Holy potatoes. Remy just hugged me! Ugh, I must smell awful. And I haven't brushed my teeth since really early this morning. I hope he doesn't notice.

If he does, he doesn't seem to care. It doesn't look like he took the time to shower either since I last saw him. "What happened to the bikes?" he asks.

"Long story," I tell him. "Did you and Bug make it to the lodge?"

"Yup. We sat there until about five, when we overheard people talking about some missing kids. So we figured we'd better let your mom know where we were. We thought that would still give you enough time to make it to your bus." He holds up his phone. "Bug loved the pictures, by the way. So did I. You're practically a park expert now, huh?"

I can feel my face turning red as Mom and Dad check with the hospital welcome station attendant. "I guess. It was kind of awesome. Hard, but I'm glad I did it."

"No one wanted to let me come here, but I told them I had to make sure you and Shiver made it okay."

He was worried about me. My skin breaks out into goose bumps. "I'm glad you're here."

"I hate that we went through all of that and you didn't get home. Not that I really wanted you to go home, but I know *you* did, so . . ." Now *his* face looks a little red.

"It's all right," I say.

And it is.

I tell him about Dad secretly taping me and about maybe getting another shot at auditions. "Thanks for all your help, even though it didn't work out exactly the way I planned." I unzip my backpack and pull out his envelope of money. "And here, since I didn't end up needing it. But thanks for letting me have it."

"No problem," Remy says as he takes the envelope. "Maybe you can come visit me in Denver the next time your family drives through?"

Something warm floods through me. "Yeah, that'd be great."

He takes my hand and squeezes it. And then he doesn't let go. Mom turns around from the information desk, but instead of saying anything, she just smiles and turns back.

And when I picture myself onstage for *Dueling Duets*, I don't see Jack next to me. Instead, behind the lights and the cameras, I see Remy in the audience, cheering me on.

As we wait for the elevator, I pull out my phone with my free hand. After I text Kenzie, I find OMGH.

Operation Maya Goes Home (OMGH)

(In time for Dueling Duets.)

Countdown: T minus 3 days

How to Get Home to Audition with Jack and Win His Heart with My Voice and Stellar Personality:

1. ~~Convince Mom and Dad this is the worst idea ever.~~

2. ~~Bertha needs major repairs~~ (tires don't count, I guess).

3. ~~K fakes lots of broken bones & needs me to spoon her soup.~~ (Not believable.)

4. ~~Walk. Phone mapping app says this will take only 253 hours. Which is like 10½ days if I don't sleep, eat, go to the bathroom, or stop at all.~~ (I don't even like Dad's 2-mile hikes, so . . .)

5. ~~Hitchhike!~~ (Shiver. Ugh. Also, scary.)

6. ~~Find ride with another RV family.~~ (Shiver. Again.)

7. ~~Buy plane ticket with Mom's credit card.~~ (Busted. And guilty.)

8. ~~Bike to bus station. Take bus home!~~

9. Two homes are way, way, way better than one. Even if one of them comes with a Frankendeer.

Acknowledgments

Thank you so much for picking this book to read! Without readers, there would be no books—and I would be very, very sad. If you liked reading about Maya, Shiver, Remy, and Bug, visit my website at gailnall.com and let me know! I love hearing from readers.

This book was inspired by two life-changing road trips I took out West. Words can't capture the beauty and immensity of places like Yellowstone and Grand Teton National Parks, the open plains of Kansas, and the colors of Hell's Half Acre (yes, it's a real place!). I'm forever grateful for those experiences and for the US National Park Service, which preserves so many of the beautiful wild places for us all to enjoy. You can learn more about them at nps.gov.

A great big huge thank-you to my ever-amazing agent, Jullia A. Weber, who (for some reason) still likes reading the crazy things I come up with, and who keeps me sane and focused. There isn't enough cake in the world for how smart and encouraging she is! Thank you, thank you, thank you (times a million!) to my savvy and hilarious editor, Amy Cloud, who not only loved Maya's story but who also helped me figure out how to make it even better. Your ideas and suggestions are everything, and if I could, I'd buy you your own glitzy tour bus (no Dirt Den included) to travel in (or to park in NYC just for kicks). And thank you so much to the entire Aladdin team—including Jessica Handelman for the lovely cover, Faye Bi for being an amazing publicist, and Katharine Wiencke for fixing all my misplaced hyphens and commas—and Eda Kaban for the cover illustration that perfectly captures Maya's story.

A special thank-you to Rae Ann Parker for schooling me on all things Nashville. Thanks for answering random text messages about the Pancake Pantry and the pedestrian bridge, and for giving me a place to stay whenever I'm in town. Another special thank-you goes to Mary Uhles, for sharing her experiences growing up in the national parks and answering all of my Remy questions. Another thank-you goes to all those full-timer RV folks out there who share their experiences online for nosy people like me to read about.

I'm a lucky writer to have so many fellow writers who kindly beta read this book for me when it was in its early stages. Ronni Arno, Brooks Benjamin, Heather Brady, Jeff Chen, Melanie Conklin, Abby Cooper, Manju Howard, Jen Malone, Dee Romito, and Stefanie Wass—thank you *so* much for your time and suggestions. Another big thank-you goes to my ever-patient critique group who read so many bits and pieces of this book—Anne Howard, David Jarvis, April Roberson, Laura Stone, Charles Suddeth, Kate Weiss, and Amy Williamson. And another thank-you to my group at the 2013 SCBWI Midsouth Revision Retreat, for all of their thoughtful comments and criticisms on this manuscript—Tricia Cortas, Kim Teter, Patricia Nesbitt, Judith Rehder, and Pat Weaver.

Thank you, thank you, thank you to my hilarious and talented MG Beta Readers group. Thank you to everyone who is part of SCBWI Midsouth. To Gretchen Kelley—thank you for our annual Mojito Tapas/writing/publishing/life meet-ups, and for being one of my very first critique partners! To Sara O'Bryan Thompson—thank you for keeping me fueled with wine and cookies and inspiration during our writing times.

Finally (but never least!), I am grateful for a wonderful circle of family and friends—Mom and Joel, Dad, Cheryl, Mike and Joann, Lisa and David, my friends, and, of course, my Eva. I love you all and am forever humbled to have you in my life.

Read on for an excerpt from

YOU'RE
INVITED

by Gail Nall and Jen Malone

TODAY'S TO-DO LIST:

☐ sync watch with Mom's

☐ buy seasick medicine

☐ pack backup bridesmaid dresses

When I peer over the boat railing, it's not like I actually expect mermaids and mermen to be bobbing in the ocean below me. Buuuuuut then again, I wouldn't put anything past my mom. If her client wants a *Little Mermaid* wedding, her client gets a *Little Mermaid* wedding, no detail spared.

My pocket buzzes and I slide my phone out.

Plz check on photog. Thx.

I weave my way through the rows of chairs sliding back and forth on the deck. The one thing Mom doesn't control on wedding days is the weather, and today isn't exactly offering ideal sailing conditions. I hope the bride has less wobbly legs than Ariel.

"Excuse me, sir, um, are you okay?" I ask a man hanging over the boat's side.

The three cameras hanging from his neck smack against his back as he straightens. Uh-oh. He does *not* look so hot. He mumbles something under his breath and I shake my head.

"Sorry. I didn't catch that. Would you mind repeating?" I ask, using my most polite voice. Mom's trained me well.

He stares at me for a second, then screams, "I SAID I'M A LITTLE SEASICK!"

Okay, so "please repeat" does not mean "scream at your highest possible volume," but I'm kind of used to the vendors treating me differently. They think just because I'm only twelve, I'm not capable of the same things a normal wedding coordinator's assistant is.

They would be wrong.

I plant my feet hip-width apart for balance and get straight to business. "I have a seasick bracelet you can wear on your wrist, and if you give me five minutes, I can grab some of the motion-sickness medicine I packed in my emergency kit. I also have a little sister who's a pretty decent photographer, if you're okay with her using one of your cameras. She could stand at the railing and grab the shots of the bride arriving by dinghy while you wait for the medicine to kick in."

His face was already turning green when I mentioned the dinghy, but he adds a look of horror to that. "I can't allow a *child* to photograph this wedding!"

I consider telling him kids can do *lots* of stuff every bit as well as any grown-up, but then the boat rolls over a large swell, and with the way he clutches at his stomach, I don't have the heart.

Between sucking in big breaths of fresh air, he says, "My assistant will take all the important shots of the bridal party. Tell your sister she can help by getting photos of the guests."

And just like that Izzy lands herself an assignment. Ick. She'll be totally annoying and gloaty about this all week now.

But the client comes first, and my job is to save the day. Good thing I really love my job, and even more important, good thing I'm really excellent at my job, even if certain people (cough, *Mom*, cough) hardly bother to acknowledge it.

Half the time she doesn't even know I'm solving a crisis, like making sure the waiter knows the groom's grandmother is allergic to wheat or scuffing up the waxed dance floor before anyone has an epic wipeout. My job is to keep things off *her* plate, and that's what I do. Always.

My phone buzzes again. On wedding days, no one besides Mom would dare text me.

Sure enough:

All handled w/photog? Bride arrival in 6 min.

Not five minutes. Not ten minutes. *Six* minutes. And you could set your clock by Mom's schedule, too. I tell the photographer I'll be right back and race belowdecks to the staging area where all the various wedding paraphernalia is located, alongside my sister, Isabelle. She's sitting on top of the backup wedding gown with her face stuck in a book.

"Izzy, you're gonna get that completely wrinkled! The bride is gonna need to wear that if she gets something on her real dress."

"Relax, Sadie. You know Mom would never let anything happen to the actual dress."

"Well, what if . . . what if a wave crashes into the dinghy on the bride's way out to the boat? How do you think Mom's gonna prevent that?"

"Umbrellas." Izzy points out the tiny round window of the cabin at a wooden dinghy motoring toward us. It's too far to make out faces, but there are definitely umbrellas bobbing along either side of one of the figures. Mom thinks of ev-er-y-thing.

I scramble back from the window and pull my sister to her feet. "Hurry up! The photographer's sick and his assistant needs your help getting shots."

Izzy squeals with excitement and follows me up the stairs. She's practically bouncing by the time we reach him. I think getting her to stop is the main reason he hands off what is probably a ridiculously expensive camera to a ten-year-old so quickly. His other hand reaches for the Dramamine and the seasick band I hold out.

He swallows the pill and then takes my advice to focus on the horizon. You don't grow up in Sandpiper Beach, North Carolina, without learning the best ways to get your sea legs.

"Izzy, head over to where the guests are and grab some shots of them watching the bridal party arrive," I instruct.

She answers with a "You're not the boss of me," but at least she does what I ask as I run to make sure the groom is in place. My favorite thing about weddings is also my least favorite: everything happens at once.

But this one is a success so far. Okay, so maybe the wedding party has a hard time getting out of their dinghies since their bridesmaid dresses have sewn-on mermaid tails, and it's true that the photographer throws up the Dramamine before it can even reach his stomach. But you can tell the bride and groom are really in love, what with the way he makes googly eyes at her as she comes down the aisle to a steel-drum version of "Kiss the Girl."

Mom slides into place beside me.

"Thanks for your help today," she whispers while giving me a squeeze around my waist.

Now it's my turn to glow. Ever since Dad died and Mom started her wedding-planning company, she's been totally pre-occupied with her business. I get the whole I-need-a-distraction-from-the-grief thing, but it's almost like she wants a distraction from me and Izzy, too. So the times when she actually notices me, it's like . . . magic. Like it used to be.

I don't have that much time to savor the feeling, though, because I need to get going on my next task. As the couple exchanges vows, I sneak belowdecks and creep over to the cage of the shaggy sheepdog who belongs to one of the bridesmaids and just *happens* to match the one in *The Little Mermaid*. I mean, what are the odds?

"You ready for your big entrance, Fake Max?" I ask, checking his collar to make sure the pouch containing the wedding rings is fastened securely around the buckle. I don't know what this dog's name is, but I've watched *The Little*

Mermaid alongside my note-taking Mom enough over the past few months to know Prince Eric's dog is named Max, so it will have to do.

He woofs at me and plants a sloppy kiss on my cheek. Ick. This job has a ton of occupational hazards, and now I can add dog slobber to the list. I secure his leash and lead him above, sneaking him around the back of the seated wedding guests.

The minister smiles at the happy couple and asks, "Do you have the rings?"

That's my cue.

And then . . . it happens.

A big plop of seagull doo-doo drops from the sky and lands directly on my head, dribbling greenish-yellowish-whitish goop down my cheek. When I scream, everyone swivels as one to face me. I freeze, horrified by both my interruption and the super-slimy, super-gross stuff sliding down toward my neck.

The groom drops the bride's hands.

I drop the dog's leash.

Fake Max goes tearing off in wild circles around the deck, barking like crazy at the circling seagull, who looks like he's lining up target practice with the top of my head again.

"Grab him!" Mom screams as Fake Max pulls up at my ankles, panting hard. But I don't grab him, because:

1) I can't take my eyes from the seagull, who looks suspiciously like he's about to dive-bomb straight for my head, and

2) I'm thinking about how I'm going to use a printed program to remove bird poop from my hair.

Fake Max is eyeing the gull too, and when the bird swoops low, the dog jumps into the air at him. Of course he misses, since his shaggy fur is probably completely covering his eyes. Landing, he then tears off across the deck in hot pursuit of the bird, who I would swear is laughing more than screeching. Fake Max runs, pauses, and then jumps, chasing the seagull straight off the back of the boat, his four furry legs still running through the air, as he drops to the water below.

His owner shrieks, "SHEP!" and shuffle-runs across the deck in her mermaid dress. She doesn't even hesitate at the railing, just goes right up and over, tumbling into the water after her dog.

"Bridesmaid overboard!" someone calls, and several men run to the stern, one carrying a life preserver.

I rush to help, but when the man with the life preserver swings it behind him before heaving it into the water, I have to dodge out of the way. I stumble back and straight into the box the steering wheel is mounted on, where my elbow connects hard with a button.

KA-BAAM! POP! POW! BANG! BOOM!

The entire ten-minute fireworks display planned for the end of the reception explodes at one time from the barge on the starboard side of us.

Activated by me.

I stand frozen in place again, my wide eyes locked with my mother's, as a group of tuxedo-wearing men haul a dripping mermaid/bridesmaid/whatevermaid and her soggy dog out of the water. At least the pouch with the rings is still attached to his collar.

But that thing I said about being really good at my job?

Maybe not so much today.

Mom likes to borrow a theater saying when she talks about her "event philosophy": The show must go on. I'm pretty sure she's never had to apply it quite like this before. I clean up belowdecks and then hang back as much as I can, trying to help without getting in the way. Mom barely even acknowledges me as she rushes around doing wedding-planner stuff, but when she does catch my eye, I see the way her lips tug down into a frown. Each time it happens, my stomach has that hollow feeling you get when you just know you are so completely in for it once everyone else leaves.

The ceremony resumes where it left off and is pretty uneventful except for Max/Shep shaking himself dry at the top of the aisle during the you-may-now-kiss-the-bride part. Luckily for us, once people get over the shock—and after Mom changes the bridesmaid into a backup mermaid dress (only two sizes too small)—things start looking up (not for me, but at least for the guests). The bridesmaid calls her mom to come to the marina, and we send the horrible-smelling wet dog back to the mainland on the dinghy. He's joined by the still-puking photographer.

By the last toast of the night, the video of the entire incident, which one of the groomsmen wasted no time posting to YouTube, has 244,365 hits. By the last dance at sunset, the bride and groom have agreed to detour to Wilmington on their way to the honeymoon in order to discuss their "hilarious wedding disaster" on the local morning show.

All's well that ends well? Not where Mom's concerned, I'm guessing. The chug of the departing dinghy signals the official end of the reception. The only people left on the boat now, besides me and Mom, are the caterers cleaning up and Izzy, who's gone back to her book down below.

Mom crosses the deck and points me into a chair near the giant Prince Eric ice sculpture.

"I'm so sorry, Mom," I say before she can get a word out.

She sighs and reaches for my hand. "I know you are, baby, and I understand how it happened."

Her smile is the kind that doesn't go all the way into her eyes, which are a little sad-looking. I stare back into them as she says, "On the other hand, I have the reputation of my business to think about, and I have to put that first."

Ahead of me?

I drop my eyes to my lap. Mom sighs again. "Sweetness, maybe twelve is just too young to be handling everything I've asked of you. Maybe we need to rethink things a little bit."

Wait a minute. Am I getting fired? By my own *mother?* This cannot be happening.

"You've been a huge help to me, Sadie. You know that. But this mistake is going to cost the company thousands of dollars after I refund the bride's dad for the fireworks show he paid for. Plus we lose any referrals that bride could have given us. I just hope she doesn't mention my company by name on television Monday morning."

She tucks me under her arm and gives me a squeeze. I keep my body stiff when she says, "I'm not mad, Sades. It's my fault for giving you so much responsibility. Summer's just starting. You should spend it doing kid stuff. Fun stuff. Not dealing with all this stress."

Does she not remember the whole reason I started working with her is because I DO find it fun? Well, at first it was just because it was a chance to be with Mom, but it turns out I'm really good at it . . . most days. I'm the one who came up with the idea for the ice sculpture to match the statue in the movie. And it was me who tracked down the sheet music for "Kiss the Girl" for the wedding band. I love coming up with fun details to make the weddings memorable and I *thought* Mom loved it too. She's always going on about what a huge help I am to her.

I didn't notice anyone *else* thinking to bring a blender for that groom who'd had emergency dental surgery the morning of the wedding, so he could still have some wedding cake. Or finding weights to clip onto the bridesmaids' dresses' hems when we had an outdoor wedding on the beach during a super-windy day. And, I mean, it's not like I haven't made some little mistakes at a wedding before. There was the time I accidentally left with the keys to the reception site and the florist couldn't get in early to do the centerpieces. But I rode my bike over as fast as I could the second she called. Maybe tonight's was a little more . . . severe, but in the past Mom's always understood that events might have wrinkles.

It stinks to be unappreciated, but what's even worse is being entirely invisible. Which is exactly what I'll be if she fires me. I'll fade back into the wallpaper like before.

I nod hard against Mom's chest so she won't catch on that I'm trying not to let the tears spill over. We're interrupted by the caterer, who needs her to sign some form, which leaves me free to slide my phone from my pocket and scroll through all my emoticons until I find the tiny pair of bat wings. I type it into a group text to my three best friends.

There. Bat signal sent.

It cheers me up a tiny bit to picture all of them heading for their bikes (or golf cart, for Lauren, depending on where she is at the marina) and pointing them to our Bat Cave. Well, our Bat Boat, if we're being technical.

I stand, cross the deck, and yell down to Izzy that I'm catching the next dinghy shuttle to shore. As I board the tiny boat, the last thing I hear is someone from the catering staff humming "Part of Your World" as she cleans up. Too bad my chance to be part of Mom's world exploded alongside those fireworks.

Real life. Real you.

Don't miss
any of these
terrific
Aladdin M!X
books.

ALADDINMIX.COM

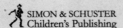 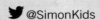

New mystery. New suspense. New danger.

NANCY DREW
DIARIES™

BY CAROLYN KEENE